# PRAISE 1

Winner of the Independent Book Publishers Association Benjamin Franklin Award - The Bill Fisher Award for Best First Book (Fiction)

Eric Hoffer Grand Prize Honorable Mention

Eric Hoffer First Horizons Award Finalist

Publishers Weekly Booklife Prize Semi-Finalist

## PUBLISHERS WEEKLY BOOKLIFE

"...Ehrlich's vivid historical coming-of-age novel...Ellis River teems with well-drawn characters and vibrant wilderness settings. A memorable proto-feminist protagonist, Ellis strives not just to reunite her family but to carve out a meaningful life. [Journal entries and letters]...lay bare the character's heart and showcase Ehrlich's sure-handed period language as she brings life to perspectives too often unexplored in narratives of the era, with empathy, insight, a touch of romance..."

Great for fans of Robin Oliveira [*My Name is Mary Sutter*] & Charles Frazier [*Cold Mountain*]

## KIRKUS REVIEW

"Ehrlich's prose is accessible and spare and particularly skillful...The story simultaneously highlights the loneliness and camaraderie that can be found during wartime. Additionally, Ellis' coming-of-age adds a personal layer to the battle-laden background...[as she] encounters previously unknown feelings. Ehrlich's story of a girl surrounded by loss and death as she searches for her family is engaging and makes for a quick, heartfelt read. An earnest and poignant bildungsroman."

## REEDSY DISCOVERY

"Loved it! ...[the] novel...will capture your attention from the very beginning...a great adventure."

# ELLIS RIVER

# ELLIS RIVER

*a novel*

NICKI EHRLICH

Bay Feather
BOOKS

*Ellis River*
Copyright © 2022 by Nicki Ehrlich

First Edition

Paperback ISBN: 979-8-9859974-0-8
eBook ISBN: 979-8-9859974-1-5
Library of Congress Control Number: 2022907883

*For my parents, who survived wars and immigration.*
*And for my daughter...and all the horses.*

*chapter*
# ONE

*Dear Daddy,*
*It's spring again, the year 1865. I never realized how*
*alive this place was when you were still here. You and*
*Walter working the horses and Mama yelling at Earl to*
*help do whatever it was he was supposed to be doing. I*
*couldn't wait to open my eyes in the morning so I could*
*breathe in the scent of horse sweat, leather and breakfast. I*
*can still hear Mama singing to herself in the kitchen. And*
*Earl's laugh, and the nickering of the horses like they were*
*laughing back at him.*

> *The morning you and Walter left with that string of*
> *geldings, headed toward Memphis, everything changed.*

ELLIS STOPPED WRITING. SHE REACHED OUT AND RAN HER
fingers along the spines of the small leather-bound notebooks
lined up on her desk. Welded horseshoe bookends held them
upright. All those years ago her mother had given her the first
diary for her birthday. Every time she filled one, some celebra-
tory event caused another to appear; another birthday, extra
chores accomplished, good marks in school. And ever since,

Ellis wrote. Doing chores or wandering the woods of Western Tennessee, she would soak up the details that would later flow through her fingers to her pen. Like the constancy of the river, a force, strong and natural, settled her at the desk, dipped her pen, and put it to paper. Her mother would tell Ellis to write down her feelings. She would never ask to see what her daughter had written. She had wanted Ellis to write freely and "get it out on paper" so she could then get on with daily life. When her mother passed, Ellis thought she'd never be able to write again. She would sit for hours at this desk in her upstairs bedroom, staring at a blank page. All she could think of was trying to get in touch with her father or find her brothers. And so, though she had nowhere to send them, she wrote letters. Perhaps someday there would be an address.

The house was too quiet, though it echoed the normal aches and pains of a wooden building. The pine stairs creaked and moaned under nothing but their own weight, reminding her of her twin brother, Earl's, footsteps as he would sneak into his room, across the hall from hers, after not showing up for dinner. The wind groaned like a twister coming through but it was only a small zephyr at worst, or an early spring breeze. Loneliness amplified.

Her bedroom window faced north, with a view of the back corrals. For a few days now, long before sunrise, an unnatural glow illuminated the horizon. And today, a shift in the wind, a distant pounding. Maybe it was just the blood beating in her head, but she got up from the chair at her desk and walked to the open window. April usually promised warmer weather and new growth, but today's breeze smelled like the ending of a story, not the beginning. She breathed in. The air, stark and barren, did not promise spring. The teeming life that once surrounded the homestead just wasn't there anymore. War does that.

Her father and older brother, Walter, had been excited when they were first made aware of what everyone thought would be a short dispute far to the east. Ellis had heard her father talking to the other men at the Society of Friends hall. Some were upset about what they were hearing, but her father reckoned selling horses to the troops would enable him to expand the homestead, finally building the ranch he wanted. And somehow he thought it would be an occupation necessary enough to the war effort that it might exempt him and his sons from the battlefield. Her father was no coward, but killing another man was wrong and this wasn't his fight. That's what he'd said. He did not hold slaves, and the community in which they lived would not allow it. But he'd traveled south and brought back stories of thousand-acre plantations that couldn't be run without them.

On the promise of a sunny summer day in 1863 he and Walter left with a string of saddle horses to be sold to the army. They said they'd be back for her birthday. She was about to turn thirteen then. That was two years ago.

Ellis returned to her desk and started to write again, … *Mama tried…*she stopped, turned to look out the window, then looked back at the paper and the ink stains on her fingers where she held the pen. Weariness slowed her hand and she leaned forward, resting her head on crossed arms.

DAYS BEFORE THE SOLDIERS SHOWED UP ELLIS HAD TRIED running the horses off into the woods, where they couldn't be found, but the well-trained equines just startled, ran around the pasture and came back. She had watched her father make deals since she was old enough to walk and ride, but she wished her brother were here to help. Most of the neighbors had started to clear out well before Earl left, her friend Prissy and her folks holding out the longest. Many headed west to the Mississippi and then north. But Mama insisted they wait for Daddy. And then Mama got sick.

At first she'd just talk to herself or to Daddy as if he were standing beside her. One night Ellis woke to a voice coming from the corral, Mama trying to rope a horse that wasn't there. And then the night it rained so hard, Mama out in the garden in her nightgown, digging potatoes. Earl had helped Ellis get her dried off and back into bed. When Ellis returned to her mother's room with tea, Earl was holding the worn paper of Daddy's letter. A letter written at least a year ago, before the war crept so far west. She saw a sadness on her brother's face she hadn't seen before. Mama had read the letter once to them, but they knew she kept it in her pocket to read over and over. Earl had tried to hide his emotions from Ellis, but the next day he was gone. He left a cryptic note about finding Daddy and Walter, but Ellis knew he hadn't a clue where they might be, or where to start looking.

Mama stopped getting out of bed. She wouldn't eat much. She would ask Ellis to read to her until she fell asleep.

Ellis didn't think Earl would have gotten too far when he left. He never did have any patience, could barely sit still for a meal, always moving. But neither one of them had been farther from home than the river, by themselves. Earl had been gone a month, now. Or was it longer.

TIME HAD BECOME GHOSTLY, JUST DARK AND LIGHT. ELLIS remembered she had been washing up in the kitchen when she heard the horses stir. The morning had been quiet; the kind of quiet like before the sky turned black, ushering a storm. The cavalry riding up the road was a small group, only five of them. But she was pretty sure there were more coming. The color blue barely clung to their faded, dusty uniforms. They flew no flag. It wasn't that they were Union soldiers, but that they were soldiers at all that unnerved Ellis. Only months before, the community had felt safe; uninvolved with the trauma of a war they thought wasn't theirs. But a troop had swept through the village a week before Earl left. Her brother had said he'd heard they wiped out the Hopkins' place. Took all but a couple of laying hens. Took two horses, their milk cow and calf. Then more news of more raids. Neighbors emigrating.

As the soldiers rode up to the front gate, Ellis stood in the doorway. Her father's shotgun leaned against the inside wall, sparking a memory of Earl teaching her to shoot. Her mother and father had argued about their daughter handling a gun. But her father wanted all of his children to be able to provide for themselves. He had taught Earl well and knew Earl had shared those skills with his sister.

The leader, a sergeant by his uniform, dismounted and walked up to the house while the other men remained on their horses. "Miss." The sergeant tipped his hat.

Ellis nodded.

"Your Pa around?" he asked.

Ellis hesitated, realizing how much more protected she felt when he had been around. "No," she answered.

She thought she saw a hint of a smile bloom on the sergeant's face and then fade away. He squinted, as if looking at her more closely, then glanced back at the others. He stepped back to better survey the house. "Your Ma?"

Ellis had buried her mother two days before, but she wasn't about to tell him that. She couldn't fight off these soldiers. She wondered what her father would do.

"I know you're here to take the horses. We don't want you to take them but you're going to anyway, aren't you." She struggled to keep her voice strong; emit the confidence she'd witnessed when her father sold horses.

"Yes, ma'am. But it's not like you might've heard. We pay good money for stock."

"We've got good stock." Ellis felt a pull in her gut, her face burned, but she planted her feet. This same feeling overcame her every time a horse left their property. She knew her father was in the business of selling horses, but she became attached to each one. Always shedding a tear when they left.

One of the other soldiers rode over to the pen and opened the gate. The horses just stood there. The sergeant moved toward Ellis. She grabbed the shotgun, trained it on him and had it cocked before he took two steps.

"Easy there, girl, I'm not gonna hurt you. Don't have the time." He smirked and checked over his shoulder. Just outside the picket fence, soldiers slumped on tired horses. One had a hand on his sidearm. The sergeant waved him off. "But we pay for what we take. Here." He handed Ellis a folded piece of paper. She kept the shotgun pointed at the soldier, but tucked it under her arm. She reached out to take the payment with her other hand, glanced at it, moving the paper with her thumb. Inside were a few Union bills. She wasn't sure how much, but they both knew it didn't matter. She uncocked the shotgun and lowered it. The sergeant watched her and she met his eyes.

She thought he'd probably been a handsome boy once. He looked like Tommy, a school friend whose family had left at the beginning of the conflict, and wondered if time and war had ravaged his innocence, as well. She wondered who was winning this war. Or if a war could be won.

"You'll take good care of them," Ellis ordered more than asked. She couldn't look at the horses. Her breath labored. In her mind she was running to them, fighting off the soldiers, pulling the trigger.

The sergeant stiffened and then looked back at the others again, lifted his chin and chuckled. "Sure, sure we will. You don't have to worry." He backed away, mounted his horse, and joined the ragged troop to surround the small herd and drive them south.

Now Ellis watched the horses go. They moved along with little agitation, the herd keeping itself together, following other horses. These were the older ones and the ones who had been too young to take before. She knew them each by name, by their face and leg markings, who in the herd they were attached to. The old gelding, Tucker, the first horse her father let her ride, was swaybacked now. Billie was just green broke.

They kicked up dust and memories of her father. She heard his voice. She, Earl, Walter and her father had moved a herd for a rancher once, an overnight drive. Earl mostly grumbled about going. Walter had told him how hard the work was. Long days in the saddle. Ellis's mother didn't think her daughter should go, didn't think it proper for a girl, but the twins were turning twelve and never got much for their birthdays. Ellis made it clear the drive was all she wanted. When she came down to breakfast that morning her mother put two packages on the table, one in front of Ellis and one in front of

Earl. The siblings looked at each other and smiled uncomfortably at their mother. They both knew it was another diary, but opened their packages feigning surprise. Ellis's package also contained a new pencil. She looked up at her mother.

"Can't be taking ink on a trail drive," her mother had said.

On the trail, Ellis had asked her father why the horses stayed with them. She was warmed by these horseback conversations as her father loaded a pipe, lit it, and smoked as they rode. They were out in the open, she had said, the horses could have run off anywhere, but they stayed together.

"Because horses are herd animals," he said with a smile. "That's what they do."

"But sometimes we have to ride out by ourselves. They don't need the herd then," she questioned.

"Well, now," he'd said, sweet smoke drifting from his lips, "sometimes they do and it'll be hard to get them away from the herd. But if you ride well enough, well, you become their herd and all they want to do is be with you."

"Like when we're working them in the round corral? When they hook-on and follow you like their mama?"

"Yep, just like that." His eyes would sparkle as he looked at his daughter, before he'd tap his pipe clean on his leather chaps, tuck it into his pocket and lope off to circle the herd before making camp.

The young mare named Billie was her father's pride and joy. She was fiery and sturdy built. She was pretty, too. A blood bay with clear black points, she'd dapple in the summer. Of course her father, Thomas Cady, cared more about bloodlines and soundness than color or esthetic appeal. When Billie was just a yearling, she'd taken to following Ellis around. Her father put a stop to it because he didn't want the young horse getting spoiled. Once he started training the horse for riding, she took a little longer on a few lessons than he had hoped. But it was because she was smart, not just stubborn. The one thing that consistently proved problematic with Billie was that she hated being tied. You could leave her untied and just drop the reins and she'd stay there all day if you didn't move her. But tie her to a hitching post and she'd find it in her to leave, every time.

Ellis's guilt at letting the horses go was only overshadowed by her relief that the soldiers left without hurting her or burning the house and barn. She'd pointed a gun at a man, but could she have pulled the trigger? They had looked spent, yet pleased with themselves. Maybe this war was coming to an end like she'd heard. But there was a sorrow or something in that soldier's eyes when he handed her the money. There were words he wasn't saying.

What remained after the soldiers left with the horses, was an emptiness Ellis had never known. Hope faded. Her mother had kept hope alive until it denied her. And then she was gone, too.

~——

ELLIS WOKE SLOWLY, HER FOREHEAD NUMB WHERE IT RESTED on the desk, her ink-stained fingers slipping from the pen. A slight breeze blew the worn curtains on the window. A soft light moved the darkness. In the pastures the gentle wind would be bending the grasses in waves. The waves on the river—Ellis stiffened, more fully awake as worry shadowed her thoughts. The river might be too high to cross now. She should have left sooner. When Prissy's family and the Carters took the riverboat up to St. Louis, they wanted to take Ellis with them. But Ellis wouldn't leave. She still had the horses then and expected Earl would be coming back. She had to be here when he returned. She listened, hearing nothing. Then a breeze stirred the silence—carried a soft nickering.

Ellis stood up so quickly that the chair fell back. She stumbled to the window, her bare feet hardly feeling the floorboards. *Billie!* The mare grazed idly on the resurgent lawn. In that second at the window Ellis felt the warmth of the horse beneath her, smelled her nervous sweat, and heard each word her father had taught her about educating horses and why this young mare was so special to what was to become the Cady brand. She remembered that morning in the barn, before the war took hold, her father had grasped the filly's halter and held Ellis's young hand, declaring, "Here is our genesis."

Ellis stepped into her brother's trousers and tucked in her father's nightshirt. As she quickly descended the stairs, scenes from the past filled her head as they did every morning. Daddy working the horses with Walter and Earl. Mama fixing breakfast. A fog hanging in the woods, cooling the morning, promising a warm day. She shook her head and didn't bother pulling on her boots before she ran out the front door and up to the grazing horse.

Ellis didn't know if the soldiers would take the time to come back for one horse, but she took Billie's return as a sign and thought now was as good a time as any to go. Something stirred her blood. She wouldn't wait any longer. She had to find Earl.

She saddled Billie and packed an extra shirt, some hardtack and dried beef in her saddlebags. She stuffed the money the soldier had paid her in her pants pocket and then thought better of it and put that in the saddlebags along with the few shotgun cartridges she had. Earl had taught her how to make a snare for rabbits and how to fish with just a line and a hook. She added those supplies, and her diary and pencils, before buckling and draping the bags over the back of the saddle. She rolled the old shotgun up in her bedroll and secured it over the bags with the leather saddle strings. When she was done, she stood next to her horse and then looked back at the house. She tied Billie to the hitching post and ran inside and up to her room. She had been wearing her brother's clothes since he left. Somehow it kept him near. She changed out of the night-shirt, holding it up to her face, and hesitating before folding it and placing it on her bed. It still held the scent of her father's pipe tobacco. She donned her trail clothes over her brother's shirt—a wool vest and canvas duster, a yellow neckerchief—and grabbed an extra pair of woolen socks.

She looked around her room, memorizing the scene; the desk, its oil lamp, years of diaries and books read and reread, her bed covered by the quilt the Friends made for her mother when she was pregnant with the twins, the side table next to the bed that her father had hewn from river driftwood, its small drawer lined with letters never sent. She retrieved an envelope from the table, backed out of the room and stepped across the hall to Earl's room. Narrow beds stood against opposite walls. Walter's was made up as if waiting for his return. Earl's looked as if he'd just been there tossing and turning. Ellis straightened Earl's bedding and placed the envelope on his pillow.

*Dear Earl,*
*I'm writing you this letter in case you come back and I'm gone. Used to be everything seemed to last forever and now it seems most folks make different arrangements.*

*I wish you wouldn't have run off like that. It's bad enough Daddy and Walter left us. Well, I hate to say it, but I didn't mind Walter leaving so much. I know he was my brother, too, but he didn't always act like it. Mama's gone. There was no one around to help with the burying. I did the best I could.*

*It's been weeks now since the soldiers took the horses. That happening after Mama died about did me in. But Billie came back and I wonder if somehow Mama had something to do with it.*

*I'm setting out to find you. I don't intend on dying along the way, but if I do, I want you to know you did everything you could to teach me how to take care of myself. I know Mama didn't like it much, you teaching me how to hunt and fish and use a knife, but I think she grew to appreciate it after you all left.*

*Your loving sister,*
*Ellis*

As an afterthought, she lifted the foot of Earl's mattress and smiled at what she found there. Earl had called it a Bowie knife. He had another knife that Daddy had given him, but he had found this one in the river when he and Ellis were cooling off on a sweltering summer Sunday. He made up stories about it, said maybe it belonged to a Pony Express rider, said it was their secret and kept it hidden. Ellis held it in both hands and ran her thumbs over the tooled leather sheath. She looped it on her belt and left the room.

Walking past her mother's bedroom door at the top of the stairs, she paused. Though she had kept the door open, she hadn't entered the room since removing her mother's body. She stepped inside one last time. As tears came to her eyes she noticed an envelope on the floor. She remembered every word of the note inside. She picked it up and put it in her pocket.

Just before she reached the front door Ellis caught her reflection in the mirror. Daddy always said she looked like her mother. Ellis just thought she looked like Earl and since her mother's death, more so. She took off her hat, wound her shoulder-length hair up and put her hat back on, pushing errant locks under it. She smiled at herself and then scowled. She'd have to remember not to smile, but then it probably wouldn't be that difficult.

Outside Billie had pulled loose from the hitching post and was grazing calmly on a patch of grass. Ellis picked up a rein and walked the horse around the side of the house to her mother's grave. It had taken her two days to dig the grave, carry the body from the house and fill in the hole again. But she didn't really remember much about doing it. She took the envelope out of her pocket, remembering the last time she had placed it on her mother's pillow and, this time, placed it by the grave marker under a large rock.

*Dear Mama,*

*I'm writing you this letter in case you wake up when I'm not here and wonder where I am. I went to get the doctor to come help you. I heard he's at the meeting hall, helping folks. I'm taking Billie because she's faster than any of the other horses. I know you don't really like me riding her, but don't worry I've ridden her before. Earl was teaching me without you knowing. Sorry, but I'm telling you now. I'm*

*worried about you, Mama. I'll be back by supper and hope*
*you'll feel like eating something then. I'll read to you from*
*Wuthering Heights.*
*Back soon,*
*Ellis*

The breeze stilled as the sun rose higher through the cottonwoods. Ellis mounted her horse and looked back one last time at her mother's resting place. Billie pranced anxiously. She hadn't been able to find the doctor.

"Sorry, Mama."

*chapter*
# TWO

ELLIS RODE SOUTHWEST, TOWARD THE RIVER AND JACK Carter's place. Billie walked out at a good pace, shying and spooking as normal, Ellis taking it in stride. It was just part of Billie's nature. Ellis hoped the mare would calm down as they went. The girl's lanky body followed the horse's every move, while her thoughts were busy calculating where Earl might be. If he had been trying to trace Daddy's steps, this is the direction he should be returning. He wouldn't know how many families had already left. The Carter farm, if not home, would be his first stop. While Ellis's heart lifted thinking of Earl's return, her body buzzed with anxiety and wariness. She worried about coming across soldiers; fighting. Was she now riding a stolen horse? How could she avoid detection when she wanted, so desperately, to find someone?

By early afternoon, the Carter's log house appeared on the rise over the Tennessee river. Dwarfed by the red barn, positioned even higher on the hill, the house looked diminutive and lonely. Ellis stopped short of the gate to let Billie graze on the early spring grass growing next to the dirt road. Listening for the possibility of company, she heard only the chirp and chatter of distant birds. A ground squirrel dodged across the road and Billie jumped sideways. Ellis picked up the reins and caught herself, sticking to the saddle. She sighed. "A squirrel. What are you gonna do when we meet something really scary?" Though she meant the reprimand lightly, her own words got her thinking about what might lie ahead. She searched down the road, then turned and looked toward the house and barn. She decided to look around this familiar place before moving on.

The barn doors were closed, a weathered board lying across the gap, suspended by wooden hooks. Just to the side of the barn was a small corral and a water trough half full of rainwater. Ellis dismounted, catching her leg on the shotgun wrapped in the bedroll on the back of her saddle. She pondered a better way of carrying the gun without a scabbard and untied it, leaning it against a post of the corral for the time being. She led Billie to the trough where the horse drank her fill, then raised her head, dripping water from her muzzle. Ellis led her into the corral, removed her bridle and hung it on the saddle horn.

"You stay here, I'll be right back. Maybe there's some hay in the barn," she considered as she secured the corral gate.

At the barn doors, she lifted the latch board and tossed it aside. One of the doors swung open part way. Ellis looked around, checking on Billie and glancing toward the house. Though the place was obviously abandoned, Ellis felt she was somehow intruding. She swung the door open farther, wincing at the drawn out screech from the rusty hinges. It opened to a ninety-degree angle before scraping against the dirt and catching. Though the back of the barn disappeared in shadows, the sun now lit the entrance through the open door. The other door opened smoothly, and Ellis hooked the chain keep to the ring on the side of the barn.

Stepping inside, Ellis sighed. The Carters had always kept a neat barn. As kids, she and Earl and Jack would play in here, jumping in the straw, chasing chickens, and petting the milk cows and plow horses. The kids were welcomed, but always made to put things away and sweep up before they left. It looked like the Carters had cleaned up before they left, too. Or someone had.

Ellis checked each stall. Though time had adorned the rafters and walls with dusty cobwebs, and mouse droppings scattered as if punctuation to some irrevocable tale, there were no sounds of life. In the back stall a small pile of straw remained clean and dry. She climbed the ladder to the hayloft and was happy to find remnants of dried alfalfa. She searched through it for signs of mold, but green as clover and sweet-smelling, it would make a fine supper for Billie. She pitched it down to the barn floor. It seemed to sparkle as it fell, the building exhaling a vacant, musty smell as it breathed in the cordial spring air.

Walking toward the house, Ellis turned to check on Billie again. The mare stood, eyes closed, head down, sleeping near the gate of the corral. Ellis watched the horse's sides flex beneath the saddle with each breath. She was glad to have this time in a familiar place before moving on. Neither of them knew what lay ahead. She saw a difference now between horses and people. People worry about the unknown. Horses, in the moment, are peaceful if the moment is peaceful and only worried if the moment is worrisome. She vowed to keep Billie's moments as peaceful as she could.

Ellis climbed the steps to the front porch and hesitated before trying the door. It didn't feel right to walk in to someone's house without an invitation, but she felt foolish knocking on the door of an abandoned home. She knocked anyway, felt a flush of embarrassment, and tried the handle. The door creaked open. "Hello," she called, because she thought she should. The echo of her voice startled her. The dust and cobwebs testified to the house's abandonment as they had the barn's.

The Carter's house was small, one-story, and solidly built from the trees on the property. The front door opened to one large room; the front was used as a parlor, the back as the kitchen. Separate bedrooms had been built onto the house on opposite sides, when Mr. and Mrs. Carter adopted Jack, a young Cherokee boy, just a year older than Ellis and Earl.

Ellis walked through to Jack's room. She wasn't sure what she expected. She remembered the room full of forked branches and pine cones, polished river rocks and mussel shells. He was always carving bits of driftwood into crude animal shapes, wood shavings and sand soiling the colorful blankets on his bed. But all that was gone. As if no one had ever lived here that she knew. Another house, too quiet.

She turned to leave the room, but paused, turned back. She lifted the corner of the mattress. Nothing. "Silly. What were you thinking…" she said to herself. But then she noticed something under the bed, a small box against the wall near the headboard. She crouched down and retrieved a cigar box, blew the dust off the top and opened it. Jack had lived here ten years, she reckoned, and there were ten carved wooden animals in the box. She laid them out on the bare mattress and viewed them as some ornate abacus. Her hand floated above them, touching each lightly: two horses, a dog, fish, cow and a fox; a snake, a cat and two birds.

A horse nickered. *Billie.*

Ellis ran out of Jack's room to the kitchen and looked out the back door at the corral. She listened for any voices or hoofbeats, but heard nothing beyond Billie impatiently pawing the ground. She ventured back outside.

"Stop that. Here, if you're gonna lay down, let me take the saddle off first." Ellis removed Billie's saddle and as she tossed it on the corral rail she caught sight of the tail of a dog or coyote, trotting away toward the river. She'd seen coyotes in the area before, but they usually kept their distance from people. "You scare that away? Good girl." She scratched the horse's sweaty back. As soon as she left the corral Billie laid down and rolled. "You don't seem too worried now."

Ellis's stomach rumbled, reminding her she hadn't eaten since a breakfast of hardtack and dried beef as she was riding. She returned to the house.

Retracing her steps, she walked back into Jack's room and scooped up half of the carvings, putting them in her pocket, replacing the others, and returning the box to its place under the bed. In the kitchen she rummaged through the cupboards, hopeful that something useful had been left behind, but found nothing but a small amount of firewood next to the stove and a wooden water bucket in the sink.

Outside, the afternoon sky was graying. A breeze blew through, announcing rain. Billie pranced around in the corral, throwing her head and whinnying. Ellis knew horses were more sensitive than people to changes in weather, predator threats and the like. But, as her mother once said, horses didn't always discern between a cougar and a kitten. The homestead had been Ellis's only security. But even home hadn't felt safe since the soldiers took the horses. She reckoned Billie was just being a mare. *"Weather changes and spring fever,"* she heard her father say. Maybe the change in the weather had Billie bothered, or she was coming into her spring heat cycle.

"Okay, okay," Ellis conceded. "We'll stay here tonight." She tossed the saddle onto the mare's back and looped a rein around her neck. Her father would not have been pleased with her methods but she was tired and reckoned it easier for Billie to carry the tack. Once the mare was in a stall, she slid the saddle off and placed it on a rack in the tack room, tossing the sweaty blankets on top to air out.

She gathered the alfalfa hay and tossed it into the feed trough in the stall as rain started tapping on the barn roof. Billie seemed satisfied with the hay and being out of the weather. But Ellis was still hungry. She closed her eyes, remembered the squirrel on the road and hunting rabbits near here with Earl and Jack. She reached into her pocket for a scrap of dried beef and sucked on that as she watched Billie chew her hay.

Her mouth watered as she remembered Mrs. Carter's corn bread and stew. She recalled the day she had been watching Earl and Jack "practice fighting." That's what they called it. Sometimes they just wrestled, sometimes they would use a knife or stick, one trying to take the weapon away from the other. Mrs. Carter had come out to the barn and they stopped, running off to the back hay stall. She had asked Ellis to come inside and help with the meal. Though Ellis appreciated the food, she didn't know why she had to help and the boys didn't. But as she was leaving the barn she heard Earl cry out in amazement at something Jack was showing him. She started to go back to where they were, but Mrs. Carter had called to her from the back porch. Later she had asked Earl what it was about. Earl had said it was nothing, just a cache Jack had dug under the floorboards in the back of the barn. "*A cache?*" Ellis had asked. "*Yeah, a hiding place, is all,*" Earl had answered.

Ellis walked toward the back of the barn and into the stall where the straw was piled. She tried to pinpoint where she had heard the boys. Sweeping the straw away from a corner, she tested the boards with her foot. One of the boards felt loose. Kneeling, she pried it up with her fingers. Two more boards came loose and underneath, a space the size of a saddle blanket and about a foot deep, held two tins of beans, one of salt pork, and a tin of corn meal. A torn sack of oats spilled its contents next to a cozy nest of newborn mice; pink, naked and squirming.

Ellis lifted the tins, trying not to disturb the mice. She took off her neckerchief, laid it out, and scooped up as much of the oats as she could, keeping an eye out for the mother mouse. She wondered if there was a father mouse, too. Where was he? She gathered up the oat-filled neckerchief and laid it out in front of Billie. Ellis watched Billie's lips discover and devour every grain. She smiled and rubbed the horse's neck. "You'll be okay here. I'll be back in the morning." Ellis collected the tins and jogged through the rain into the house.

Placing the tins on the kitchen table, Ellis opened the stove door. If she was going to stay the night, she'd want to light a fire. Have a hot meal. She remembered Jack talking about his adoptive parents' room; how Mr. Carter had added a fireplace so Mrs. Carter would be more comfortable. Ellis had never ventured into Mr. and Mrs. Carter's room, and even now felt she was intruding, but she needed kindling and more wood. Their door was closed, and she opened it reverently. The room wasn't much different than Jack's. A little bigger, furnished with a large bed frame, a desk with no chair, and a tall, empty wardrobe. The fireplace centered the wall oppo-site the bed frame. Cold ashes lay thick in the firebox. Ellis knelt and moved her finger lightly through the ash. It was all that remained. She stood and stepped toward the desk, where she opened each drawer in turn. The side drawers were emp-ty. The flat, top drawer stuck and she jiggled it loose, pulling it out farther than she had planned. The back corner hid a small leather-bound bible. Ellis stroked its embossed cover and picked it up. She flipped through the pages, back to front, and the book fell open on the first page of Genesis, where an inscription had been written. It read simply, "I hope you will change your mind."

Ellis stared at the worried writing. Who wrote it? To whom? And why, what did it mean? She wondered if her find-ing it now meant that she should change her mind. But about what? About leaving the homestead? Certainly not about finding Earl.

An eeriness crept over her. Her skin crawled. She snapped the bible closed but kept it and left the room. The house felt unwelcoming to her now. In the kitchen she took off her coat, spreading it on the table. With some urgency she packed the tins of food and the bible in the water bucket, placed the fire-wood on the coat and folded the sides over, tying the sleeves together. She lifted the bundle with one hand, grabbing the water bucket's rope handle with the other, and hurried out the back door.

The rain lifted to a cold drizzle. Ellis pulled the half-open barn door closed behind her, leaving the other open for the little light it afforded. Untying the coat sleeves, she dumped the wood, shook out her coat and, shivering, put it back on. In the center of the aisle she used her knife to dig out a shallow hole in the dirt. She picked up the bible, held it in her hands for a moment, looking out the door up to the gray sky. "I hope I'll be forgiven for finding an alternative use for your word," she mumbled, as she tore out pages, wadded them, covered them with some dry straw and small pieces of kindling. She heard Billie nicker.

"It's okay, girl, I'm staying out here with you." She struck a match and felt the tiny spark of warmth comfort some small corner of her heart.

She kept the fire modest, but enough to heat a can of beans, which she opened with her knife the way Earl had taught her, and set it in the flames. She was too hungry to wait long, and with gloved hands was able to snatch the blackened can from the fire without burning herself. She let it cool for a moment while she fished a spoon from her saddle bags. The tepid beans and hardtack satisfied her, but she thought tomorrow she would hunt. Drinking from her canteen she realized Billie might need more water. She emptied the bucket and looked it over, seeing no gaping holes. At the door of the barn she paused, watching the rain turn to snow. She ran to the trough, dipped the bucket, and saw the shotgun she had leaned there and forgotten. The metal burned cold against her fingers but she grabbed it in one hand, the bucket in the other, and hurried back with the heavy load.

"There you go, girl." She placed the bucket in the stall with Billie. The horse looked at her, sniffed the bucket, and finally drank. Ellis rubbed the horse's neck and warmed her hands under her mane before leaving the stall and settling down by the fire. She leaned against the stall door and spread the blanket close by, hoping the meager heat would help it dry. She took off her hat and closed her eyes, trying to obliterate a desperate feeling of loneliness. Billie hung her head over the stall door and huffed. Ellis felt the horse's breath ruffle her hair. She carefully reached up and touched Billie's nose.

"That's why I'm staying out here with you," she mumbled, as a tear pooled at the corner of her eye.

Though it was only late afternoon, Ellis was exhausted but couldn't sleep. She heard noises at the back of the barn near the hayloft. Then the soft whir of a barn owl. She watched it flit through the shadowed rafters, land on the loft, and fly back up with something in its talons. A mouse. One of the unlucky ones.

Ellis rose quickly, ran back to the cache and peered inside. A beam of daylight struck the hole, just to the side of the mouse nest. The mother lay there with her babies. Ellis sighed, relieved the owl had found some renegade mouse, and replaced the boards.

She found an old rag, shook it out and settled back by the fire to wipe down the shotgun. When she was done, she took her journal and pencil from her saddle bag and found the letter she had started writing to her father. She hoped she'd find him before she ever had to tear these pages from her journal. For now there was nowhere to send them, but a letter made her feel like there could be someday.

*...I'm not sure how to talk about what happened after you and Walter left. For a while things carried on the same. Earl worked the corn fields, Mama tended the garden, I helped them both where I was needed and as I could, but mostly I tended to the horses. We had good, green pastures for them. Sparky and Flame were hearty stock and good behind a plow or wagon. I continued to ride*

*Billie around the fields, fixing fence and moving the cows. I never worked her too hard, like you said, because she was young. Mama didn't want me to ride her at first, she was afraid I'd get hurt on a young, green horse, you know how she was, but Earl thought I could do it and learn a lot on the way. I did that. It's easy to love riding a horse that's well trained. But Billie taught me to sit a horse not yet steady. "If you can sit her shenanigans, you can sit anything," Earl would say.*

*Mama read your letter over and over and always kept it in her pocket. She kept expecting another, or for you and Walter to show up one day. We got word of battles, heard about Franklin, and hoped you weren't there. Prissy's family packed up and headed north. Then other Friends followed. They heard stories about troops coming through and taking their sons. Some of the men just went without being asked. Mama tried to hold on to Earl, but you know how he is. All you had to say was 'don't' and he would. I kept expecting Earl to come home. I hope he found you.*

*Mama got sick. I'm sorry to tell you, Daddy, but she died. She'd been feeling poorly, but still working the garden. I read to her that night. I wasn't sure she heard me, but she kept mumbling, repeating some of the words in the book. She didn't wake up the next morning. A few days later the soldiers came through and took the rest of the horses. I'm so sorry, Daddy. But Billie came back and now we're out looking for you and Walter and Earl.*

*Mama kept saying, "Look forward. Nothin' worth thinking about behind you." How is it I can be looking forward to something and not know what it is? But I do.*

*It's like an itch. It's like knowing the horses need fed and watered. Did you teach me that or did I just always know to do it?*

*Daddy, it was so quiet for so long. I couldn't stay there and just hope, any longer. Though I do still hope and pray to see you again.*

*Your loving daughter, Ellis.*

*chapter*
# THREE

THE NEXT MORNING, ELLIS ROSE AS THE LIGHT CREPT through the barn door. The ground outside proved damp, but the snow had been temporary. It happened in the spring sometimes. She thought about rekindling the fire, but was afraid of staying here too long. She had to move on.

Ellis recalled hunting these trails and woods many times with her brothers and more recently by herself. Herds of white-tailed deer, so plentiful just a few years ago, grew scarce as hungry troops traveled through. A stillness permeated the woods now, in contrast to her childhood memories of chittering birds, cooing doves and human laughter. Even the river seemed to flow tentatively, as if wanting to fade, unnoticed, into the background.

The Carter place had been on the outskirts of land occupied by folks known to her. Once, she and Earl had explored the ruins of the Henshaw place, a half days ride south along the river, from the Carter's. Mr. and Mrs. Henshaw had been the most recent settlers to move out from the east. Word was Mrs. Henshaw had come from wealth and couldn't accustom to the life. She lost a baby and they moved back east, abandoning their land.

Toward late afternoon, Ellis reached the trailhead to the Henshaw homestead. A small covey of quail scattered across the trail. Billie flinched half-heartedly and Ellis praised her. "There you go, good girl," she said, glad that the horse seemed to be calming down. Though the Henshaws never finished their house, she remembered they did have a corral where she and Earl would leave their horses while they hunted and trapped. She urged Billie down the trail. They'd need another place to stay for the night.

As they got closer, the dilapidated ruins of the house came into view. The place looked worse than she remembered. The house itself looked as if it had been purposefully demolished. A partial stone fireplace stood among saplings and weeds, the chimney still reaching twenty feet toward the sky. She and Earl had camped here under a roof and between partial walls. Any boards that had been there then were gone. A corral stood nearby with a few top rails missing and the gate open, daring entry. Billie stopped and raised her head, unsure. A breeze stirred a smell of raw nature and old smoke.

Ellis dismounted and led Billie into the corral. The rails that remained would be enough to contain her, as bluegrass and clover grew inside. She unsaddled and unbridled the horse, tossing the tack onto a low rail, and untied her bedroll which blanketed the shotgun. She fished four brass shells from her saddle bags, all that were left, shouldered the gun and hiked toward the spot where she had seen the quail. Though he'd taught her how to shoot, Earl had usually carried the gun and the heft of it still felt foreign to her.

Walking past the remains of the house, Ellis noticed burnt boards in the fireplace. She wandered up and poked around in the ashes, scattered by rain and wind. She ambled on, past the house, noticing indentations in the tall grass. Tufts of fur stuck to nettles. A wet-dog smell of coyotes. A short squawk startled her and she aimed quickly as three quail took wing.

The discharge of the shot shook her. Its thunder, so much louder than she had remembered, echoed like shattered glass against the silence of this abandoned landscape. One quail dropped, boosting her emotions for a moment; her mouth watering, an iron taste, flavored by the smell of gunpowder. As she retrieved the bird, she heard Billie whinny and hurried back to the corral. Running and bucking in the corral, the horse calmed as Ellis came closer.

"It's okay, girl," she said, looking around. Billie snorted and came up to Ellis. "It's okay, I'm here," she whispered, rubbing and petting her horse's head and neck. Ellis's gaze searched inside the corral. The mare had rolled in two spots, crushing the grass and weeds and gouging the soil where she struck her hooves getting up. She had cropped most of the sweet grass inside, leaving clumps of weeds, and had reached her head through the rails for grass that grew outside the enclosure, losing strands of mane on the rough wood. This evidence told Ellis that Billie had been relatively comfortable. But there was also a beaten path impressed along the rails where Billie had run in circles. At some point she had taken up a nervous posture, not wanting to be alone, or had been frightened by something.

"I'm sorry, girl. It was just the shotgun." Ellis held up the dead quail. "See? You've had your supper, now it's my turn."

Ellis gathered wood, thinking she would start the fire in the old rock fireplace. But the distance away from Billie bothered her. The horse's agitation had triggered a new wariness in Ellis. She stood by the gate looking back at the stacked rock, finally deciding to clear a space next to the corral. She figured smoke would be less obvious from a campfire without a chimney.

Before building the fire she led Billie down to the river to let the horse drink. As she was filing her canteen she spied an old rabbit trail under the brush. She crouched, still, watching but not seeing any sign of movement, and upon closer inspection found no fresh droppings. Though she wasn't very confident about catching one, she decided to set the snare overnight.

ELLIS PICKED AT THE CHARRED QUAIL. SHE ATE PATIENTLY, layer by layer, as she held the skinned and skewered bird over the fire. The meat was peppered with shot, even though she had tried to aim at the head. But she was able to avoid the pellets as she peeled away the sweet-tasting seared meat. Satisfied, she leaned against a corral post, as Billie grazed behind her. Rays of setting sun washed the grasses in a pink glow. She stoked the fire, releasing sparks like summer lightning bugs. As dusk's color faded, an overwhelming weariness wrapped its arms around her as she pulled her blankets close.

Sometime during the night, Ellis thought she heard a strange squeak. Her first thought was of Billie and the hinges on the gate. She wasn't sure if she was dreaming or awake, but she sensed the horse still sleeping behind her, standing, head relaxed, in the corral. Ellis returned to a sound slumber.

The next time she woke to silence. Trees silhouetted against dawn's early morning blush. It seemed as if opening her eyes signaled the birds to morning song. The air was crisp, and she wrapped the warm blankets around her shoulders as she found a place to relieve herself. She saddled and bridled Billie and walked her to the river.

Suddenly Billie startled, planting all four feet as if not knowing which way to bolt. Ahead at the edge of the water, a coyote lapped at the stream while another kept its eyes on the approaching duo. Ellis moved for the shotgun, which she had replaced on the back of the saddle. Untying the bundle, she moved stealthily, not taking her eyes off the pair of coyotes. She cocked the gun, aimed and fired. Billie jerked at the empty click, but the gun had misfired. One of the coyotes grabbed what was left of its furry meal and they both ran off across the stream into the woods. Ellis thought she heard them laughing.

She remembered the snare. The squeak she heard during the night.

"You're welcome!" she yelled at the coyotes. "Enjoy your rabbit stew!" Her voice echoed down the river. Tears burned behind her eyes as she took up Billie's reins. "Probably for the best. Lord knows where you'd be if the gun went off."

Finding the place she had set the snare, she searched but couldn't locate the wires. They could have been dragged anywhere. They might still be on the rabbit. She opened the shotgun and rubbed a finger on the firing pin, noticing the metal was cracked. She checked the shells and found them damp. The rain and cold had taken its toll on the tired firearm. Not wanting any more trouble than she could handle, she laid the shotgun on the ground and covered it with leaves and pine branches. She felt like saying a prayer.

LATE MORNING AND WELL PAST FAMILIAR SURROUNDINGS, Ellis reached a fork in the trail. The wider path provided clear landmarks; rocks, hills, a lone stand of cottonwood. Distance and daylight could be more easily calculated. Time might seem more stable. But a passing notion of finding company gave way to yearning for the security and secrecy of the woods. She didn't know from whom she should hide along the way. So far, the land had seemed deserted. After leaving the Henshaw place, the scattered homesteads she passed lay empty. One looked like the family up and left but could return any moment. Gates were latched on the corrals and barn doors stood open. No noise. No farm chatter. Not even a rooster crowing. Familiar sounds she paid no attention to before, now she noticed missing.

Ellis kept close to the woods and the river. The repetitious days confused her sense of time. She supplemented the preserved food she had found at the Carter's, with small fish; trout and bass, caught with worms easily scratched up from the fertile woodland floor. Daylight focused her attention on riding. She searched for her brother, her father, someone familiar; while hiding from the unfamiliar, from trouble. Each night her mind wandered in the dark; flickering like flames between memories and possibilities. Huddled by the fire she would hold her pencil above the page, waiting to attack a thought, but that enemy never showed and her journal remained mostly empty. Sometimes she would start a letter, as if soon she might have a place to send it, "*Dear Earl,*" but stoking the fire, checking on Billie, quieting her anxious awareness took precedence, bleeding energy from anything but survival.

The warm afternoon found Ellis napping sporadically in the saddle. Billie stopped short. Ellis shook off her drowsiness and searched her surroundings. The horse's neck stiffened and her ears pitched forward, she let out a worried snort. Ellis felt her own nerves catch. She tried urging her horse ahead, but Billie wouldn't take that step and started to back up. Ellis relaxed as much as possible in the saddle until Billie stopped. Dismounting, she rubbed the horse's neck to calm her. The edge of the forest offered a clear line of sight up to a point. Dense trees stood before her, seeming to gather closer the deeper she searched. Ellis watched for movement. The scent of poplar, fir and something she couldn't quite place, something slightly sweet, hung in the still air. Leading her horse, she continued on the trail, trying to keep her nervousness from the reins.

Behind some trees, just ahead, a patch of ground had been cleared. New grass peeked through drying mud left by winter rains; those same rains had washed away the topsoil from shallow graves. Fragments of bone and skull escaped earth's hollow grasp. Unrecognizable as men any longer, soldiers had died here, away from home and family. Ellis thought there were maybe a dozen, but as she walked and coaxed her skittish horse along the trail, the remnants of battle spread like a blighted corn field on all sides of her. Beyond the graveyard, a field of small mounds caught her eye. She squinted, trying to make sense of what she was seeing. A large ribcage, still covered by thin hide. Another and another. She turned her face from the dead horses and watched the ground at her feet as she walked. That pungent sweet smell, like the smokehouse, evoked visions of hanging pork and venison, drying animal hides. She remembered the weary soldiers herding the last of her horses away from home, swallowed by their own dust. She touched Billie's nose. Her stomach lurched as she quickened her step. Earl's ghost stories rang in her ears and she couldn't quite shake the feeling of being followed.

Once past the charnel grounds, Billie seemed calmer and less likely to bolt. Just before mounting, a flash from the side of the trail distracted Ellis. She knelt and picked up a gold button, still attached to a scrap of faded cloth. Along the edge, a thick crust of reddish brown clung tenaciously. Ellis's thumb traced the object, trying to read its story. The cloth was neither blue nor gray. Just faded and torn. If she and Billie had ventured here sooner, would they now be lying beneath the forest floor? And Earl... She suddenly gagged as if the story reached her throat. She dropped the button, wiped her hand on her pants, mounted quickly and loped away until she no longer felt her skin crawling.

Nightfall brought a noisy silence, the stillness interrupted by the crackling of the campfire and her own breathing. The occasional hoot of an owl, normally a melancholy note, played a harsh chord on her nerves as she thought of what might lurk in the darkness. She focused on the small campfire. Staring at the flames dried her eyes, felt like it dried her very soul. Again she tried to write, but her thoughts dulled like the tip of her pencil. She heard her mother's voice but couldn't make out the words, kept trying, forced her hand. She thought of the shallow graves she had passed today, and the one she had dug for her mother. The tip of the pencil broke away. Empty pages reflected her hollow feelings.

Another owl hooted. She jerked awake and stood. Alarmed by the silence, she drew her knife. Earl's knife. Heard the flapping of the owl's wings, his flight swallowed by the darkness.

She sat and sharpened her pencil with the knife, stroke by stroke, enough to make a point without taking too much. Slowly the wood peeled away. The graphite dust blackened the steel of the blade, blew off with a whisper and left no stain.

ELLIS DECIDED TO TRAVEL ON THE MORE OPEN TRAIL THE next day, for a change of scenery if nothing else. Since she hadn't seen another living person since leaving home, she wasn't sure hiding in the woods was necessary. But here, out of the protective cover of trees and bush, blew an incessant wind. She knew she needed to relax but, like the horse, found herself spooked at everything. She longed for the farm. Familiar things. Alone out here, she heard things and saw things and so did Billie. When the horse flinched, she flinched and sometimes the other way around. But they kept going. Movement, travel, made it all more bearable somehow, like they were making progress. Distractions formed a heightened sense of purpose—the cry of a hawk, a breeze tickling cotttonwood leaves, squeaking saddle leather—comforted her.

They hadn't been back on the trail long, but Billie was fidgety and Ellis felt like walking. She stopped the horse, swung her leg over and slid off the saddle. They'd been following the river, the deciduous landscape both familiar and foreign.

"Oh, Billie," she said as her feet hit the ground and she rubbed her horse's neck. "Where on this earth are Daddy and Earl?" She stood and looked into the horse's eye as if waiting for an answer. She saw her own reflection there as her hands soaked up the horse's warmth. Billie nuzzled her. "Daddy always said not to let you horses do that. That you'd get pushy.

But I don't mind so much." She held her hand out to the soft nose and let Billie nuzzle her again, calming them both for a moment. She turned to search the trail ahead and walked on, leading Billie.

Days filled with hours of walking and riding, mounting and dismounting, strengthened Ellis's body and her determination. The forest floor and dusty trail cushioned their steps. Finches and buntings hid on branches in the thickets. The horse's sweat and breath were constant companions. She could taste the pungent pine and oak in the air, and along the creeks the dogwood started to bud. Ellis could feel Billie through the reins as she led her, but now and then she'd glance back, just to make sure the horse's expression hadn't changed. Billie, too, seemed strengthened by the journey and grew more trusting along the way. As sharp as Ellis's senses seemed to be, she knew Billie's were even keener. A horse didn't always see so well, but they could hear and smell things miles away. Survival.

"That's why your ears are so big and your nose so long," she said aloud, just to hear a voice. Billie twitched an ear toward her. Ellis mounted and rode on. As dusk settled she searched for a place to bed down for the night. Easing down a gully, Billie stopped short, flaring her nostrils. Ellis slid forward in the saddle. "What…?" Then she smelled it, too. Something burning. A campfire. She patted Billie's neck to urge her forward and then thought better of it. A campfire meant people, and she longed for people. Good people. But she didn't know if there was anybody left but soldiers. What would they make of her? Blue or gray—did it matter? Would she be safe?

Before she got to the light of the fire she dismounted and tied Billie to a sapling. She edged toward the campsite, hiding behind brush until she saw movement. She ducked down. She could see just one person and a horse. She moved a little closer. A man in tattered clothing huddled close to the fire. She couldn't tell if he was wearing a uniform or discern the color of his clothing. Perhaps he was someone like her, trying to leave the area or find his way home. Dare she believe this could be her brother? Thin, dirty and clutching his side with one hand, he held a stick in the other, poking at the burning wood. Ellis wondered how a soldier could escape the killing fields.

His horse didn't look much better. Still saddled, the animal stood quietly, tied to a bush, grazing his surroundings. Ellis froze, wanting to rush in for the company and run the other way for safety. The horse sensed her presence and let out a low nicker. Unalarmed, the man stood and shuffled to his horse. Ellis could hear him talking to the horse in a low voice, but couldn't hear what he was saying. Then the man reached out and rubbed his hand over his horse's eye. The horse lowered its head.

Ellis remembered watching her father showing her and her brother how to calm a horse by rubbing it and wiping a hand over an eye. Her father had said a horse's thought went to the feel of it and took away the sight of it, which calmed them.

Ellis heard a cracking branch behind her as Billie's whinny flooded the foggy dusk. The horse by the fire answered. Ellis's head snapped back toward Billie and then toward the man at the campfire drawing a pistol and shouting, "Who's there?"

*chapter*

# FOUR

MILES OF DUSTY HOOFPRINTS TURNED TO MUD IN A PASSING spring shower, leading her memories back to the homestead. Warmer days watching her father train colts, bits of their winter coats lofting in the placid air. Sunday afternoons riding to the river with Earl. "Earl!" Her brother's name unfurled from deep inside her gut. She heard the hollow click of the hammer as he pulled the trigger, but the gun was either empty or misfired. He threw the weapon aside and drew his knife. His horse jerked but stayed put.

"Show yourself!" he demanded.

"Earl, is that you? It's me, Ellis." A quick doubt flashed like a spark, but she carefully stepped forward toward the fire. The man kept the knife trained on her. "What…? El… Ellis…?" He stood, squinting, trying to make sense of the hazy image emerging from the campfire smoke. "Is it really you?" He sheathed his knife.

Ellis walked closer to the fire and Earl walked closer to Ellis. "El, what the…what are you doin' out here?" He moved to put his arms around his sister.

Ellis could feel the bones of him through his clothes. As she embraced him she felt him flinch, but they held on tight to one another.

Her muffled words fell on his shoulder. "You feel like you haven't had a meal for a while." She thought she heard Earl sob and he hugged his sister harder. Ellis closed her eyes for a moment to relish her brother's embrace. The sight of him drawing his pistol, the sound of the vacant click, flashed in her mind. She opened her eyes and her gaze fell to his empty holster.

Earl put his hands on her shoulders and held her at arms length. "What are you doin' out here? Why'd you leave the farm? Ma must be worried sick." He stopped. He saw it on her face. "What's happened, El?"

Ellis couldn't stop staring at Earl. Dirt filled deep lines on his face. His eyes were those of an older person. His youth had been sharpened like his breath. He looked sickly…like those last days. He looked like Mama.

"Mama…died," she uttered slowly, watching Earl's face. His expression stayed the same. Sad and troubled.

"How?" But Earl knew the answer to his question.

"When you never came back it was just me and Mama working the farm, taking care of the horses. You know how sickly she was. How she acted crazy sometimes. I guess that's why you left, but…" Images of the past few months mixed with the emotion of seeing her brother again. Words caught in her throat and escaped through silent tears. Her voice cracked. "I took care of her best I could. I tried…I…"

"Oh, Elli." Earl again wrapped his arms around his sister.

Something cracked behind the trees and Earl pushed Ellis behind him and again drew his knife.

A horse nickered and his nickered back.

Ellis put her hand on Earl's arm. "Earl, put your knife away. That's just Billie," she said. Billie stepped in closer and put her head down. Earl walked toward the horse, picking up his discarded pistol on the way and holstering it.

"Billie? Our Billie?" he asked.

"The army came through again. After that first time. After Mama died. And took the rest of the herd, even Billie. But seems she escaped. She came back to the farm."

Earl stepped up to the bay mare and rubbed her neck. "Never could keep her tied," he smirked as he admired her. Ellis looked down at the ground and then up at Earl. "Do you know where Daddy and Walter are?"

Earl hesitated, bowed his head. "I found Walter after I got swept up in some fighting out by Pickwick. He wanted me to go home but I didn't want to leave him and he wasn't sure which would be safer." Earl paused, sighed. "He caught a bullet, but he kept fighting." Earl stepped back to the fire and sat next to Ellis on a log. His hand moved to touch his ribs. "We ended up in a camp where, hell, it was bloodier there than—" Earl's speech slowed, his eyes fixed on the fire. A vacant gaze. "—on the battlefield." He stopped himself and looked at Ellis, then at Billie. "Shit, El, you don't need to hear this."

"Go on," muttered Ellis. She'd seen what war could do.

Earl took a breath. "Walter got sick. He died, El. We buried him at Shiloh."

Ellis watched her brother slowly shake his head. She thought there might be a lot more he wanted to say. His eyes focused on the night, and dark yesterdays.

"What about Daddy?" asked Ellis.

"I don't know. Walter said they got separated a few weeks in. He heard Pa got sent east. I don't know why. You know he wouldn't fight. I heard there was more fighting there than we saw, and we saw plenty. I don't know, El." Earl bent forward to toss another log on the fire, and grimaced.

"Are you all right?" asked Ellis, glancing at the side he'd been holding when she came across him.

Earl straightened, put a hand to his ribs again and stood up to stretch. "I'll be okay." He tried to smile. "But what am I gonna do with you?"

"What do you mean? I'm goin' with you wherever that is, I guess."

"Elli…" Earl shook his head.

"What? You gonna tell me it's too dangerous?" Ellis stood, picking up a twig, pointing it for emphasis. "I've been riding for weeks looking for you and Daddy." She broke a piece off the twig and threw it to the ground. "Were you even on your way home? To me?" She broke the twig in two and threw it into the fire. She looked around in the darkness. "Where are we?"

Earl stepped toward her, put his hands on her shoulders. "I was, Elli. I was on my way back to make sure you were all right. I swear."

Ellis shrugged his hands off halfheartedly. Earl dropped his hands but didn't move away. Ellis reached out and touched her brother's chest, just over his heart.

"I'm so tired," she sighed.

Earl took Ellis's hand and hugged it to his chest. "Look, I think we're pretty safe here tonight. Let's talk more about this in the morning." He looked up at the horses, now standing together. "Looks like Billie and Smokey are getting along." Ellis looked over at her bay mare and the gray gelding standing calmly together. She raised her eyebrows. "Smokey?"

"No, it's not our Smokey, but I thought he looked a bit like him. And it reminded me of home calling him that. I got him off a dead Reb…" Earl frowned and seemed sorry he'd said that.

Ellis gave Earl's hand a squeeze and moved toward the horses. "I'll unsaddle Billie."

"No need." There was an abruptness in Earl's command. "That is, you best just leave her saddled. In case we have to leave fast."

"I thought you said it was safe here." Ellis sensed something was very different about her brother.

"Safer than most, maybe, but Elli, no place is safe in this country anymore." He looked proudly at his sister. "Seems you're strong enough to know that, now."

Ellis took the look as condescension. "Earl Zephyr Cady, I'm the same age as you and you know it. Just because I'm a girl…"

"Which no one would ever know looking at you in those duds. Is that my shirt?"

"No, it's one of Walter's. I couldn't work the farm in dresses and sure didn't want to ride out here in one."

"Yeah. You'll be better off that way." His smile turned to a grimace. "Did you happen to bring a gun?"

"The only gun left in the house was Daddy's old shotgun. I left with it, got some quail, but Billie about went crazy. Then it misfired when I went after a couple of coyotes that stole my snared rabbit." She didn't want to tell Earl she'd left it out in the rain. "Only had two damp shells left. I didn't want the trouble of it." She looked at the ground. "I kept thinking of Mama. You know how she felt about guns." She looked at her thin brother. "You eating okay?"

"Still got some deer jerky. Snared a rabbit, squirrel. Caught a fish yesterday."

The twins looked at each other, each with a different untold story they were too tired to tell.

Ellis untied her bedroll and saddle bags and loosened Billie's cinch. She looked over at Smokey and saw some dried blood at the side of his mouth, maybe from a hard jerk on the bit. He looked like a gelding of some breeding, though he was boney and lack-luster. Ellis took off Billie's bridle and hung it from the saddle horn. She tied one end of a lead rope around the mare's neck and the other to the same branch Smokey was tied to. She spread her blankets, dropped the saddlebags, and sat on the ground next to her brother, leaning against a log.

"Billie looks pretty good," Earl said. "A little on the thin side, but nothing like the bags of bones the Rebs are using. Now the officers, they take pretty good care of their mounts. They rotate them and let them rest. But the soldiers—they just keep moving."

They sat in silence for a few minutes, watching the fire. Earl glanced over at the horses. Billie was grazing, already untied from the branch.

"Why do you keep tying her up when you know she's just gonna pull loose?"

Ellis smiled, absentmindedly picked up a stick, scribbled in the dirt by her feet. "I overheard Mama and Daddy, once. Mama seemed upset about something one of the young horses had done. She said she felt like takin' a two-by-four to the colt.

Knock some sense into him. Daddy said, 'Mother, you can't force education. You just have to be consistently persistent.'"

Earl chuckled, sighed. "Yeah, I remember him saying that a lot."

"Well, I know Billie doesn't like to be tied, I'm just trying to be '*consistently persistent.*'" Earl joined his sister saying the last two words.

Earl smiled and looked at Ellis.

Ellis looked back at him. She thought she saw that familiar twinkle, a devilish spark, in his eyes. She tried to stay there, not look at the rest of him, the aged whole. She looked away, down at her boots, threw the unproductive stick to the side. "Yeah, well, turns out Mama wasn't talking about a horse." She looked sideways at her brother and he looked back at her. They smiled in tandem.

Earl chuckled and nudged his sister. "Hey, still writing in your diaries like you used to?"

"Well," said Ellis, extracting a worn journal from her saddlebags. She yawned, flipped through the pages. "After Mama died I had a hard time. It was hard to write, you know?" Earl looked at the ground, nodded. "But I started writing letters to you all. Here's one for you." She handed the open journal to Earl. As she watched him reading, she grew weary, her eyes heavy. Here, with her brother, she felt more at ease than she had in a long time.

*Dear Earl,*
*I can't believe you left us! Mama tells me to write to get my feelings out, well, I guess I really need to write this! I want to say I hate you for leaving, but I know you were itching to go for a long time. It's just you left me and*

*Mama here alone! You said it wouldn't be for long and it better not be. Right now I hate you, Earl, but, mostly, I miss you.*

*Your angry sister, Ellis*

"Ha…yeah, sorry Elli. Really, I thought I'd be able to find Pa in a day or two. I thought they'd be on their way back and I'd run into them on the trail and make you and Ma so happy to see us all back again." Earl sighed. "I thought I'd be the hero." He paused and a pained look shadowed his face. "I was on my way back when I got swept up in a sea of cavalry. I can't explain how it happened, but it was like I was riding along and a storm came up behind me and the next thing I knew I was in the middle of it." Earl looked down and shook his head.

Ellis moved closer to him. Touching, side by side.

"I didn't even know who we were fighting. Everybody's clothes were so dirty and faded you couldn't tell who was who. I just kept my head down and tried to stay to the back. They shot my horse out from under me, which might've been for the best 'cause I was able to fall back and hide." Earl looked at his sister. Her eyes were half closed, but her brow wrinkled. "It wasn't Blaze. I lost him a few days before. He might be roamin' around out there, still." Earl looked at Ellis again. She closed her eyes and swallowed hard. "I was out of lead and had nothin' to fight with but my blade…I…" Earl stopped. "I never joined up, El, I was just…" Earl slumped, empty of words. Silently, they faced the fire and soon Ellis's head bobbed against Earl's shoulder. He moved carefully, covered her with her bedroll blanket, stoked the fire, and then sat down beside her, picking up the journal that fell from her hand. He carefully plucked a pencil from her breast pocket and pulled his own blanket over the both of them.

*Dear Elli,*

*Forgive my writing. Haven't done much of it for a while. I tried keeping a journal when I first left. For a few days it kept me company. I dreamed of finding Pa and Walter. We'd ride home and you and Ma would meet us and I would let you, only you, read about my adventures. But after a while one day just faded into the next. Cold mud at our feet, the ever-present smell of gunpowder and worse. There's no silence anymore. My ears ring with the screams of bullets, dying horses and men. We walked, rode, fought. Seldom did we eat or sleep. I don't even know if I escaped or got lost. One day I just found myself on my own. I look at you now and think about that day I found you and Walter at the river. You in that pretty dress Ma had made you. I know you hated it, but didn't let on for her sake. The way you were yelling at Walter and hitting him. Something bubbled up inside me from a place I didn't know was there. I never thought I'd punch my own brother, but something was wrong and you were mad, so I had to be, too. The next day Pa and Walter left. I didn't know what to make of it all, and you and me never talked about it. When I found Walter, he tried explaining. He wanted you to know he never meant to hurt you. I remember saying, "She knows how it works, Walter, she's grown up on a farm." But right about then the fighting started and me and Walter were in the thick of it together. We ended up at the field hospital and never spoke of it again. When you're in a place like that, it's hard to remember anything that happened before. You just get lost in the nightmare, trying to find a reason to breathe. These are things I don't know if I'll ever be able to say to you. So I'm writing them here in the back of your journal. Maybe you'll find this later. Maybe we'll be able to talk about it someday. But I want you to know I'm so glad you found me. Even now. You brought me back home.*

Earl lay next to his sister. They had been born together, grown up together. No mean thoughts or feelings about her would ever enter his mind. He turned to look at her sleeping, the firelight playing off her face. He reached up and touched her hair, wiped his thumb against her cheek.

He tucked the blankets around her before bedding down on the other side of the campfire.

*chapter*
# FIVE

Just before dawn Ellis woke to a familiar smell. Earl crouched by the small fire. He held a tin cup in one hand, poked at the fire with his knife in the other. He looked up when she stirred and offered her a cup of coffee. The aroma of the brew reminded her of the cattle drive when Daddy first offered it to them. They hadn't appreciated the taste then, but they drank it just the same. She remembered Earl back at the farm, after Daddy left, trying to help by making breakfast for her and Mama. She and her mother never had the heart to tell him his coffee was awful. They would just look at each other, take the cups he offered, and choke it down.

"Do you still drink this stuff?" Earl queried as he held out the cup.

"Yes." She didn't expect much, but she was delighted to have real coffee and wondered where he got it. "But I ran low on coffee a while back. Had to cut it with chicory and then ran out of that, too." She put on her hat, tucked her hair and welcomed the cup Earl offered. She sipped the hot beverage. The familiar bitter taste and the heat soothed her as she breathed in the cool morning air.

"If you're going to ride with me, you're gonna look the part," Earl said. He pointed his knife at her, rose and stood there staring. Something in his gaze unnerved her.

"What?"

"You got your hair tucked under that hat. But if your hat comes off, and it might, you don't want to be found out that easy. They might take you for a Jayhawker, but might not. Come here." He stood by a tree stump and motioned for her to sit.

Ellis took off her hat and stepped toward the stump. "What's a Jayhawker?" she asked.

"Renegades. Wear their hair long and their guns cocked. They say they'll cut their hair when the war's won." Earl chuckled and then got serious. "I met a few that were gentlemanly, but others that were mean son's of bit…well, were down right mean."

Ellis had no fondness for wearing her hair long. It got in the way of work. She always kept it tied up or stuffed under a hat. When her mother got sick and didn't know the difference, Ellis would tie it in a ponytail when it was long enough and cut it off with her mother's scissors.

"You ever cut hair before?" she asked.

"Sure. Cut my own a time or two."

Ellis looked at her brother's disheveled head. "That ain't sayin' much."

Earl smirked, ran a hand through his hair. "Sit." He pointed to the stump with his knife.

Ellis sat on the stump in front of Earl, sipping her coffee as he cut. She could hear the knife blade rip through her hair. It pulled and smarted now and then, but something about it felt good, too. She stared at the waning campfire.

"Earl, Mama started telling me the story again about how she named us. She'd been poorly and hadn't talked much for days, and then just started talking like she was at a Sunday meeting."

Ellis had heard it before. The children were given middle names matching the four elements: Walter Hill Cady, Earl Zephyr Cady, Ellis River Cady.

"Do you think she was sad about not having a fourth baby?"

Earl smiled, "I asked Pa about that once. Know what he said? He says, 'Earl, your mother named the first colts born on our place. Three of 'em. Guess which ones.'"

Ellis thought back to the older horses at the homestead. "Blaze…Flame…"

"And that crazy pony they gave you…"

"*Sparky!*" they chimed in unison and laughed.

When Earl was done, he pulled a small piece of broken mirror out of his saddlebag and held it up for her. From what Ellis could see, he had done a good job with the knife. The clothes she was wearing and the short hair made her look like Earl's identical twin. Her otherwise sullied appearance added to the disguise. She stood and ran her fingers through her hair, shaking out the loose strands, then smoothing it back she replaced her hat. She looked at Earl watching her with a smile on his face.

"You'll do. Come on, then." He gathered up the hair on the ground and tossed it into the fire. It sizzled and smelled, reminding Ellis of graveyards and branding calves. Earl wiped out the tin cups and handed Ellis some deer jerky he had stowed. He kicked dirt on what was left of the fire, stirred it around with his knife and kicked more dirt on it.

They tightened the horses' cinches and Ellis bridled Billie. Earl mounted Smokey and started out.

"Hey, where you going?" asked Ellis.

"We're heading west," ordered Earl.

"West? Why? I thought we'd go north or maybe east to find Daddy, or…home…" said Ellis.

"El, we can't go that way. I'm hoping Pa will come find us, but there's still fighting going on there. I've seen enough. We've got to get across the Mississippi."

"The Mississippi? How are we gonna do that?" Ellis didn't understand and sure didn't want to get that far from home now that she had found Earl. "Can't we just go home?" But she knew they couldn't, saw it in her brother's eyes. She had left because the fires were coming closer. She doubted there was anything left to go home to by now. She'd have to make her home with her brother. Wherever they could.

Earl looked at her, paused, then moved his horse forward. "Let's go," he said.

Morning light began to filter through the trees. The day dawned through a weary mist.

They rode most of the day at a slow but steady pace. Smokey continued plodding along, as enervated as Earl. Billie stayed behind them, almost too close. Now and then Smokey would pin his ears, but he never offered to kick. Ellis would pull Billie up a little, but the young mare kept creeping up on Smokey's tail, in need of support, Ellis thought. When the trail widened they rode side by side and the two horses kept pace well.

Billie slowed, put her head up and pricked her ears forward. Something or someone was up ahead. Earl stopped short about the same time Ellis heard muffled voices. Earl motioned to Ellis to be quiet and move off the trail. They dismounted and led the horses deeper into the brush. They waited silently and hoped the horses wouldn't give them away by nickering to other horses. Ellis imagined the trouble Earl could be in should any soldiers find him—the Union thinking he was a Confederate soldier and the Confederates thinking he deserted with one of their horses. And as willing as Earl had been to keep her in disguise, now they would see her as a soldier if she wasn't discovered as a girl. Neither of those revelations would end well.

Through the rhododendron and blackberry they could see a group of three men on foot. They wore dusty blue uniforms and carried rifles, two with bayonets attached.

With a finger to his lips, Earl again cautioned Ellis to be quiet. Agitation at her brother's bossiness wrestled with acknowledged fear for their safety. Her skin hurt.

The group of soldiers kept walking. Ellis heard one of them say, "I thought the war was over. Where are we going?"

Ellis silently turned to her brother, his expression dire, unchanged. Had she heard correctly. Did the soldier say the war was over?

"We're supposed to meet up with the regiment at Brownsville. You wanna get paid, don't ya?"

"Sure do. I'm gonna get back home and marry that girl, Virginia."

"Marry? What do you want to marry her for? You'll get all tied up with that rich family and end up having to do what her Daddy wants you to do."

"Naw, I'll have my own place and we'll be going there. I'm gonna raise some cattle...and some kids!" They all laughed and kept talking, making too much noise to hear Billie's low nicker. Ellis stroked Billie's nose to calm her, but kept watching the men. One of them seemed to look right at her. She couldn't see his face, but his hat was different than the caps the others wore. It had a full brim, one side pinned up with a metal ornament.

"Did you hear something?" he asked the others. They stopped, tightened grips on their weapons. A crow flew over the brush toward the men.

"Don't be wastin' your lead on a crow there, Wilson." The men laughed anxiously and moved on.

When they couldn't hear the voices any longer, Ellis followed Earl out of their hiding place. They mounted up and continued on the trail.

"We'll have to keep an eye out for more of them if they're meeting up in Brownsville. We need to get to the river and find a good place to cross," said Earl.

"Earl, didn't you hear? They said the war was over. We could go home. Maybe Daddy…"

"Yeah, I heard. But there's folks out here that haven't and they're not gonna take our word for it. Let's go."

———

A DEEP RUMBLE SCATTERED A FLOCK OF PARTRIDGE. BILLIE shifted sideways, Ellis gripped with her legs. "Shit, Earl, what was that?" They saw movement in the trees; men running.

"Cannon. Here, take this." He handed her a pistol from the back of his belt.

"What about you?" Ellis questioned. Looking at the gun, she winced. "Are there bullets in this?"

"One. I found it in my bedroll this morning." The horses pranced in panicked excitement. Earl reached behind him in his saddle bags and came up with another service revolver and a leather sheath. He tucked the revolver in his belt, checked the one in his holster, and tied the extra knife onto the front of his saddle.

"Where did you get that?" asked Ellis.

"Never mind." He paused a second. "Do you know how to use that?" he asked, nodding to the pistol.

"Well, I used to carry one hunting, you know that."

"Yeah but have you ever used it?"

"Well..."

"I mean on a person."

Ellis looked stricken, but resigned. She remembered the soldiers at her front door. "I guess I can if I have to." She looked at her brother and pulled the Bowie knife out of the sheath on the back of her belt. "I also have this."

Earl looked at his sister, smiled weakly and nodded. "Yeah, you'll be okay." Another loud boom and some rapid gunfire drove them into the woods. The brush grew too thick to pass. They found a good place for the horses where they wouldn't be discovered and tied them, hoping they would stay there, but aware they may not be able to keep them near if the fighting came their way. Earl pointed at a tree hollowed out by a wildfire. "There, you get in there and stay still. Don't come out until you hear the fighting's gone past, understand?"

"But..."

"You look like a soldier, Elli—no more than another target."

"What about you?" Ellis asked, her voice now fearful.

"I'll find another one. I'll find you after this is done, you hear? Stay there." Earl ran off and Ellis heard the pop of the intermittent gunfire coming closer. The dusky woods fogged over the nightmare. For a moment, quiet. Then, like an approaching storm, the shouting and gunfire intensified. The smell of sulphur and sweat in the foggy air engulfed her. She tried to sink deeper into the tree, imagining she was invisible and safe in its dim decay. She thought of Billie and hoped just this once she'd stay tied and out of harm's way. Noises echoed in her head. Then quiet again, like a train gone by. She stayed still and held her breath to listen. A twig snapped to her left. She inhaled sharply, hoping she hadn't made the sound.

She heard water running, and a grunt. She turned her head slowly and through a hole at the bottom of her hiding place, two boots appeared under the lower half of a male body. From her crouched position she could only see this half of him, his male part free from the confines of his trousers. When she realized how close he was, she tried to quietly shrink back, but it was too late. He saw her. She smelled urine. Not attempting to put himself back together, he pointed his revolver at her and said, "Come out of there now or I'll shoot!"

She tried to will herself to move or speak, but couldn't. She heard a gun discharge nearby, commanding the man's attention. He must have looked up and she felt herself move, twitch, nothing more. Another shot rang out. The man twisted and dropped. She looked at her hand, holding the smoking pistol, the one Earl had given her. What had she done? She heard only distant gunfire now. Her legs tingled. She crawled out of the tree stump and looked at the dirty blue uniform, the muddy boots. His hat clung to his head, its brim pinned on one side with a brass eagle. Her ears rang.

"Good shot, boy!" crowed a man walking toward her. Where had he come from? "Come on, let's go!" The man pushed her forward, but she stopped herself; stepped back to the dead body, unable to take her eyes off the hat, but not looking at the dead boy's face. She watched her hands reach down and pull a tin portrait from the brim. On the back, the name Virginia. *"...I'm gonna get back home and marry that girl, Virginia."* Her hands tucked the portrait in her shirt pocket as she joined a herd of mangy soldiers stomping through the woods.

Where was Earl? She had to find him. Had to find the horses. She stepped over and around bodies. Some wore rumpled blue or gray uniforms, others did not. Here on the spent battlefield they lay together, as if in death they got along. She searched vacant faces and bloody clothing for Earl, and was relieved not to find him. Had he really escaped? They all looked alike. Dirty, tattered, stained. Some of the soldiers scavenged through the remains, taking weapons and ammunition. She saw bullets; on gun belts, in dead hands. And like she was watching someone else, she started gathering what she could; loading her gun and putting extra ammunition in her pockets. How would Earl find her?

"Over here, boys," said the man. A group gathered. "Who we got left?" he asked, but didn't care about an answer. Some of them seemed to know one another, some didn't. They were talking nervously. Sometimes giggling. Two of the boys were talking as if they were waiting for the schoolhouse doors to open; wild-eyed, eagerly telling tales.

"We got a place a couple miles up," one of them said. "Just me and my Ma left. Heard about Yanks coming through here and decided to join in. My brother's out there somewhere, fightin'."

"Who's your brother?" one of the others asked.

"Jeb Williams," he answered.

"Never heard of him," the other mocked, and a few of the others laughed.

"If he was south of here and not with us, he's either dead or skedaddled. Either way he's dead," another said. Some grumbled.

Ellis kept quiet. She wanted to run away; she had never felt more like running, but knew she couldn't. She felt gritty, sick. She was terrified of being found out by these foul men, and horrified to be one of them. She stared at the ground, watched a black beetle crawl toward the shelter of a rock. But images of hands holding guns, the smell of urine, hot metal and gun powder; were clearer in her mind than the struggling insect on the ground. She tasted fear and betrayal. She thought of Walter that day by the river, years ago. What he was telling her—showing her—and how Earl had stopped him.

She had always fought to be on equal ground with her twin brother, but it was true; Earl had always protected her. Now she didn't know where he was or if he was even alive. She had to trust he'd find her. They'd find each other. If she ran from these men they'd shoot her for deserting. If she revealed herself as the only girl in the camp, well, she'd heard their rude talk.

"I think we can head back down now," announced the sergeant. "We chased most of them back and we should be just about at the border. Let's go."

The men collected their gear; hunting rifles, canteens and bedrolls. Ellis's only option was to follow them. Maybe somewhere along the way she'd fall back and be able to find Earl. Maybe he had the horses. She walked on, her feet marching forward, her thoughts drifting.

She stayed to the back as much as she could. Didn't talk to anyone, though she realized some of these boys weren't much older than her—their whiskers not yet visible, some voices not yet changed—a ragged Confederate regiment comprised of children now aged too quickly.

She remembered a red fox in the woods where she played when she was little. She watched it raise a family of kits and teach them to hunt. One night the fox got into the chicken coop. The next night Daddy and Walter camped out with shotguns. Ellis cried, watching out her bedroom window. Mama tried to explain to her the fox had to go. Once the fox had a taste for blood, it wouldn't quit until it got them all. It was either the fox or the chickens.

chapter

# SIX

ELLIS'S BODY ACHED. EXHAUSTION ACCOMPANIED THE troops' footsteps like a fog, the silence broken only by an occasional clank of metal on metal, an empty canteen swinging into a rifle barrel. No one spoke during the long trek back to a clearing in the woods. There, a wagon leaned against a tree, its team of horses long gone, one wheel shattered, leaving that corner to droop down into the weeds. A couple of the men threw back its canvas cover while others kindled the fire and set up a metal tripod holding a large cast iron pot. Ellis witnessed everything in slow motion. She lowered herself onto a tree stump and watched as corn and potatoes from the wagon were peeled, cut and tossed into the pot.

As the ringing in her ears subsided, the muffled voices of the men mingled with her muddled thoughts. The voices grew louder as her hearing returned to normal.

She counted thirty-two men, most of them not much older than her and Earl. They squatted near the fire and slumped onto bedrolls. A few were being bandaged and tended to by others while some were left to stanch the blood of their own wounds. Few spoke, but they swore and belched and farted offering no excuses.

The captain, she guessed about Walter's age, was the only one mounted during the foray, though he had walked his horse once the battle ceased. Four gaunt pack-horses stood tethered to a rope strung between two trees. The Captain untied a worn flour sack from one of the packs and poured grain into muzzle feeders for the horses. He tossed a couple of handfuls and some water into a small bucket and carried it over to the fire where he added the mix to the black cook pot.

Ellis's gaze fell back on the horses. She closed her eyes and prayed that Earl had found Billie and Smokey. She was certain Billie would not have stayed tied where they left them. Not this long. But if Smokey had, maybe she'd stayed with him. She had to believe it. Nothing would assuage her guilt if anything happened to Billie.

A weathered soldier declared the stew done by ladling it onto tin plates and into cups. Each man stepped toward the fire to claim his share and a piece of stale bread. Ellis got in line, kept her head down, away from the light of the fire. The stew smelled good and didn't taste bad, though it was hard to guess the ingredients in the lumpy brown mud; potatoes and small bits of meat. The meal emboldened some of the soldiers to conversation.

"Did you find water?" a soldier asked another.

"Yep, a stream about a quarter mile west."

"Hey, where's Jimmy?" asked another of the soldiers.

"I don't know," said another. "I don't know who's here anymore and who's not." He took a bite, spoke with his mouth full. "I hate leavin' the field like that. Where we can't even bury 'em, you know?" He shook his head, swallowed. "It's not right."

"Yea, Captain doesn't even call roll anymore. What's the point."

"I just keep wakin' up wonderin' if I'm dead or alive." He looked down at his plate. "It's hell either way." Some of the soldiers chuckled at that.

Ellis kept glancing up, searching the faces, none of them Earl. She hoped she hadn't missed him in the mud of the battlefield. But she felt he was alive. He was out there looking for her, but she was too tired to figure out how to get to him tonight. She finished her meal and wiped out her cup with the last bite of bread. Blankets were rolled and stacked by the wagon. She wondered about the fate of the soiled wool's previous owner as she took one.

She searched for a place to bed down on the perimeter of the camp, as far as she could without looking suspicious, though she noticed most of the men were either already asleep or lost in a private world the size of their blanket. She walked past a soldier leaning against his bedroll, writing on a scrap of paper with a stub of a pencil. Another soldier gingerly unfolded a worn letter as if he was afraid it would crumble to pieces and blow away.

A man with a bandaged head looked around shyly before taking a small picture out of his shirt pocket. Ellis looked down so as not to intrude. She touched the picture in her own pocket and removed it as she dropped her bedroll and sat down. She held the piece of tin, searching the face of a young girl, long hair, fancy dress, a smile of privilege. *Why had she taken it?* she wondered. She looked up and saw the soldier, still holding his portrait, looking at her. His eyes found his picture again for a moment, and then looked back at Ellis. One side of the young man's mouth twitched a fast smile which faded quickly into melancholy. He nodded, and laid down, putting the picture in a vest pocket and placing his hand there, over his heart.

Ellis nodded back and returned Virginia to her pocket. She started to lay down, but a ghostly chill crept up her spine. She glanced quickly in the other soldier's direction making sure he was really there. He snored softly.

Ellis couldn't remember ever feeling so spent. Her body, mind and soul begged sleep. She laid down, closed her eyes. Exhaustion engulfed her, but sleep refused the reluctant soldier. In that twilight between wakefulness and dreaming, memories seemed the only safe haven.

THE CADYS ONLY WENT TO CHURCH ON SPECIAL OCCASIONS. It was a long ride into town, but Ellis's mother always made sure they rested some on Sundays. They would get up early to tend the livestock, then on warm summer afternoons Ellis and Earl would head west to the river, sit under the big oak tree and contemplate that wide expanse of water.

"You think the horses could swim across?" Earl said one day. He looked at Ellis as if he already had the answer.

Ellis looked at the horses' big bodies and skinny legs, sharp hooves. "I don't think they're built for it exactly."

"But?" he jeered.

"Well, but we're not exactly built for it either, are we? And we swim."

"Exactly!" Earl jumped up and started unsaddling his horse.

"What are you doing?"

"Goin' swimming."

Ellis wondered what Daddy would say about her taking his young mare into that muddy river. But Earl's enthusiasm was contagious and Ellis's curiosity spurred her to unsaddle Billie.

"At least if you fall off here, it'll be a water landing," Earl taunted and jumped on Flame bareback.

Ellis had ridden bareback plenty but not on Billie. She really wasn't supposed to be riding the spooky young horse at all. A saddle at least gave her some stability. Although her father knew she'd been sneaking in some rides and thought it good for both of them, her mother wanted to keep her daughter safe and reasonably intact for marriage.

Ellis led the unsaddled mare up to a rock to climb on gently and not frighten her right from the start. Easing down onto her back she used the reins to turn her head both ways just to make sure she was still relaxed enough. Then she followed Earl to the river's edge.

It didn't take much coaxing for Earl to get Flame into the river.

"You've done this before," Ellis said.

"Yeah, once or twice, with Jack," Earl teased.

Billie had walked easily toward the water, but the soft mud and sand under her feet at the water's edge made her unsure. As Flame entered, the water splashed at her legs. Billie jerked to a stop. Ellis pitched forward, but caught herself.

"Come on, girl, you can do it," Ellis coaxed. Billie took a step forward and then one backward. Ellis held on tight to the horse's mane, let the reins slack and rubbed Billie's neck. She tried to calm her own body like her father had taught her. Flame waded into the water, up to her belly now, and as much as Billie wanted to follow, she was nervous and twitchy. Ellis's father had told her it was like that with horses sometimes.

They saw things differently or maybe they saw them more clearly. Maybe to Billie it looked like the river was swallowing Flame, or had bit off her legs, at least. Up to her knees in the river, the mud giving under her feet, Billie started to act up.

"Hang in there, El," called Earl. He was watching them as Flame stood still in the river.

Ellis coaxed and kicked and pushed at Billie and she finally took another step forward. Earl moved Flame forward and suddenly they were swimming.

"There's a hole here where they can't touch bottom. No time to write a letter, it's sink or swim, sis. You can do it!" Earl swam Flame across the hole and walked her out onto a sandbar.

Ellis sensed Billie's dilemma. She didn't want to be left behind, but she didn't know she could swim. It was up to Ellis to help her make up her mind.

"C'mon," Ellis urged and kicked with all she had. Ellis felt Billie gather herself up and after a split second's hesitation, explode into the water, smack in the middle of the hole. They sunk in over their heads and then bobbed up, Ellis's legs still hugging the horse, her hands still tangled in her mane. She could feel every contraction and twitch of the big horse's muscles. A few more strokes and they both calmed into the flow, the horse pawing with her front and kicking with her back. Soon she was able to touch bottom again and walked out to where Earl and Flame were. For a minute they just stood there dripping.

"Gee, you should've seen that!" Earl laughed.

"Don't laugh too hard or you'll fall off your horse," Ellis sneered.

Billie let out a grunt and shook herself like a wet dog. The vibration traveled through Ellis's body as well, causing her to tighten her grip and Earl to laugh even harder.

"So, smarty pants, now how do we get back?" Ellis asked, hoping it wasn't the obvious answer of "same way." She took off her shirt, wrung it out and put it back on.

"C'mon," Earl said and started riding up the sandbar. A few yards up he turned back into the river, but here it was much shallower and the horses crossed easily, the water just up to their knees.

"Damn it, Earl, you knew all along there was an easier way across," Ellis scolded.

"Don't let Ma hear you talk like that," Earl teased with a wicked smile.

"Shit," Ellis said.

By the time they rode back to their saddles, the heat of the summer afternoon had dried and relaxed them. Billie walked calmly as they neared the farm. Looking back on it, Ellis realized Billie hadn't spooked at all on the way back. She'd pushed her to the deep end of the river and had come out alive.

------

ELLIS WOKE WITH A START. THE NIGHT HUNG STILL AND dark over the quiet company of battered soldiers. Sweet memories had guided her to a deep sleep. Pungent dreams lingered thick on her skin. She heard one of the men get up and walk to the far edge of the camp to relieve himself. He returned to his blankets, collapsing back to sleep. She waited for a few minutes to make sure no one else was up, and then she rose slowly. As quietly as she could, she gathered her things, slung her bedroll over her shoulder, and disappeared into the dark woods.

Just before sunrise, she heard the pulsing of the river. Brush grew thick on the high bank. Early blackberries ripened at the top of thorny vines. She carefully pulled a branch down and picked a handful. Bracing for the unripe tartness, she stuffed them all into her mouth at once and grimaced as she chewed. She hurried to the narrow, swiftly running stream to rinse her mouth and search for a place to cross. A deer trail led down along the bank and Ellis followed it to a low spot. There, not only deer tracks but the hoofprints of two shod horses crossed at a shallow spot, then disappeared on the other side. She crossed there and searched the woods. A cool quiet pervaded. The rushing river behind her and her own footsteps offered the only sounds until a Blue Jay flapped its wings just above her head. She looked up and saw a broken branch an arm's length up a river birch. She looked down and saw another hoof print. She smiled and followed.

"It's about time," said a voice behind her. She swung around, dropping her bedroll and going for her knife, before she registered her brother's voice.

"Whoa there sis, it's me."

"Holy shit, Earl." She ran to her brother and embraced him.

"You gotta quit swearing like that, El." He smiled at her.

"Actually, if I'm going to fit in around here, I'm gonna have to swear quite a bit more than I do," said Ellis.

"Yeah, you may be right."

"Where are the horses?"

"Up that ridge. C'mon." Earl started up the hill and then looked back at Ellis. She stalled, staring, still seeing the soldiers bedded down at the camp and lying on the battlefield. "You okay, El?"

Ellis shook her head, "Yeah, I'm coming." She followed her brother up the ridge to a small clearing. He had made camp here last night and the horses were grazing calmly. She walked up to Billie and put her arms around her horse's neck. Billie put her head back down to graze and Ellis kept rubbing her.

"You're gonna pet the hair right off that horse if you keep rubbing her like that," Earl said, sounding like their father.

"Where did you go?" Ellis was looking at Billie, but then turned to her brother. "Where were you, Earl?"

"The horses got scared off and I went after them. I caught up with them a ways down the river." Earl poked at the fire with a stick, threw on some kindling. He looked back at his sister. "What happened to you? I went back. Nobody had come to bury—." Earl looked back down at the fire. "Somehow I knew you were okay."

"I…" Ellis didn't know how to describe what happened. She could feel it, but couldn't quite put it into words.

"What. What happened, Elli?"

Ellis's legs felt weak, thinking about it now. She combed her fingers through Billie's mane and hooked her hands there, dropping her head between her shoulders. "I think I killed a man, Earl. A boy, really. I think it was one of that group we ran into on the trail. He was…" She shook her head slowly. "I thought I was still. Invisible. But…" she paused. "My gun went off. I hadn't thought about pulling the trigger, but I guess I did." Ellis raised her head but kept looking at Billie. "It wasn't like shooting a deer or a rabbit, Earl. It was different. He could've been you, or Walter or…" Ellis stopped speaking and just stared at her hands tangled in Billie's mane. Everything that happened yesterday was as if she read it in a book. Observed pictures of somebody else. She reached in her pocket and touched the tin portrait.

Earl moved closer and eased his arm around her. "It's okay, sis. You had to do it. It was you or him. I know. It's hard, but it'll get easier."

Ellis looked at her brother's face. Although his eyes still had a softness for her, she saw a hardness cast from them, too. She had learned to look into a horse's eye to see if they were in pain or not. In such a sensitive and forthright creature, it was easy. But people could hide things. You might see that in their eyes, that they were hiding something, but you couldn't always tell what it was they hid. Her brother had that cold look now. A painful mask.

"Easier—"

"You're all right, that's what counts, El." Earl looked off into the distance.

"What would Mama say?" asked Ellis.

After a pause Earl said, "She'd tell us to write it down." He and Ellis looked at each other and smiled through the pain. "I think you're the only one that ever actually did it." He took his arm from her and held his side for just a moment.

"Are you okay?" Ellis asked.

He straightened back up and said, "Me, yeah, I'm fine. Got jostled in between the horses coming up the ridge." His breath caught and then he breathed out.

"Sometimes I still write to Mama. I don't know. Maybe she'll know somehow. Do you think she will? Know what's goin' on here even though she's…"

Earl looked at his sister. "Yeah, I think she'll know. I just hope she doesn't see everything. But I think somehow she's protecting us. I don't know. Jack said our dead ancestors protect us in battle. But…all those bodies on the field. No one protected them." Earl searched through his saddlebag. "But then I went through fights I just shouldn't have come out of alive, but I did. It's confusing. A man would protect a man by killing another man. Somehow out there when it was happening, it made sense. But now…" Earl shook his head. "Hey, go write your letter and rest up." He held up a coil of wire. "I'll see if I can snare us some supper."

"Shouldn't we be moving on?"

"That troop you were with is goin' the other direction. I think we're clear for now. We'll rest and get an early start tomorrow." Earl turned away from his sister, again touching his hand to his side.

"Earl?"

"Just keep an eye out, okay? I won't go far."

Ellis tossed her blanket and saddle bag next to a birch. She took out her journal and noticed the pencil had come loose from the string tying them together. She reached back into the bag for the pencil. It had been broken in two, barely held together by splinters of its own wood. She tried to straighten it, jamming the two halves together, but the pressure separated them for good. She put one half back in her bag, sharpened the other half with her knife. A sunbeam stabbed through the trees, glinting off the blade, flashing images through her mind. She tried to stop them, tried to put the point of her pencil to paper, but there was too much to write.

She looked at her knife again, changed her grip on the handle so that the dull edge of the blade leaned against her forearm, like Earl had shown her, like Jack had shown him. *This is how you hold a knife to protect yourself*, Earl said. He had learned this and so much more from Jack, his Cherokee friend, the boy he'd sneak off to play with when he was supposed to be doing chores. The one who disappeared when more families from back east moved into the area.

~~Dear Mama,~~
*Dear Daddy,*
*I just want you to know Billie's all right. I found Earl and we're riding together now. We hope we'll find you somewhere soon. I had to do some things I didn't want to. I wish I knew where you were. I don't know what else to say.*

Ellis closed her eyes and nodded off, waking when Earl returned with a dead rabbit in his hand and a pained smile on his face. After all he'd been through, she wondered if he was still troubled by killing game. She watched him butcher the rabbit with a strange eagerness.

chapter
# SEVEN

THEY LEFT THE MEADOW CAMP EARLY THE NEXT MORNING. Here the woods grew thicker and the ground sprung softly underfoot. The eerie echo of a bird call touched the air.

"You hear that?" asked Earl.

"A loon," breathed Ellis. They rode along the top of a bluff. Earl dismounted, tying Smokey to a tree. He took a spyglass out of his saddle bag. Ellis dropped Billie's reins and followed Earl on foot. They climbed up a berm and laid on their bellies, looking over the ridge.

Through the trees and brush they could see the wide, muddy river. Five or six men stood around a fire pit. A small cabin nestled against the hill, wispy smoke escaping its chimney. A wagon sat empty attached to calm horses. A Union flag hung limp on a flagpole at the ferry landing.

"Looks like they're waiting on a supply boat. They own the river now." Earl watched through the spyglass. "Let's stop here for the night. We'll make camp down the hill and then see what we're dealing with in the morning." He took one more look through the glass, lowered it and scowled, searching the same direction.

"What is it?" asked Ellis.

"Not sure. It looks like the flag is at half-mast. Here, take a look." He handed her the spyglass.

"I think you're right. Maybe because the war's over?"

"Maybe."

If the war was over, couldn't they just be on their way home to find Daddy? Wouldn't things be back to normal? But she had just seen battle, killed a Union soldier herself, though she would have never considered taking sides. She wasn't sure what Earl had done before she found him, but now she reckoned she was as much an outlaw as her brother. Weren't they deserters? Horse thieves? Even if the war was over, it didn't seem to stop the fighting, no matter which side you were on.

There was a burned-out tree at the bottom of the berm. Earl built a small fire in the portal, which kept the smoke from showing. They ate a meal of cooked rabbit and blackberries; placed their bedrolls close to the fire. Earl was right. No place was safe.

⌒——

"ELLIS, WAKE UP…" EARL GENTLY SHOOK HER. SHE STARTLED.

"What?"

"We gotta go." Earl had already packed up his bedroll. The fire was cold.

"Where?" Ellis wasn't sure if she was asking where they were going or where she was.

"A riverboat just left the dock down there. Took on everybody but the ferryman. I think we can get across now without too many questions."

"Ferry across, with the horses?" Riding on a ferry platform across the river would be a new trick for Billie.

Earl was rubbing Smokey, staring into his eye.

"Earl, what are you doing?"

"We can't take the horses. Smokey's a Reb horse. See that brand?" He nodded at the horse's shoulder. "They didn't do a very good job of it. You can really only make out the 'C.' But I get caught with him and there will be questions."

"But Billie?" Ellis tried to think what her father would do. He could get Billie to get on the ferry and stay still. Other horses must be able to do this. "We can do it, Earl, we can get them on the ferry."

"No, El, we can't. We gotta leave them here."

"No." Ellis couldn't believe her brother would do this. "I'm not leaving Billie."

Earl knew how stubborn his sister could be. "Look El, I can't stay here another minute and lookin' like that you can't either. Another boat comes down that river and we're dead. I've been watching them all morning, more Union troops are coming. They're gonna sweep this whole area soon." Ellis had never seen Earl this scared and anxious. He wasn't just running from the war. There was something else.

"Why, what did you do, Earl?" Ellis was seeing another side of her brother. It frightened her.

Earl glanced at her and leaned against his horse. Staring at the brand on Smokey's shoulder he explained, "I'm wanted by both sides, El. The bluecoats want me because I fought with the greybacks and the greybacks want me because, well, I helped some Negroes through a rough spot."

Ellis looked at her brother. "You what?"

"You didn't see it, Elli, you didn't see what they were doing to them. It wasn't right. I know I hardly went to meetings, but Ma and Pa were right to believe the way they did. I just hope I'll be forgiven for what I've had to do." He gave her a pleading look and then changed back to all business, tightening his horse's cinch and tying on his bedroll. He looked back at Ellis, then bent down and clawed at the ground, picked up a moist handful of dirt, mixed it with horse manure, and smeared it on Smokey's shoulder over the brand.

"You know, it might be better if you don't come with me now. I'll tell him I'm a messenger needing to get word to a regiment across the river. If he's getting paid by the army maybe that ferryman isn't going to ask any questions." Earl picked up some leaves and rubbed them between his hands to clean them.

He continued, "If it looks like it's working, come on down and join me and we'll go together. If not, make sure I get across and then you can follow. Say you were supposed to be with me but we got separated. We'll meet up on the other side of the river and then head north to St. Louis." Earl checked his cinch again.

"But Earl..."

"It's a big city we can get lost in, Elli. Maybe even head west from there, join up with a wagon train. I hear they're headed west in droves." Earl seemed lost in what he was saying. He mounted Smokey, clutching a hand to his side on the way to the saddle. He looked at his sister. "Elli, I'm sorry, but if the tale doesn't work, we might have to leave the horses. Here, take this." He handed her the spyglass. "Once I get across then come down and sell Billie to the ferryman if you have to. It's the only way. We've got no money to pay him to take us all across."

"But..." Ellis tried again.

Earl didn't hesitate. He kicked his horse forward and trotted off.

"Wait, Earl!" But the gray horse carrying her brother was already halfway down the slope. She checked her saddle bag. Reaching deep down she felt a damp bundle of paper. The money was still there.

"Damn it, Earl, can't get a word in edgewise," she mumbled, hearing her mother's voice, seeing her father shake his head and smile. For a moment she thought about turning around and heading home. Maybe her father had found his way back. But she'd learned without Earl around half of her was missing. The miracle of their reunion wasn't lost on her. She had to go after him.

"Don't worry, Billie, I'm not leaving you." Ellis rubbed Billie's nose and gave her a soft pat on the neck before mounting. She rode up to the ridge and watched the river below. With the spyglass Earl had given her she watched him ride to the cabin, talk to a man on the porch steps. Then she witnessed Earl handing over Smokey's reins to the boatman. He tied him to the post in front of the cabin. As Earl tried to unsaddle Smokey, the boatman grabbed his arm and shoved him toward a large skiff. Ellis breathed in sharply, lowered the spyglass and rubbed her arm. Though he seemed to be okay, Earl had left Smokey and all he carried behind as the boatman rowed toward the far shore. Seeing no other signs of life at the cabin or the landing, Ellis urged Billie down the steep bank to the river.

At this bend in the Mississippi, the still water resembled a lake. Ellis searched for a shallow entrance and urged her horse to step into the water. "That's it, that a girl," she urged.

Billie seemed fine to walk in, but when the water touched her belly, she balked. Ellis urged a little more. "Come on, girl, you can do it." But Billie hopped around and Ellis didn't want her to panic, so she rode her back out.

A large platform raft tied to the dock floated empty. It looked stout enough for horses and wagons. She searched the river for Earl and the boatman, but the expanse was wide here and curved around a point covered in thick shrubs. She couldn't see where they had gone. She wanted to try loading Billie onto the raft before the boatman returned. She led Billie onto the short dock and urged her to step onto the raft. It took a little coaxing, but finally Billie followed her aboard.

"That wasn't so bad now, was it girl?" She smiled and rubbed her horse's neck. Looking over Billie's withers she saw Smokey, still tied in front of the cabin. She glanced back at the river crossing. Maybe she could get them both across. Then she and Earl would have mounts on the other side. She knew Earl really liked the gray gelding. And Smokey was a good horse. He just needed some good feed and fewer battles. She dropped Billie's reins and hoped she would stay still. She carefully stepped back onto the dock, trying hard to keep the raft from moving. She untied Smokey and led him to the dock. The gelding surprised her by loading easily. He had obviously been trained well. Now that she had them both on the raft, she couldn't see getting them off to wait for the boatman and having to do it all over again, so she decided to wait, as they were. She reckoned she had plenty of money to buy Smokey back and pay for all of them to cross.

Both horses raised their heads and looked up at the ridge at the same time. Mounted soldiers were coming toward them.

"Shit." She looked out along the water but still didn't see the boatman. Another look up the ridge forced her decision. She untied the raft, picked up the long pole that laid on the dock, and pushed off. Thrusting the pole into the water, she strained her body against it. With all that effort, she still didn't feel them going anywhere. She pushed again and realized they were moving, floating. The horses shifted a little and she tried to calm them.

"It's okay, you two. Just keep your heads down and keep still." Smokey was standing stock still but Billie started moving around some. The more she moved the more the raft tilted. Ellis gave the raft one big push with the pole, set it down and stepped up to Billie to calm her. She rubbed her and whispered to her. The horse relaxed some and stopped moving. Ellis took up the pole again and pushed some more, using the rudder tied to the back of the raft to steer. They were almost around the bend.

"Hey! Get back here, now!" The command came from the east shore. Ellis looked back and saw the mounted soldiers, but wasn't sure if they were the same ones she had seen on the ridge. She couldn't have turned around if she'd wanted to. Just as she reached the bend she saw the boatman rowing back toward her. He was alone. He stopped rowing and stood up in his boat when he saw Ellis and the two horses on his raft.

"Who the hell are you?" he shouted. He sat back down and rowed quickly toward her, the raft drifting toward the point. Not wanting to get stuck on a sandbar, Ellis pushed on the pole as hard as she could. She couldn't see the far shore but she hoped Earl was there waiting.

The ferryman fought a current, rowing viciously, making his way around an eddy and back toward the raft. He inched closer but had to keep rowing to stay in one place. He fumbled shipping his oars, catching one between the boat and the raft. He drew a pistol and grabbed the raft rail at the same time. "Stop! You Rebel thief!" His yelling and cursing, and the sudden movement from him trying to climb onto the raft, troubled the horses.

His gun fired, Billie reared up, Smokey moved sideways and the raft flipped. Ellis felt the cold swallow her. A jumble of hooves, flared nostrils and panicked wild eyes met her as she surged in the wake. She felt the current pull her down again, the chill push precious air from her lungs. The muddy waters obscured her vision like a dust storm. She couldn't die like this. Without seeing Earl, without knowing her father's whereabouts.

Her foot found something hard and she pushed off. The current released her and she resurfaced, disoriented at water level. Coughing and treading water, she searched around her. Her hat floated an arm's distance away and as she grabbed for it she saw Billie. Head stretched toward shore, Billie swam with a wild look in her eye. Ellis dove toward her, kicking as hard as she could. She grabbed the horse's mane and urged her on. "Come on, girl. You can do it. Swim!" she sputtered. Eventually she felt Billie walking instead of swimming. Ellis pulled herself up onto Billie's back and rode her to the west shore.

As they climbed out of the river, Billie stopped and shook off the wet. The leather tack squeaked and rustled and Ellis hoped it wasn't ruined. She thought about how angry Daddy would be that she didn't have any saddle soap to clean it and couldn't take the time if she did. Her only concern now was to find Earl. She didn't see anyone on this side of the river but Smokey had made it across and was grazing by the riverbank as if nothing had happened. She walked over and picked up his rein. Quiet amplified the dripping water spilling from her and the horses. She searched up and down the shore for Earl, but didn't see him anywhere. She looked back and saw that the boatman had secured the scow to the raft and was making his way back to the east shore of the river. He wasn't coming after her, but that army group worried her, though it would take them a while to cross the river, if that's what they intended.

A distant steamship whistle broke the silence. She could just make out the soldiers and their mounts on the eastern shore. Yes, that was what they were waiting for. She felt a little safer thinking they wouldn't be too concerned with one person, even though she did steal her way across the river on that raft. "Stupid way to haul things across water," she mumbled as she dismounted and did what she could to wring some of the water from her belongings. "Seems somebody could come up with a better idea," she muttered aloud to Billie. She mounted again and picked up Smokey's reins, but the horse balked when she tried to set off and she had to coax him. "C'mon, boy," she urged. But he wouldn't move.

She dismounted, approached Smokey and rubbed his neck. She ran her hands down each of his legs and lifted his feet. He still had all his shoes. There was a deep scar on his rump, which she hadn't noticed when he was dry. But it didn't seem to be bothering him now.

"What's wrong, boy?" She looked around. The small landing dock was near where they emerged from the river. She walked over to it and searched the water. Is it possible Earl never crossed? But she saw him in the boat with the boatman, didn't she? She turned back to the horses and noticed something on the edge of the dock. Something round and shiny. Earl's watch. The one Daddy had given him before he left. She picked it up. A smudge of dark red came off on her finger.

"Earl," she whispered. "Earl!" She yelled into the silence.

chapter

# EIGHT

*THINK, EL,* SHE HEARD EARL SAY. "THINK, ELLIS," SHE MUM-
bled under her breath. She got back on Billie, put the watch in
her vest pocket and now, perhaps feeling her urgency, Smokey
led willingly.

Cottonwood owned the shore, shading a tangled under-
brush of scrub and grasses. The garlic scent of skunk cabbage
wafted low to the ground. A wide road stretched north and
south along the river. Ellis spotted a game trail snaking under low hanging limbs. She dodged the brush from horseback,
branches scraping against her legs, and looked for footprints or
any sign of Earl. But it was all she could do to keep the horses
moving ahead. Eventually the trail widened and cleared. She
stopped to listen. Searched the ground. Held the horses still.
"C'mon, Earl, where are you?" she whispered.

Ellis remembered playing hide-and-seek with Earl and
Jack when they were little. Even as they got older, they would
hike into the woods and try to cover their trails to avoid detection. Once, she was the seeker and spent hours trying to find
them. They had climbed a tree together and were watching her
search the whole time. She had been looking for footprints,

but Jack had brushed them away with a branch before climbing the tree. Jack had been a skillful opponent and Earl had admired and imitated him.

A bird flew from a low bush and Billie flinched. Ellis heard a soft groan. She rode carefully in that direction.

Beaten and bleeding, her brother crouched against a tree.

Ellis jumped off Billie and dropped the reins, hurrying to her brother. "Earl."

Earl jerked back, then looked up at Ellis through swollen eyes, his face streaked with blood and dirt. "Hey," he said weakly. "How the hell'd you get the horses...?" His voice caught. I thought you were—I thought if you hadn't drowned the ferryman would'a killed you." Tears mixed with the blood.

"Earl, God Earl, you're hurt." Ellis held her hands out toward her brother, wanting to assess his injuries, trying to help, but not knowing what to do.

Earl tried to get up but thought better of it and slouched back against the tree. "That boatman didn't buy my story. Tried the truth, told him I was from Tennessee, but he had it in his head that was still Rebel territory." Earl coughed. "He's working with the Union. Said the war's over and they won. Said some coward killed President Lincoln. I told him I didn't know anything about that." Earl leaned his head back in pain, his hands moving from his head to his side.

"Earl, you're bleeding." Ellis took off her kerchief, folded it and held it against the gash on Earl's head.

"Yeah. Check my saddle bags. See if you can find the coffee. It's in a tin and might still be dry." He took the kerchief from his head, paled at the sight of it, and put it back.

"Coffee—?"

"Just do it, sis. Quick."

Ellis found the tin wrapped in a damp shirt. She hurried back to her brother's side.

"Open the tin," he said. His face looked gray. Ellis held the container and forced the lid off. Earl scooped a handful of coffee grounds and took a pained breath. "I saw them do this in the camp. It's supposed to stop the bleeding." His red eyes met Ellis's horrified gaze. In a quick motion he removed the cloth and pressed the coffee grounds against the wound. He swallowed a scream. It broke like a whimper as he slumped, semi-conscious.

Ellis searched her brother's face, looking for a smile, a word, anything that said he'd be okay. He took a shallow breath. With her knife, she cut the sleeves off the damp shirt and tied them together. Earl came to.

"What are you doing?" he said. His voice was groggy, his eyes half closed.

Ellis tied the lengths of cloth around Earl's head, keeping it taut over the coffee grounds and makeshift bandage. Earl winced, but didn't move. He opened his eyes wider.

"I'll get the canteen and clean up your face," said Ellis.

"We gotta move," said Earl. He tried to get up but swooned and sat back down with Ellis's help.

"I think we can rest a little while. Those soldiers were waiting for the river boat. The ferryman went back after the raft flipped. He didn't come after me." She looked at Earl. The drying blood painted his face like a grotesque mask, but she thought the bleeding had stopped. She tore another piece of cloth from the dismembered shirt and began cleaning Earl's face. "He did this to you?"

"I offered up Smokey for fare across, but when I tried to take my saddle he got rough. When we got to this side he saw Pa's watch and said he'd take that for the rest of what I owed him." Earl waved Ellis's hand away. She stopped dabbing at the dirt and blood. Earl nodded, defeated, and shivered through a warm breeze.

"I told him he had my horse and saddle. That watch—made it through all those bloody battles. It was my good luck charm. I wasn't about to give it to him." Earl put a hand to his wound and winced.

Ellis nodded at Earl's wounded head. "How'd that happen?"

"He started to fight me for the watch and then we saw you on the ferry raft. He swung an oar and hit me in the ribs, I remember that. I don't remember him hitting me in the head, didn't see it coming. I saw you rounding the bend on that raft." Earl coughed. "Geez, El, I couldn't believe what I was seein'. I don't know, everything happened so fast. I must've blacked out. Next thing I knew I was here, wonderin' what was real and what wasn't." Earl paused, looking confused. "I lost the watch."

Ellis tried to read her brother's face. He looked distant. She reached into her vest pocket and pulled out the watch, handing it to him. "No you didn't, brother." She smiled at him and then noticed his blood-stained hand holding his side. "Let me look at that." she said.

Earl examined the watch, gripped it in his hand, then squeezed his eyes, trying to clear his head. "Naw, it's okay, I've seen lots worse than this." Ellis helped him up, one hand on his arm and the other around his gaunt torso. He was unexpectedly light, like Mama had been.

"Are you sure you can ride?" asked Ellis.

"No choice," said Earl.

Ellis helped him onto his horse. She wasn't sure he would stay there, but he was right, they didn't have a choice. Whatever it was Earl had done over the past few months, he considered himself an outlaw. And now Ellis had stolen a ferry ride, maybe a horse, and was riding beside her outlaw brother. War or no war, she reckoned that made her an outlaw, too.

THEY RODE MOSTLY SINGLE FILE, EARL FIRST SO ELLIS COULD keep an eye on him. His horse was pretty good at picking out a trail. These looked like animal trails, deer and their predators probably, not like trails a human would follow. Toward nightfall they made camp between some tall brush and a small, clear stream. They hadn't seen any signs of men or horses since they left the river, but they should be well hidden here if anyone did come along.

Ellis helped Earl off his horse. He was trying to stay strong, but he was unsteady on his feet. She felt her own legs shaking as she helped support her twin.

"I think we're safe to make a fire. Just keep it small." Earl shuddered as he leaned against a tree.

Ellis caught his arm. "Sit down. You're looking like a newborn colt."

Earl shook her off, weakly, dropped to his knees and retched. He held his head in his hands and fell forward onto his elbows.

"Earl, what can I do to help?" Ellis knelt beside him and draped an arm over his back, trying to support him.

"I'll be okay, just…" He waved his hand dismissively, crawled back to the tree and sat.

Ellis decided to leave the horses saddled. If they had to leave quickly it might be all she could do just to get Earl up onto Smokey. Earl shivered a little when she put his damp bedroll blanket around him.

"Don't worry," he said, "I just need some rest."

Ellis loosened the horses' cinches and tied up their reins. There was plenty of forage here so she figured they would stay put, but she kept a close eye on them as she hunted down some more firewood. She thought there must be something more she could do for Earl. She thought of Mama. She gathered wood and built a fire.

Ellis was stoking the fire when Earl said, "You remember how I taught you to make a rabbit snare?"

"Sure. I used it a lot on the farm after…after you all left. I brought one with me." Ellis remembered the coyotes. "But I lost it."

"Well, this seems a likely place don't you think?" Earl's thin, dry lips spoke slowly. "There's one in my saddlebags."

"I'll get to it. You rest."

She gave Earl the canteen and struck out to find a rabbit trail. It didn't take long. It looked like they had camped in the middle of a warren. She set the trap and went back to check on Earl.

He had fallen asleep, his face now flushed and damp. His brow wrinkled in pain and his perpetual smile flattened. His head wound had stopped bleeding. She carefully lifted his shirt to see what he'd been trying to hide from her. A deep purple bruise the size of her hand spread over an area of his lower ribs. He was thin but the ribs weren't showing like she thought they should. On the edge of the bruise she noticed a bump the size of an acorn under a pink scar.

Earl stirred. With half-opened eyes he mumbled, "Get that rabbit?"

Ellis looked away from her brother's pained face. "I'll go check the snare." When she started to leave, Earl clutched her arm.

"I'm sorry you've had to see this. I'm sorry I've had to… see things."

"We'll be okay, Earl. Now we're together."

"You remember Pa talking about his brother William? Our uncle?"

"He didn't talk about him much."

"Yeah, but he did say he lived in Missouri. Some little town where their Pa settled. Walter told me. That's where you should go." Earl tightened his grip on Ellis's arm. "Don't go north, go west."

"Okay, is that where we're heading?" Ellis felt the pressure on her arm, but didn't want Earl to let go.

Earl's face changed. He paused, seemed anxious. "In the camp, the men pleaded for a coffin. They wanted a marked place so family could find them."

"What? Earl…?"

"Worst thing they thought was to be left all tangled on the battlefield, not even laid out. No dignity in that."

"Earl, what are you talking about?"

Earl brightened and looked up at his sister. "Oh, hey, I'm okay, that rabbit done yet?"

Ellis scowled, scared, but hoped Earl wouldn't notice. "I'll go check the snare. You rest. I'll be right back." Ellis watched Earl nod his head and close his eyes again. She watched his chest move with breath before she left him.

SHE HELD THE SKINNED RABBIT, IMPALED ON A GREEN STICK, over the fire. It was well-charred by the time Earl stirred again.

"Smells good," he said.

Ellis brought the meat to her brother and sat beside him. She tore hot pieces of flesh from the carcass and ate, handing pieces to Earl that he mostly declined.

"I made some more bandages out of your other shirt." She nodded at his head. "Maybe we should change that now the bleeding's stopped."

Earl moved to stop her, but both strength and intention denied him. Ellis untied the bandages and carefully removed the cloth sticking to the wound. His hair was caked with dried blood and coffee grounds, but there was no fresh blood. With the canteen, she wet a clean piece of cloth from the torn shirt and gently cleaned Earl's face, this time finishing without protest. She carefully swept away the coffee grounds and washed around the wound the best she could. Earl's face was drawn and hollow.

"Should I use more coffee?"

Earl smiled a little. "I think it's done its job. You might need it in the morning." He touched his side, gingerly.

"What about that?" Ellis nodded at Earl's hand.

Earl winced and scowled, lifted his shirt. Ellis touched the scar next to the bruise. Earl twitched and gasped.

"I think you got some broken ribs. What's that scar from?" asked Ellis.

Earl sighed. "I took a ball a while back. They were too busy hacking limbs off soldiers back at the camp where Walter died. And I was too worried about him to think much of it then. We had to scramble to leave camp, but one of the surgeons there told me it would work its way out eventually." Earl let out a sharp breath with a chuckle.

"What?" Ellis didn't know whether to be worried or encouraged.

"I was just thinking, if only that ferryman had aimed for that ball and split me open, he might of done me a favor." A weak smile faded. "Is there still water in the canteen?"

Ellis poured what was left in a tin cup and gave it to Earl. She picked up both canteens. "I'll go fill these and be right back. You need anything else?"

Earl shook his head and closed his eyes.

The canteens full, Ellis checked on her brother. She tucked both of their blankets around him. He stirred, smiled and mumbled something about Daddy and Walter and he'd tell her more later. She made her bed closer to the small fire. Earl's face looked peaceful now, and unafraid. In the still air she heard only the trickle of the stream and an occasional frog jump toward an unsuspecting insect.

The pages of her journal were wavy on the edges, but they had dried well.

*Dear Earl,*

*When you recover and we're at Uncle William's place or wherever we're headed, we're going to remember these nights in the woods. We always did think about living like this. On the horse drive, when we went with Daddy, I remember you saying how you loved sleeping under that canopy of sparkling stars. And Daddy joking, then why did he work so hard to give us a roof over our heads. He always tried to scare us, just a little, to keep us appreciating what we had. Like telling us a rattler wouldn't cross a horse hair rope. So after everyone was asleep you went and got his new lariat and strung it out around our bedrolls.*

Ellis put her journal away, stoked the fire and laid down. Though she was exhausted, sleep didn't find her. She glanced tentatively at her dozing brother, watching his chest move with each breath, but not wanting to see too much; his pale skin, his pained expression—those last days with her mother.

She watched the shadowed forms of the horses, wondering what it was like to sleep standing up. Smiling to herself, she retrieved the rope from her saddle and moved her bedroll closer to Earl. She laid the rope out around their sleeping place. She stoked the fire and laid down on her blanket. The horses wouldn't wander far. The tall grass and quiet night kept them near.

*chapter*
# NINE

SHE AWOKE NOT TO LIGHT, BUT TO A SOUND. ONCE AWAKE
Ellis couldn't figure out what the sound had been. Perhaps
just a fading dream. She lay still listening, getting her bearings.
The fire was out, yet the air carried the promise of a warm day.
Billie stood close by, nuzzled her foot and went back to graz-
ing the new grass. Earl was still asleep. That wasn't like him.

She could see a bit of light in the patch of sky through the
trees. She got to her feet slowly, watching where Earl slept.
A chill, edged in hope, coursed through her. She had never
wanted more to be wrong. Earl was lying flat on his back. He
had pulled his hat down over his face and when she lifted it,
she saw his peaceful expression, eyes closed, the smirk he com-
monly wore, now on his pale lips. Like he'd been dreaming her
dream. She pulled the blankets from him slowly, with rever-
ence. His hands were folded together on his belt and he held
their father's watch. His gun and holster lay by his side. She
looked back up at his bloodless face, collapsed to her knees
and wept.

As she raised her head, Ellis noticed a corner of paper
protruding from Earl's torn vest pocket. She blinked away

tears as she moved her hand slowly toward the paper; a moment's thought that Earl could be playing with her and might suddenly slap her hand away. But as she carefully slipped it from his pocket, she noticed his utter stillness. She unfolded two ragged pieces of paper. Her father's handwriting flowed over the pages, worn and faded. She recognized the letter her father had sent her mother. So many times Mama had read those words out loud to keep him near. But she had never shared this other letter. The beginning was clear:

*I fear this letter may never reach you, I hope the others did. The train was stopped before Nashville. There was awful confusion...*

Ellis skipped down to the last paragraph where she saw her and Earl's names.

*I trust you and the twins are handling things on the farm. I know Earl can be strong-willed, but he's tough bodied and kind hearted. His "other half" is his equal, if not his superior, I believe. Even though of the female persuasion, Ellis can outride and outwork him, as you know, and as I've told you after our drives. Try not to hold her back. She knows her mind and is a good girl. She takes after her mother.*
*Your loving husband, Thomas*

Billie suddenly turned her head and pricked her ears back toward the trail. Someone was coming. Memories flooded Ellis's mind as tears streaked her face. Hide-and-seek. How could she leave her brother like this? But she had to disappear.

A breeze blew through the edge of the forest. She thought she heard Earl's voice.

Ellis tucked the letters into her pocket, grabbed the watch and put Earl's hat back on his face. She picked up the holster and, after a moment's hesitation, looked at her brother's body and strapped the worn leather belt around her. Her legs stung with scratches from yesterday's ride through the brambles. She tightened Billie's cinch and readied her reins. Then she tied Smokey to a nearby sapling. She ached to take him with her, but she had to make it look like Earl was alone. That there was no one else to follow. And she could move faster by herself. With a branch, she swept away as many of her own footprints and Billie's as she could, mounted and rode deeper into the woods.

Although they had been headed north to St. Louis, Earl had said to go west. It seemed to Ellis that the soldiers at the ferry landing had been heading upriver to the city. West did feel safer.

Her stomach queasy and mind unsettled, the thought of leaving Earl and Smokey tormented her. She watched and listened through hours of riding, finally believing there was no one on her tail. She hoped whoever found them would bury Earl and give Smokey a good home. Earl would have made her leave. He would have wanted her to protect herself.

Ellis rode on alone, heeding the landscape, and feeling an almost unbearable heaviness. Weighty thoughts of Earl, the one who always protected her, showed her how to take care of herself, and how to have fun. She had found him and lost him again, forever. *Just keep riding and remember we're brothers if someone comes along. It'll be safer that way.* That's what Earl had said.

The wind chastised her, driving relentless tears down her face. She labored to remember the good times with her brother. After Daddy and Walter left, her mother said, *"Just remember all the good times we had together and they'll be back before you know it."* But they hadn't returned and the memories of good times faded. That finally got the better of Mama. *Mama.* Earl and Walter had called her Ma, and Daddy, Pa. Ellis thought about all the other differences between what she did and what Earl had done. The way they talked. His jaunty step. His confident seat on a horse. As she rode on alone, she practiced being Earl.

She patted Billie on the neck. "Just you and me now." Wiping her eyes and searching ahead, they traveled through a valley, following a stream. Hills rose before them and Billie was alert to the upward sloping ground. "We just need to find a place to cross these hills." Ahead, a rock formation leaned over the trail. Ellis stopped and looked around. There was no place to go but under it. She rode on cautiously, but curiously. With the overhang just behind them, Billie quickened her step. "Easy girl," Ellis said, though the rock overhead had unnerved her, as well. On the other side the trail split. Checking the direction of the sun, Ellis chose a path. "Let's try this way, Billie."

They climbed for about an hour and soon stood at the top of a rise. When the trees cleared, they stopped at a high point overlooking a small mountain range. "Well, look at that, Billie," Ellis whispered. From this vantage point Ellis could see almost three-hundred-sixty degrees. The beauty lay in the natural stillness. The breeze, birds raiding berry bushes and the soft creaking of saddle leather were the only sounds. Ellis ached for her brother. The two of them, lost together in that forest was his dream. Soon, however, clouds began to darken and build. Colors turned the gray of evening though it was still just mid-day.

They started down the hill as the rain began. Ellis dismounted and walked closer to the rocks. A sudden wind came up and the rain pelted harshly, just as she found the mouth of a cave. The opening was big enough for Billie, so Ellis led her in. The horse balked, chuffing and flaring her nostrils, but finally relented, following closely. If this had been a predator's home, Ellis knew Billie would resist more convincingly. She rubbed the horse to help quiet them both, glad for the shelter as the hard rain erased their tracks.

Her eyes adjusted to the dark of the cave and Ellis could see the back wall. The chamber wasn't deep, but the solid rock was perfect weather protection. She found the scattered remains of a fire ring, and judged it hadn't been used in quite a long while. "We might as well stay for the night, Billie," she said. After gathering some twigs and bark that had remained dry under the shelter, she lit a small fire with one of her few remaining matches.

She sat on her haunches by the fire, put her head between her knees and wept. A sadness and lethargy overwhelmed her. But soon she stood, drank from her canteen, and walked to the edge of the cave. Rain dripped from the rocks overhead. She stepped into it lifting her face to the turbulent sky. She closed her eyes, breathed in the freshness, and let the rain mix with her tears and quench her despair.

She wished this rain could wash away all traces of war. Dissolve it like it did the hoofprints. It could make crops grow and rivers run, but it couldn't bring back the dead. It couldn't reunite families. It couldn't ease her anger.

Billie nickered. Ellis straightened, felt the wet creep down her neck. She shivered and sunk back into the cave to stoke the fire. Picking up a bit of old charcoal, she started drawing on the wall, letting her hand do what it would. Black lines became a rudimentary horse. A warmth washed over her; something primal. She stopped, dropped the charcoal and stared at her hand, stained black. Billie breathed out, sighed like only a horse can. Ellis thought she heard her mother's voice surfacing, felt her brother's embrace. She remembered a phrase from the book she read to her mother. "Haunt me…be with me always…drive me mad." Her stomach growled and ached, but she ignored it as she sat down by the fire with her journal.

*Dear Mama,*
*I never thought I'd be glad you weren't around anymore,*
*but I confess to you I am glad I don't have to tell you this.*
*Earl is dead. I still don't know about Daddy.*

Remembering her father's letters she'd taken from Earl, Ellis reached into her pocket and unfolded them, reading them slowly, by firelight.

*My dear Tess,*
*I trust this journey will be quick, and soon Walter and*
*I will be back at the ranch with you. With the mon-*
*ey we bring back from this sale, I can buy the stud colt*
*from Bill and finally get the last link to the bloodlines we*
*need to breed the best horses in Tennessee. We have been*
*re-routed from Memphis to Nashville. Got word from a*
*cavalry messenger at the river crossing. But that should*
*put us back home even sooner than I planned. So far the*

*journey has gone well. Our eldest and I should be arriving*
*in Nashville with all stock in good condition. We should*
*advance our planned schedule, returning home by the end*
*of next week.*
  *Your loving husband, Thomas*

Ellis heard her mother's voice reciting her father's words.
She unfolded the second letter and was surprised at how clear
the ink was upon the page.

*My Dear Tess,*
*I fear this letter may never reach you, I hope the others did.*
*The train was stopped before Nashville. There was awful*
*confusion and Walter and I were separated in the hoards*
*of soldiers and civilians. I had told him, if this was to*
*happen, to meet me back at the depot or at Wilson's Ranch,*
*where we planned to leave the horses. I waited two days,*
*but he never arrived and there was no word.*
  *I was asked to accompany the horses to Richmond.*
*"Asked" is not the exact word. I was compelled. It was*
*made to seem my duty and for it they promised they would*
*find Walter and reunite us. I offered them the required sti-*
*pend to keep myself and Walter from fighting, but the offer*
*was refused. They knew my faith would not allow me to*
*fight, but they did not want a soldier so much as a wran-*
*gler. Since much of the trip would be by train, I thought*
*it might not take much longer, but the rails have been de-*
*stroyed in more than one place it seems, and we have had*
*to drive the horses through spent battlefields and wilder-*
*ness. Although I have not yet seen the fighting, we have*
*been able to hear the percussion in the distance on many*

*occasions. I try to think of it as thunder, but no lightning or rain has accompanied the rumbling din so far. As soon as I get to the city I will send word by telegraph. I hope Walter has found his way home as we have not yet been reunited, as promised.*

*I trust you and the twins are handling things on the farm…*

"Mama, why didn't you tell us?" Ellis whispered. She carefully folded the letters and put them in her pocket where her fingers found Jack's carvings. She took them out one by one, rubbing each between her fingers as she thought about her family. The bird reminded her of her mother, eloquent but fragile. She stood and placed them in a small niche in the cave wall; the bird, horse, snake, cat, and fox. She picked up the bird and held it in her hand as she returned to her journal.

*Earl found Walter but he was wounded and died back in Pickwick. They buried him at Shiloh, Earl said. Earl hadn't found Daddy and was pretty sure you'd be seeing him before we would. Now Earl's gone I guess you're all together. I wonder why I'm still here, but I know you wouldn't want me thinking that way. I've got Billie to think about and something in my gut telling me to keep going. And there's your words, and Daddy's, making me want to believe in something bigger than all of us; something or someone that maybe has this all planned out. I guess I'm still trying to figure out what I believe, but if you are watching over me, I hope you'll point the way when I need it.*

*Your loving daughter, Ellis.*

After replacing the tiny bird carving in the niche with the others, Ellis heated water in a tin cup, for coffee. She dug into her saddle bag for some dried rabbit meat she had saved, folded in a cloth. She held the meat in front of her face for a moment, her movements in the slow motion of dreams. As the rain poured down outside the cave, Ellis remembered when she and Earl had snuck out for a ride the night after their tenth birthday. She wrote:

*The full moon was so bright it might as well have been daylight. We rode and raced, talked and laughed. We'd headed out to Jack's place, but when we got there Jack said he wasn't about to go gallivanting around in the storm that was coming. "Storm! Can you not see what a gorgeous night it is, Jack? There's no storm!" Earl had said. Of course we knew it might rain, but it was a warm night and we didn't mind getting wet. Well, Jack stayed home that night and we kept riding. It wasn't but a min-ute after we turned back that all hell broke loose. The rain came down in sheets until the wind came up and blew it sideways. We couldn't see our horses heads in front of us. Earl yelled over the deluge, "Just give him his head! He'll find his way home!" I was riding old Sparky back then and as scary as it was, sure enough he found his way home. We were in a lot of trouble when we got back, as Mama and Daddy had been looking for us. The storm woke them up and when they checked on us and we weren't there they considered the barn thinking we might be smart enough to be making sure the horses were okay. When our horses were gone, too, they were all but frantic. I know they were glad to see us back home safe, but after we rubbed down the horses and fed them, we were made to sleep in the barn with them that night. They brought us towels and dry clothes. "Can't have you catching your deaths," Mama said. "Doctors cost too much and undertakers aren't much cheaper." But after a while she did bring us some hot stew. Her stew never tasted so good as that night. We vowed to our parents we'd never do anything like that again. But Earl and I agreed later, it sure was fun.*

*chapter*
# TEN

THE NEXT MORNING LOOMED GRAY AND EERIE. SOUNDS CON-
fused the ear. Bird calls and dripping water rang louder in the
thick fog. Ellis could tell Billie was troubled by it, too. But
a horse has some other way of knowing what's out there. A
"sixth sense" her father called it. Earl had made her promise
to find her uncle's place as soon as she could, but he never
got around to telling her how to get there. She knew he was
just trying to keep her safe, but she wasn't sure she would feel
safer in a town with people she didn't know. She thought Earl
might like living on the trail just fine. The more she thought
of Earl, the more she wanted to be him.

The embers from last night's fire were cold. She thought
about rebuilding it and staying until the weather passed, but it
was no longer raining, and something was telling her to move
on, as if the spirit of the cave were pushing her out. Billie
seemed restless, too. She saddled her horse and looked up to
see Jack's carvings sitting in a line where she had put them.
She grabbed the tiny horse carving, put it in her pocket, and
left the shelter.

As they rode down the mountain the fog billowed across the trail and thickened. She strained her eyes, watching between Billie's ears, trying to keep track of the trail. Then she took a deep breath, loosened the reins and kept her eyes on that spot. "It's up to you, now girl. Keep us on the trail."

The fog hung like sheets on wash day, obliterating sight and rendering sound contradictory. Ellis's legs hugged her horse, the only thing grounding her in the present. She concentrated on riding, staying in stride with Billie; being soft and feeling each footfall, each muscle contract and relax. She tried to see and hear and smell what Billie saw and heard and smelled. She felt that someone else was moving her. Someone else was doing all the work of being her as she sat there watching the gray-white nothingness. Watching the ears, feeling Billie's careful, calm footsteps as they touched and released the ground.

Billie grew more confident. Ellis would have thought the horse would be beside herself, spooking at every little noise or smell. But though Billie quickened her step at times, she kept steadily walking out, her ears pointed forward mostly, but flicked back to Ellis now and then, as if checking in. Ellis talked to her, whispered, "I'm still here, and you're doing fine."

Her whisper was loud to her own ear. Ellis felt she was floating, Billie had grown wings, nothing was real. The feeling jolted her, like falling or waking from a dream. Her eyes hurt from staring into white. Just as she felt the wave about to engulf her, a breeze flew by and the fog lifted. They had reached a plateau where the view was breathtaking. Without any signal from Ellis, Billie stopped at the edge of the trail. They stood looking straight ahead. The valley loomed before them for miles. Clouds still ghosted about in the gray-blue sky, but the weather was clearing. The sky lightened. Reality returned.

The path led off to the left and down a hill. Green sweetgrass grew on the side of the trail and Ellis discovered a blackberry bush, the fruit closest to the sun, just ripening. She dismounted and let Billie graze. Approaching the brambles she heard a faint rattling. *"Make sure you check for snakes before you get too close to those berries,"* her mother would warn. She backed away from the bush, led Billie farther down the trail, mounted, and drank from her canteen. She reckoned the berries weren't ripe anyway. Praising her horse, she rubbed Billie's neck. Ellis took the spyglass out of her saddle bag and searched the horizon. Within the vast wilderness, she saw something that didn't quite fit. There was a faint movement, like the twinkling of stars. She wondered if it might be a town. Torn between fear and excitement, she justified staying on the trail but keeping a close watch.

They rode steadily all day but seemed to be making precious little progress. The trail was rockier and hillier than it had looked from the top of the mountain near the cave. The activity she thought she'd seen through the spyglass, flashed in and out of sight as they traveled.

By late afternoon they came to a clearing where a small stream ran through a meadow. Deep woods flanked the grassy lowland. Ellis stopped and listened. She rode Billie toward the water where the horse put her head down to drink. The gurgling of the stream was all she heard, which unsettled her somewhat. But she was hungry and figured Billie was, too. She dismounted and let Billie graze while she made camp.

ELLIS OPENED HER EYES BUT DIDN'T MOVE. SHE FELT A tremor of dawn. Billie nickered softly nearby; her neck tense, head alert. Ellis didn't hear or see anything, but she could feel it, a vibration. She quickly rolled her blankets, tightened her cinch and bridled Billie. She and her horse both looked in the same direction at the same time. Someone was coming and they were coming fast.

She climbed on Billie as the horse pranced in excited circles. Looking for a direction, Ellis saw her saddle bags on a tree stump next to where she'd been sleeping. Billie jerked forward, needing to run. Ellis let her go, grabbed on to the saddle horn with one hand and leaned out, snatching up the bag with the other as they galloped past. She straightened back up into her saddle and positioned the bag in front of her. She gave Billie her head and rode.

The cavalry seemed to come from all directions, and suddenly she was engaged in the group energy of the herd and men. They were riding hard all around her, no words uttered, the energy a moving heat in the cool air. They galloped out into a clearing where, she realized, another battalion was riding toward them. The ground rumbled, hooves pounded, the wind muffled other sounds. Then one of the soldiers riding ahead of her pulled his revolver and shot over his horse's head. That shot transformed the silent dream into a raucous nightmare.

"You there!" someone yelled. "Fall back and reload!"

Was he shouting at her? Reload? She hadn't pulled her gun yet; Earl's gun. But she wasn't going to miss her chance to get to the rear of this foray. She checked behind her to make sure it was clear so she could rein her horse in, but Billie was running with the herd, heedless of flying bullets. A horse went down in front of her. Billie jumped it, and the effort helped to slow her down so Ellis could turn back.

Billie was a mass of hard, nervous muscle. Ellis clung to the saddle as she spun in circles, trying to get the horse stopped. Gaining control, Ellis looked toward the front lines. Through the skirmish, she watched as horses went down, leaving their riders less powerful foot soldiers, if not also injured. A few unscathed horses, having lost their riders, were high-tailing it into the woods.

She was about to join them when a soldier rode up next to her, his yell losing its tenor in the din of battle. From his mount, he reached out and grabbed Billie's bridle, dragging her along in the direction of the fray. Ellis struck at his hand with the end of a rein, but the soldier held on. As she reached for her knife, the soldier's horse went down, rolling with its rider still attached. His grip on Billie's bridle pulled the horse to her knees and Ellis flew off over her shoulder. The bridle dropped from Billie's head and the saddlebag tumbled to the ground as the horse regained her footing, jerked sideways and ran after the other loose horses.

Dazed and disoriented, Ellis grabbed the saddlebag and ran to a fallen tree. She dropped behind it for cover and drew her gun from its holster. In front of her, men were running in all directions. Some lay still on the ground. She meant to point her gun and shoot, but instead, she covered her ears, the noise vibrating in her head. Someone ran up from behind her and dropped next to her. She pointed the gun in his direction. Blood painted his shirt in shades of red and brown. He smelled like gun powder and rank mud. She thought of Earl.

"Don't shoot, I'm on your side," he panted, voice raised above the din.

He was a young, smooth-faced man, not much older than herself. Was he smiling?

"This is gonna be a good win. We got twice as many men as they do. C'mon!" He got up to forge ahead and Ellis almost followed him, but he dropped not ten yards from where she was. She ducked when he was hit and started looking for a way out toward the woods. She raised her gun, to peek over the log, but the fighting seemed to be moving in a swarm away from her. She waited. *Wasn't the war over?* she wondered. Maybe they'd been wrong.

Soon she heard only random pops from distant gunfire. She stood up slowly, and could barely take in the carnage before her. Bloody bodies of men and horses, still and stagnant. Her ears rang, but at the same time there was an eerie quiet. Stunned and sickened, she heard a soft moan. Could any of these torn bodies still be alive? How was she still alive? A whimper and movement came from the young boy who had hidden behind the tree with her. She ran to him and dropped to her knees. His chest and stomach were so bloody she couldn't tell what his injuries were. She had to stop the bleeding. She ripped open his shirt.

"Where are you hit? What can I do?" her voice a choked whisper. She searched his torso for a wound, and froze.

"Can't do anything for me, darlin', but you get yourself into those woods and disappear. And take my gun with you. I was out here fightin' with my husband until he got killed." Ellis stared at the soldier, another woman like her, caught up in this battle. The soldier's voice gurgled and she choked back a cough.

"What?" Ellis asked, stunned.

"We were headed north, toward Kansas City. I thought once I was there I'd be safe. But..." she winced. "Damn, the war's supposed to be over. This wasn't supposed to happen." Her gun was still in her hand. She gave it to Ellis. "You may need more fire power than you've got. Learn to fight like you look. They find a girl out here and no tellin' what will happen to you. You hear?"

"How did you know?" Ellis looked at the blood-stained gun. Then she looked back into the woman's face. "My brother—," she started, but the woman stared past Ellis, like she was looking at someone behind her. Ellis felt a presence and turned, but no one was there.

Ellis's mother had died slower, easier, and Earl, well, she hadn't seen him go. She guessed everybody died differently. Maybe because of how they met their end, maybe because of who they were.

Her body tingled, energized, alert. She rubbed at a heat in her shoulder. Her hand came away bloody. Everywhere she looked there was blood. She saw movement ahead and thought some of the soldiers were coming back. She grabbed the extra gun and tried not to look at the dead woman's face as she said a silent 'much obliged' and ran toward the woods. Stumbling, she almost fell, but caught herself. She felt a distant pain, like it didn't belong to her. She glanced at the ground and saw the bodies of a dead soldier and horse. They lay there, sideways and muddy, but as if they were still running. In his hand, the soldier gripped Billie's bridle. She watched the horse's ribs , but saw no movement. Picking up the bridle, she pried it from the dead soldier's grip. She wondered if she'd be able to find Billie or if Billie was even still alive—or injured. One way or another, she had to find her. Slinging the bridle over one shoulder, saddle-bags over the other, Ellis took cover in the woods. She hid on top of a knoll where she could watch the battlefield.

Some of the soldiers did come back, maybe to see if there was anyone alive. They walked among the scattered bodies, checked pockets and grabbed spent weapons. Ellis couldn't help but wonder if there were other women, girls like her, scattered on the blood-soaked ground that once was no more than a corn field or winter pasture. A wagon showed up carrying three men with shovels and they started digging. She wanted to get as far away from there as possible. She put the extra pistol in her belt and headed off on foot through the woods.

She finally got far enough away that she couldn't hear the digging or the voices anymore. Though she would hear them again in the quiet hours of night, for now, the silence of the woods was welcome. She stopped to listen, to see if she could hear a horse's footsteps or the chomping of grass. But all she heard was the natural rustle of leaves and branches in the trees and the occasional bird call over the dull ringing in her ears.

Her body numb, she strained to put one foot in front of the other for the longest time, staring down at the ground in front of her and occasionally looking up to scout the distance. She walked and watched, smelling the decaying forest floor, and taking comfort in the damp air. She could hear her own breathing and now and then her eyes closed for a moment, though she kept walking. She yearned for those peaceful moments with closed eyes, and they would close for longer and longer periods. The day fading behind her.

She forced herself awake, trudging through a meadow, knee-high pasture slowing her steps. From the evening's dusk a tiny yellow glow blinked in front of her. She wouldn't allow her feet to stop. Another blinking light, and another. Lightning bugs surrounded her like stars, as if she were in heaven. Earl had named his pony Firefly. She felt her twin's absence keenly and as she struggled forward, steps burdened, she thought of the letter she would write him when she finally stopped walking.

*Dear Earl,*

*I got caught up in a battle again today and I swear it felt like that time we tried playing in a dust devil. You remember that? You said you'd done it lots of times and it was fun, so I ran over and jumped in. Before I knew it my eyes were full of sand and I could hardly breathe. It knocked me down and moved on without me. I remember how dirty I felt and you falling down laughing. Today was nothing to laugh about, but I felt just as dirty. A lot of horses went down. Hey, did you know Billie can jump? There was a boy, Earl, a boy like me. She was so excited about the fighting that I started getting excited, too. For a moment I wasn't scared anymore, just excited. Then I saw that soldier fall. It wasn't like Mama's dying, a steady weakness; and it wasn't like you, not waking up. She was talking to me, words flowing with the life blood pouring out of her. She was telling me her story and then just stopped.*

chapter

# ELEVEN

ELLIS DREAMT A HAWK FLEW DOWN AND LIGHTED ON HER shoulder. The raptor's talons gripped her and it tried to fly, but the weight was too great for the small bird. Yet the bird kept trying, ripping and tearing at flesh and muscle, unable or unwilling to fail.

Through the blur of partially opened eyes, she looked through tree branches, felt herself laying flat on the ground, covered with a blanket; felt something soft under her head. She sensed warmth, smelled fragrant smoke. No sounds. She surrendered to unconsciousness.

She thought her eyes were open, staring into a thick fog. The call of a distant bird; not a hawk, but the chirrup of a Blue Jay. Water splashed. Rain? The river. No, water meeting metal. She felt a gentle touch on her shoulder.

For a moment she thought she might be in heaven. But the moment faded into visions of smoky gunshots, screaming horses, flowing blood. Pain, the hawk again, and a surge of panic. This must be hell. Her eyes flew open.

The face in front of her bore a dark countenance. Bronzed skin, black hair, a grim seriousness. Was this the devil laying a hand on her shoulder; not the one where the hawk perched? But the touch was cool and calming. Ellis tried to jerk away, but her body resisted her. She squinted through the fog and searched the sullen face. In it, she saw her mother, then Earl, then the dead soldier's stare. As those faces and her vision cleared, she felt as if she was floating; back into herself. The eyes watching her now, were dark not only in color, but in the magnitude of what they held. Like looking into a deep black lake where joyful memories sunk into recent sorrow.

"Hey, you okay?" someone asked.

Ellis startled into a sitting position, dizzy, and reached for her knife. It wasn't there. Neither was her gun. In fact, other than tattered long johns, even her clothes were missing. She clutched a blanket around her shoulders and leaned back against a tree.

"Whoa, there. It's okay, I'm not gonna hurt you." A woman's voice, deep and tranquil. "Nobody here but me. Do you remember what happened? What's your name?"

Ellis's mind cleared slowly. The battle. Billie running away with the other horses. The dead soldier. All the dead soldiers. The horses. Watching the wagons return. Men and shovels.

"I just—took off on foot." Her own voice echoed in her head. "Billie…"

"Billie—that your name?"

Ellis stared at the dark-eyed woman. Shaking her head in slow motion, words escaped her mouth. "Ellis," she said, though she wasn't quite sure. "Who are you?"

"I'm called Libby. Some skirmish happened about five miles back; a couple days ago looked like. Were you with them?"

Ellis scanned the woman slowly. At first all she saw was Libby's determined face, then a felted wool hat on her head, a turkey feather in the brim of the hat. She blinked and noticed the woman's shirt sleeves billowed as her arms worked. Blinked again. Leather lacing twined like snakes, securing moccasins over woolen trousers.

Ellis wanted to move, run, but her body felt trapped in a dream. A rabbit in a snare. "Didn't mean to be. Just got swept up, I guess." She felt around for her clothes. Looked sideways at Libby.

"Your clothes are dryin'. I washed them." Libby rose and walked toward the fire, where she had constructed a makeshift drying rack out of branches.

"You took my clothes off?" Ellis asked.

"I did. You had blood all over you. I couldn't tell where you were injured. Other than some bruises, turns out it was just your shoulder and that's a clean graze."

Ellis felt her shoulder. The one the hawk had a hold of. Her hand touched a thick bandage.

"How's it feel?" Libby asked, scrutinizing Ellis's face.

"A little sore. Doesn't hurt much." Ellis's brow wrinkled. "Was there a hawk?"

"What?"

Ellis shook her head; pressed her fingers to her forehead. "No. Nothin'."

Libby rose and walked to the fire. She removed Ellis's clothes from the drying branches and brought them to her. "You were out when I found you. Another day after that. I'm waiting for my...friends. I gotta say, you surprised me. I didn't know you were a girl until I got your clothes off." She smiled at Ellis. It wasn't much of a smile, but Ellis figured it might be as much as you'd ever get from this woman named Libby. "Don't worry. I won't let on. The folks I'm traveling with won't mind, but if you feel safer that way, you keep it up."

Ellis started to stand, but the dizziness stopped her.

"Here, easy now," cautioned Libby. She helped her up and stood next to her for support while Ellis dressed herself.

Ellis first noticed the folded cloth between her legs when she lifted a foot to put her pants on. Her hand went to the cloth, she looked at Libby.

"I thought you were wounded worse than just your shoulder until I figured it out." Libby smiled that slack, comfortable smile again.

Ellis thought about it, felt a twinge in her gut, and blushed. She remembered her Mama's embarrassed but proud face when she'd found Ellis crying, the young girl thinking she'd injured herself riding. They had laughed and cried together, an intimate celebration of mother and daughter.

She finished dressing and sat down, exhausted. Libby, a petite woman, a few years older than Ellis, stirred something in a pot over the fire. She poured a hot liquid into a tin cup and offered it to Ellis.

Ellis took the cup. The liquid had a pungent, weedy smell.

"Go on," urged Libby. "It'll help."

Ellis's movements were slow and stiff, but she sipped from the cup and was surprised by the sweetness.

Libby brought her a plate of beans and bread. "Drink it all before you eat." Ellis finished the tea and ate hungrily. She watched Libby walk up to a small black horse, grab a handful of mane and vault onto the horse's back. Her movements were practiced and fluid. She looked down at Ellis.

"Where are you going?" Ellis was feeling dizzy again, but a peaceful fog enveloped her.

"You stay put. I'll be back," Libby said.

The words echoed as if spoken across a canyon. As Ellis tried to figure out if she was dead or alive, she heard a hawk screech. She looked up and then back in the direction of Libby's departure. Her mind fogged, but she finished her meal before falling into a sound sleep.

———

ELLIS FELT THE WARM GROUND BENEATH HER AND SMELLED smoke from a campfire. She heard low, muffled voices. She struggled to open her eyes and sat up too quickly, feeling faint. Libby was already at her side.

"It's okay, this is my group."

A black man stood next to Libby. He was just a head taller, with broad shoulders. He wore the same kind of clothes as Libby, suspenders holding up worn dungarees. His un-dyed shirt needed washing. He looked at Ellis with wary, but kind eyes. He spoke to Libby. "Good to see he's awake. We'll have to move out soon."

The wooziness dissipated and Ellis sat up slowly. The man held a plate of beans and hardtack in front of her. She wondered how long it had been since Libby had fed her a similar fare. She must have slept through the night. Morning light streaked through the pine and elm. She took the plate.

"Wait before you eat." He then offered her a tin cup. The liquid smelled like the drink Libby had given her earlier. She breathed in its aroma. "It'll help you keep that food down. Your stomach might not take to it otherwise."

This meal had some meat mixed in. It smelled good, reminding Ellis of a venison stew Mama used to make. Ellis was hungry, but waited, warily watching the others. The black man, now sitting next to Libby, raised his fork, smiled and began eating. Libby lifted her fork and nodded to Ellis. Ellis didn't know why this woman had helped her. But somehow she trusted her, even though she wasn't sure about the others. The two men sitting on the other side of the fire didn't seem interested in Ellis. They ate and kept their heads down. Didn't talk much. Their hands appeared dark and weathered, like they'd waved a thousand goodbyes. When they all finished eating, Libby gathered the tin plates and handed them to the man next to her. He washed them in a bucket of water.

Libby kneeled in front of Ellis, blocking the men's view. "Let's look at that shoulder," she said. She reached toward her in a slow and skilled manner that reminded Ellis of her father working with a young horse. "*You don't want to scare them with quick movements, but you can't be too timid either,*" he would instruct. "*If you treat them with respect and confidence, that's what you'll get out of them.*"

Libby seemed to be working from the same book. She unbuttoned just enough of Ellis's shirt to allow access to the shoulder wound. Ellis couldn't see the men on the other side of the camp, but could tell from the muffled sounds and low talking they were stowing gear and preparing their horses.

The herb mixture, with which Libby had treated the wound, seemed to be working. The shoulder was still sore, but clean and dry, and overall Ellis felt better. Libby re-bandaged the wound and helped Ellis button her shirt and pull on her vest and coat.

The man who had been sitting close to Libby, crouched by the fire. He scraped dirt from the ground and tossed it on the flames; stirred the coals with a stick and added more dirt, putting the fire out slowly. When he looked up, his eyes met Ellis's. His face remained stoic and unsmiling. He looked at Libby and his eyes softened, a hint of a smile touched his lips. Looking back at Ellis he said, "My name's Abe. Like Mr. Lincoln, God rest his soul." Abe looked down and shook his head, then looked up again. That there's George," nodding to a taller, well-built man wearing spectacles, "And that's Miles," nodding toward the third man who looked older than the others, yet tough and poised.

Both of the men glanced at Ellis when introduced, but continued tightening cinches and packing saddlebags. Miles tied a bedroll onto the back of his saddle, his horse's gray rump toward Ellis. Her gaze took in the color of the horse, followed its movements.

She rose slowly and walked up to the gelding. She brushed away the dirt on its left shoulder. A scar shaped like a "C". *"C, for Cady,"* Earl had boasted. *"He's supposed to be with me."*

"Where'd you get this horse?" Ellis asked. Miles looked at her and then at Abe. Ellis moved her gaze to the horse's head. "Smokey." She stroked his neck. "Where'd you get him?" She felt a rage bubble up in her; a storm of guilt return. "This is my brother's horse." The accusation rose in her voice putting Miles and the others on edge.

"Where'd you get him!" she snapped. "What did you do with my brother!" She moved aggressively toward Miles. He drew a knife. Ellis stopped. In her mind she saw Earl drawing his knife, a stick that he had carved to look like a knife so he could teach her what Jack had taught him. How to defend herself.

"Hey now," said Libby, stepping between them. "Take it easy." She held her hands out motioning to Miles to put the knife away. She spoke calmly to Ellis. "We found the horse a couple days ago. We—buried the man. Didn't feel right leavin' him. Nobody else around. We reckoned no one would miss the horse."

"Was Earl—the man, was he…" Ellis choked on the question she wanted to ask about her brother's body. She had suffered over not being able to bury him. Knowing that the beauty of the wilderness could betray its own cruelty.

Miles spoke. "He was still pretty much in one piece. We buried him the best we could."

Libby gave Miles an annoyed glance, then looked at Ellis's fretful face. "He's at peace now. You got nothin' to worry about."

Ellis wasn't listening. Her mind took her back to that place where Earl had died. Their last day together. She had wanted to stay with him, bury him, but something had scared her off. The ferryman, the soldiers? Or was it this group?

"I've gotta go back," Ellis mumbled, still looking at the ground. She looked up at Libby. "I've gotta go back."

"Nothin' to go back to. You don't wanna go back now," Libby said.

Ellis heard her mother's voice. *"Look forward. Nothin' worth thinking about behind you."* Defeated, she stood next to Smokey. Hands on the horse's neck, she closed her eyes and pressed her forehead to his warm hide.

"I ain't no horse thief," Miles said. "Your brother—well, I guess if it was your brother's horse, he's yours now." Abe added, "Look, we're headed north and you're welcome to join us. I figure you might want the company. But if not, that's okay. It's a free world. Well, at least it's gettin' more that way all the time. That's what we're headed for."

Ellis listened to Abe's words, sifting through information and possibilities. Earl was buried, Smokey was safe. Billie might still be out there somewhere. Then her thoughts caught on something Abe had said. "So, it's true—about Mr. Lincoln? Somebody killed him?"

"Yeah. Not a week after Lee surrendered. Country didn't have enough goin' on." Abe shoved supplies in a leather satchel; shook his head again, slowly. The others nodded, still and reverent.

Ellis surveyed the group and asked the question before thinking much about it. "Are you runaway slaves?"

Abe and the other men looked at one another. Libby looked at Abe, then lowered her eyes.

Abe explained, "Son…Ellis, ain't it? The war's over but the battles are still happening. We fought when we had to but we don't wanna fight anymore. We were already up north. George there, he was a teacher in St. Louis. Miles fought some, took care of Union horses. Those that did stay south don't have it much better than they did before. For most of them, the land they were given got taken away again. You got people down there so mad they're meaner than ever, and some have a right to be." Abe continued to pack up belongings. Ellis realized Abe was the only one of their group on foot.

"We're trying to put our families back together and head up toward a peaceful life. We helped out some other folks along the way. Me and my wife—" he looked at Libby, "—we studied all we could about treating what ails folks."

Ellis heard George and Miles snicker.

"Yeah, well, Libby's better at that than me, but I make a better stew," Abe said and he turned to smile at Libby. "I didn't have a Cherokee Mama and Grandma to teach me such things."

Libby acknowledged him with a glance, and swung up onto her horse. Ellis thought Libby was beautiful; an elegant rider, her face fine featured and smooth skinned, yet hard to read. The little black gelding wasn't a handsome horse, but he had a sturdy mustang build. Together they looked confident and powerful.

"She rides better than me, too. Better than most, for what it's worth. We got higher aspirations than share-croppin'."

Ellis's heart warmed. She knew Libby was right, just like Mama had been. There was nothing to go back to. And yet she worried about going forward with this group. She felt comfortable with them now, but...

"But—I'm white," Ellis said under her breath, as if she was thinking out loud, as if it was a secret. She heard a chortle from George. He and Abe exchanged a look, a smile. "Why would you want me with you? What if..."

"You don't have to be black to want your freedom," Abe continued. He looked at George. "There's some white blood underneath some of this dark skin." He turned back to Ellis. "Kid, I don't know why you were fighting with that bunch, but we kind of figured you just got caught up. We seen it before. You're not in any uniform, so you're a free agent. Just like we are. You can tell us your story if you want, but for now we gotta get movin'."

Ellis scrambled up and packed her bedroll. She knew what it was like traveling alone.

George mounted his horse. Miles held out Smokey's reins to Ellis, but she shook her head. She stroked Smokey's neck. "I think I'll walk a while," she said.

Libby rode off on the black, ahead of the group. Ellis watched her ride away.

"She'll be back. Just likes to scout ahead for us sometimes," explained Abe.

"Where'd she learn to ride like that?" asked Ellis.

Abe smiled, looked at the ground before glancing at Ellis. "Well, just born to it, I think. Then she did a lot of it. Worked for the Pony Express. You heard of 'em?"

Ellis looked at Abe. "Heard of them, sure."

"Well, she wasn't much older than you when she rode for them. Cut her hair short and rode hard." He smiled to himself. "Huh, went by 'Elby' then. No one ever knew."

"Elby?" questioned Ellis.

"Her Indian name is Little Bird, L.B."

Ellis locked eyes with Abe. She felt vulnerable and safe at the same time. Abe smiled and Ellis looked away.

*chapter*
# TWELVE

THEY TREKKED FOR HOURS AT A PRETTY GOOD CLIP, TAKING turns on foot and horseback. Along the way they chewed on a dried food made from meat and berries. The salty-sweet taste was pleasant enough. Ellis felt tired, but not as fatigued as she had been. Libby rode back and slid gracefully off the black horse, handing the reins to Abe. He jumped on and stayed at the back of the group. Libby walked with Ellis.

"What happened to the rest of your horses?" Ellis asked.

"We were all on foot in the beginning. It was easier to hop trains and find lodging and safe houses without them. But now that we're headed back, riding's faster. We've found bands of abandoned horses all along the main trails and scattered in the woods." She motioned to the black gelding Abe was riding and the brown Miles was on. "We came across those two near a river a few weeks back. And, well, then the gray. We're bound to find more. Some of them rally after being let go. Some don't." She looked at Ellis. "You've got that bridle and saddlebags. What happened to yours?"

Ellis didn't want to think about that day, but an urge to explain herself surfaced. "I came off her and she ran off with some others. The way they were shooting at the horses—I'm glad she got away."

Libby watched the ground as they walked.

Ellis stared ahead, remembering that moment, trying to squeeze the images from her mind. "I hope—" Ellis blinked away the heated pressure of tears. "If I'd have tried to ride off they would've shot us both for sure." She looked down at the trail.

Libby nodded. "Well, hope your horse made out better than you did."

"Or at least as good," Ellis muttered. She longed for Billie, but was glad for company.

Suddenly, George stopped his horse and raised his hand. The others paused and hushed. He motioned to Libby to come forward. In front of them was a small herd of horses, a couple grazing beside the trail, others lying down.

Ellis started to follow Libby toward the herd. When she came alongside Abe on the black horse, he reached out a hand, touching her shoulder to stop her. They were all watching Libby.

Ellis scanned the herd as Libby moved forward toward them. A skinny but well-built sorrel raised its head and nickered. A brown mare stepped in close to it, then limped away. One of the horses that was lying down got up and followed the mare. Ellis couldn't see them all for the trees and brush. She wanted to get closer, but joined the others watching Libby's slow, supple movements.

Libby walked a few steps closer to the sorrel, the horse watching her but not moving. The woman stood still with her hands open as if offering something. The sorrel looked at her, put its head down for a bite of grass, watching her while he chewed. Libby didn't move. Soon the horse raised its head, leaned in her direction, took a step. Libby backed up slightly, slowly knelt on one knee. The horse put its head down and walked toward her. It reached its nose out, and Libby offered her palm. The horse lowered its head again, as if thinking. Then it took another step toward Libby and nuzzled her fingers. Libby touched the horse's nose, then rose slowly and continued to rub and pet the horse. She drew a length of leather from her waist and put it around the horse's neck.

Ellis walked slowly toward them. She untied Billie's bridle from her waist and held it out to Libby.

Libby shook her head. "I got a rope. You keep that handy."

Ellis nodded. She stroked the horse, admiring its red coat, thankful there was at least one in relatively good shape. Looking over its back, she noticed the brown mare standing next to a horse struggling to get to its feet. It seemed undecided whether to get up or lie flat, but a saddle kept it from doing either. Ellis froze, staring at the struggling bay.

Abe brought Libby's rope to her and she fashioned a halter and lead for the sorrel as she followed Ellis's gaze. "Looks like there's a saddle needs to come off one," she said to Abe, handing him the sorrel's lead. When she turned back, Ellis was running toward the struggling horse. Falling to her knees beside it, she put her hands on the horse's neck and closed her eyes. Libby and Miles walked up beside her.

"I thought it was Billie, but..." Ellis whispered.

Miles looked toward the other horses. "Now and then one escapes a battle, but these others—throw-aways," he scoffed. "They get too tuckered out to go on and the soldiers trade 'em for fresh mounts and keep going, leave 'em behind to fend for themselves."

"Let's see if we can get him up. We can use the saddle and he'd be better off without it," Libby said.

Each time the horse attempted to stand, the three of them pushed with his effort. The bay gelding finally succeeded in getting his feet under him.

"That a boy," said Ellis, rubbing his neck. Now that the horse was standing, it didn't look much like Billie after all. He was thicker, less refined, and though covered with mud, both front feet were white up to the fetlocks.

Libby's hands searched the horse's body, feeling down each leg and lifting each foot. "I think it's just fatigue." She carefully lifted the saddle off. The thin blanket stuck to the horse's back. She gradually peeled it off, taking patches of hair and hide with it.

Ellis felt sick. She wondered how long this horse had been suffering under that saddle. "Is he gonna be all right?"

The horse walked away from Libby. His movement was slow, but he seemed unbothered. "He might be, might not." She checked the saddle over. It was a western saddle, not a McClellan like the cavalry used. The leather was scuffed and worn. One stirrup was broken, but the leather covering held it together. The wooden tree was still intact. Libby checked the cinch, laid it out on the ground and rubbed it clean of hair and blood. Picking it up, she tossed the cinch over the saddle and held it out to Ellis. "Here, take this." She nodded toward the sorrel. "Saddle that one and we'll go check on the others."

Ellis accepted it. The saddle was light, but the weight of her thoughts grew unbearable.

"Don't worry," Libby said, as she shook out the thin blanket. "Your horse hasn't been out there that long." She refolded the blanket and handed it to Ellis.

Ellis glanced at Libby, hoping to see the truth in what she said. Taking the blanket, she nodded slowly. "What about those others?"

"They'll work with nature. In a few years there'll be some nice herds of tough mustangs out here."

Abe held the sorrel attached to Libby's rope, as Ellis saddled the horse. George fingered the leads of the other horses as they grazed. Once saddled, Abe led the sorrel to a tree stump and tried to mount, but the horse kept moving away. Libby and Miles returned from checking on the rest of the herd. They all watched Abe's efforts, but didn't offer any help. After leading the horse up to the stump for the third time, Abe looked at the other men. "If he won't stand still this time, I'm walking." Libby smiled and looked at the ground.

Miles walked over to the stump, leading Smokey. "Here, this one might suit you better. He's well-trained and steady." He offered the reins to Abe.

"Well, Red," Abe said to the sorrel, "you're in for it now." He traded reins with Miles but before mounting he looked over at Ellis, his eyes asking her permission. She was looking down, grasping the bridle she wore across her chest. She looked up, caught his gaze, nodded.

Miles stroked the sorrel's neck, led him around in a few circles, grabbed the saddle horn and swung himself gracefully into the saddle. The horse stood still while Miles rubbed his neck. He regarded Abe on Smokey.

"You make sure you stay on that horse, now, Abe," Miles teased, and he and George laughed. Abe smiled, looked at Libby and cocked his head, raising an eyebrow as if to say, 'well, I tried,' before he fell into line behind the others.

Libby jumped on the black horse and gave Ellis a hand up to ride double. "He can handle both of us for a bit."

Libby and Ellis rode in front of the group, setting a slow but steady pace. Ellis's thoughts were on Billie. She tried to erase the visions of the battlefield. The screaming men and tangled hoofbeats, screeching metal swords, deafening explosions. The acrid smell of gunpowder, blood, and Billie stumbling. She looked behind her at the sorrel Miles was riding. If that horse could live through it, surely Billie could.

⁓

AS THE EVENING LIGHT DIMMED, ELLIS REALIZED THEY had been riding in a comfortable silence. The muscular black horse was a hasty walker and they often found themselves having to wait for the rest of the group to catch up. Searching the countryside, Ellis had been able to leave behind some thoughts of loss, as she moved with the horse and the rider in front of her. She felt a calm from both and she wondered if Libby was calming the horse, or the horse's quietness was calming Libby. In this moment Ellis felt soothed by them both and contemplated how she got here from the tumult of the battlefield.

"Why—" Her voice came out as a whisper.

Libby turned her head. "You say something?"

Ellis cleared her throat. "How did you find me? Why did you help me?"

Libby looked ahead. She sighed. "We've helped others. Most of them on the run from one battle or another. Can't blame 'em. Did what we could."

"My brother—before he died, he said he'd helped some folks—some Negroes. He didn't say much more about it, but…"

Libby stopped her horse, turned to look behind her for the others who had fallen back. "Let's wait up here, give him a rest," she said, patting the horse's neck. She offered Ellis a hand down, then swung a leg over and dismounted. She led the horse to some grass on the side of the trail where he put his head down to graze.

Both women remained silent as they watched and considered the terrain. Now and then a breeze moved a leaf high on a sweetgum or flickered through the weedy grasses. They listened to the peacefulness. Libby reached for her canteen.

"I knew him," Libby said, taking a drink. She offered the canteen to Ellis.

"What?"

"I knew your brother."

Ellis, her brow furrowed, looked at Libby.

"I didn't know his name. Wasn't even sure where he came from, but he helped us move some folks to a safe station. I recognized him when we found him…buried him." Libby glanced at Ellis, again offered her the canteen.

Ellis took the canteen, drank and handed it back.

"When I saw you, I thought I was looking at a ghost. You looked so much like him. Thought I was seeing things." She paused, searched Ellis's face. "Nobody talked much about family. Reckoned if you didn't talk about people they stayed in your memory the way you left 'em, you know?" Libby tied the canteen back on her saddle; glanced at Ellis, who was looking at the ground.

"The people he helped," Ellis queried, "did they make it?"

Libby nodded, "As far as we know, yeah. He followed them north for a ways. We had to go a different direction with another group. When we came back we followed his tracks for a while, but lost him near the Tennessee border. He knew the area better than us and he was riding hard, like he was trying to get somewhere."

The women's eyes met. The silence was broken by the rhythmic hoofbeats and low voices of Abe, George and Miles as they rode into sight. Libby mounted her horse. Ellis stared off into the woods. She heard Earl's voice. *I just hope I'll be forgiven for what I've had to do...I'm so glad you found me. You brought me back home...I was on my way back...I swear.*

"C'mon." Libby reached down, offering a hand. "A little longer and we'll make camp."

Ellis grabbed Libby's arm and swung up behind her, onto the black horse. A sadness turned wistful. "Home," she whispered.

Libby turned an ear toward her. "What?"

"He made himself out to be an outlaw. But he was a hero." Her voice cracked. "Earl was headed home."

# chapter
# THIRTEEN

THE MORNING SHADOWS DISAPPEARED, MIDDAY CARRYING the scent of horse sweat and storm clouds. Crickets chirped in loud symphony and the horses swished their tails in rhythm against the flies. Moving water chattered just ahead of them, lifting the heads of the horses and the spirits of the riders.

They dismounted by the stream, spread out, and let the horses drink. Ellis knelt to splash her face. She untied her neckerchief and wet it in the cool water. The cloth had been washed of its past by rivers and rain. If only her memories could be cleansed as easily. Raising her head, she wiped the back of her neck and looked across the creek. Hoofprints. The grassy riverbank rose abruptly on the far side of the stream. She stood, but couldn't see beyond the top of the bank. Stepping into the water she rushed toward the slope. Abe came up behind her, grabbing her around the waist to hold her back.

"Wait," he warned, releasing his grasp. We don't know who's up there."

Libby crawled up the embankment, keeping her head low when she reached the top. She slowly stood and waved the others up.

An emerald meadow spread before them. Oak and cottonwood trembled in a moist breeze. A dozen or more horses grazed and lounged. One stood saddled. Ellis moved forward, trying to keep quiet. She squeezed her eyes shut, opened them again. "Billie," she said, a question, a whisper of hope. Abe reached out to stop her, wary of the surroundings, but she pulled free and ran out into the meadow.

As she got closer, she slowed her step so as not to spook the horses, and for one woeful moment she thought maybe it wasn't Billie, maybe she just wanted it to be, maybe hope would escape her once more. The bay mare looked up at her, nickered, and put her head back down to eat. Ellis stopped, watched the horse, smiled. The horse looked up again and walked toward Ellis. Trembling, the girl stepped forward and rubbed Billie's neck and shoulder as she grazed. She buried her face in the mare's mane. She had found Earl, and now Billie. She felt the weight of the odds and mourned the balance of life. Maybe it was Earl looking over her now. Maybe it was her father. Maybe it was just coincidence. Maybe there was no balance. Would luck run out on the next battlefield?

Ellis loosened the saddle's cinch and lifted it off the horse's back. Before removing the blanket, she felt under it with her hands. She carefully slid the blanket off. Dark patches of sweat showed the outline of the saddle, and hairless patches of hide on the withers had been concealed by the blanket, but no sores were present. Billie's right shoulder had suffered a gash that was now scabbed over.

Libby, leading her black horse, walked up to Ellis. "You gonna bridle that horse?" she smirked. Ellis looked at her and smiled. It sounded like something Earl would say. She bridled Billie, then rubbed her back with a handful of dried grass.

Once re-saddled, her belongings secured, she reached into one of the leather pockets of her saddle bags and felt her journal, held her hand there while thoughts played in her head. She heard a horse nicker and looked back at the group. They stood on the edge of the meadow, watching her.

Ellis and Libby walked back to the group, leading their horses. Billie nickered and Smokey nickered back.

Abe chuckled and said, "Well, didn't we get lucky running into you."

Ellis smiled, mounted Billie and patted her rump.

"Too bad we can't take more of them," said Miles, looking toward the herd.

A pair of hawks circled over the meadow, as it started to rain. The shower was brief, leaving steam rising from the grass, a heady smell in the air. Ellis leaned forward, touching her face to Billie's damp neck, breathing in her wet-horse scent, feeling her warmth. Billie's presence nourished Ellis like the spring rain nourished the trees. One of the hawks cried out as the other landed on a high branch. The herd watched the riders pass; a tranquil snort, a contented swish of a tail. Then, heads lowered, they returned to peacefully grazing.

ELLIS FELL INTO THE NATURAL RHYTHM OF RIDING BILLIE. She fit the horse and rode as if Billie's stride was her own. Her legs melted into the horse's sides. Flesh, leather and hide moved as one being. The sway of the saddle became her own jaunty cadence. Without effort, she rode as if in a dream. And yet, if this dream were a picture, it would show a fuzzy dark edge. As the group rode on in silence, that edge crept farther into the serene image. The beauty of a burgeoning spring of new leaves and early grasses turned monotonous. Ellis heard whispers. Startled, she looked at her traveling companions. Abe rode beside her on Smokey. She looked at the horse's calm face, made eye contact with Abe, and the whispers stopped. Perhaps she had fallen asleep, she thought.

She urged Billie into a trot to catch up to Libby, and rode beside her. Libby acknowledged Ellis and returned to her forward gaze.

"Do you know where we are?" Ellis asked.

"We'll be passin' some homesteads in a day or two. If the folks stuck around, that is." Libby kept her eyes searching ahead. "There were some good people around here. Helped us out before." She waved a fly off her horse's neck. "We'll be getting close to a town after that." She turned her head toward Ellis. "You okay with that?"

Ellis watched the trail ahead of them. She hadn't thought about it for a while, what it might be like to be in a town. She suddenly felt dizzy, colors dimmed, that dark edge creeping into the picture. Her hand felt for the tintype of Virginia she still had in her vest pocket. She reached in and pulled it out. Looking at the young woman's face, she saw her own. She imagined wearing that stiff dress, the freshly laundered smell of lye and starch. She quickly pocketed the photograph. Gripping Billie's mane in one hand, to steady herself, she closed her eyes. The image faded and she breathed in the smell of sycamore and George's pipe tobacco.

Trotting up on the other side of Libby, George took the pipe from his mouth. "Isn't that lake around here somewhere?" he asked Libby.

"A few more miles, I think," Libby answered.

George's eyes flitted between Libby and Ellis before he turned his horse around, returning to the back of the group.

Libby scrutinized Ellis. "Are you okay?"

Ellis opened her eyes. The ground flashed beneath her as if she were still and it was moving. Then it slowed and the whispered voices returned. "I—," she started, but heard Mama say, "...*look forward, there's nothing behind you...*" Earl said, "*If you're gonna ride with me...*" The bleeding soldier said, "*...keep those boy duds on...no tellin' what will happen to you...*"

Billie slowed to a stop. Ellis stared straight ahead, her face pallid. Libby turned her horse and jumped off. She hurried to Ellis's side and laid a hand on her leg. "Hey, look at me," she said to Ellis, but Ellis didn't move. "Hey!" she said louder. Billie lifted her head and moved away from Libby as she caught the reins.

Ellis looked down at her friend. "What is that...?" whispered Ellis.

"What is what?" said Libby.

"The voices...the whispers..." She looked around, disoriented.

The others had caught up and stopped their horses. "What is it?" asked Abe.

"I think we need to stop and rest a while," said Libby, helping Ellis off her horse.

George relit his pipe, leaned on his saddle horn. "We got another couple hours of daylight, if..."

Libby looked up, stopping George in mid-sentence.

Miles rode up next to George. Their eyes met in an unvoiced understanding.

"I think it's hit her," George said to Miles in a low voice.

"Over here," called Abe. He had ridden through a break in the woods and found a small clearing. "We can rest a bit."

Ellis felt heavy, each footstep straining to find the ground. *"Keep moving...stay there...I'll find you..."* The voices grew louder. She covered her ears.

"Make them stop," she cried.

Libby guided her to a tree and helped her sit, leaning against it. Ellis thought she said something to Abe, but the voices and distant screaming filled her head. When her eyes were open, Ellis's world spun, but when she closed them she saw fire and blood and Virginia's dress burning. A girl, waiting for her love to return. A girl whose future Ellis had destroyed. She opened her eyes to the spinning forest and then closed them entering a darkness that held her mother's tears, her brother's bloody face, her father's gentle hands. She stared at those hands as they turned into Libby's, who offered something to Ellis.

"Here, chew on this. Don't swallow it until you've chewed it good," Libby instructed.

The bitter-sweet grassy flavor was not unpleasant. She saw herself as a horse, nibbling hay. As she chewed, the voices began to still, the images faded. Ellis felt her muscles relax. The voices she heard now echoed soft and clear.

"...just a boy."

"I've seen it before...nostalgia..."

"Keep an eye on him...wounded..."

"...the body...healing well. The mind..."

⌒

WHEN ELLIS WOKE, EVERYONE WAS GONE BUT MILES. HE SAT on a rock next to her, whittling on a small piece of wood with a hunting knife. She felt groggy and looked at him warily as she sat up. She sensed it was morning, but didn't remember much from the end of the day before.

"You there now?" he asked.

Ellis was silent for a moment, then as if it was someone else speaking, "I'm—sorry, I don't know what…"

"It's okay." Miles wiped his knife on the leg of his trousers and continued to whittle. "You and me, we've seen a lot. Things no man should have to." He searched her face. "You're young for doin' what you had to. I saw younger and lots older. Some of them that survived seemed okay, but none were joyful comin' off the battlefields."

Ellis's mind cleared and Miles seemed to sense it. He slid down from the rock he was sitting on and leaned back against it, pushed his hat back from his forehead and kept whittling. "Lots of 'em drank to get those sounds and sights out of their heads. I did for a time, myself. But then I figured the Good Lord didn't have me go through all that just to become a drunk."

"How did you…" Ellis started, but wasn't sure how to ask.

"I headed west. Thought I'd go somewhere new where nobody knew who I was, what I'd done. But then I found George and Abe. They had plans to help folks." Miles stopped whittling and examined the piece of wood. "I'd fought hard for the Union, but never felt I helped more than I hurt. I didn't see what good I'd done, except maybe prove a black man could be a good soldier."

Miles stopped whittling and looked into the distance as if he saw something. Ellis followed his gaze but saw nothing.

"All those boy soldiers. Your age, younger. Smooth-faced." He looked at Ellis.

Ellis met his gaze and looked away. She felt exposed, naked.

Miles sniffed and spat. "Look, I don't know where any of us are gonna end up. But I know I did some good now along with the bad. I reckon I'm about even with God. That's all we can hope for. If you're gonna make it, you need to snap to. Those voices you hear, those pictures in your mind, they'll pass. You need to ride strong, ya' hear?"

Ellis listened to his words. She looked around. The sorrel horse and Billie were standing together, each with a back foot cocked, resting. The silence enfolded her like a soft blanket at dusk. Yet it held the weight of sadness, guilt and shame.

"Where are the others?" she asked.

"They went scouting for a trail they knew from the last time through here. There's a lake where we can wash the dust off us. And, if we're lucky, they're huntin' some grub. A venison steak would sure be nice, huh?"

Ellis didn't feel hungry. "Thanks for staying with me."

"Libby makes some strong potions. Never know how somebody's gonna take to 'em." Miles stood and sheathed his knife. "Most people come out the other side better off, though." He looked at Ellis, a hint of a smile on his face. "You ready to ride?"

Ellis forced herself to stand and walk up to Billie. It was all she could do to mount her horse, an overwhelming sadness gripping her bones. Her blood felt thick and stagnant.

"Ride strong," Miles said again, as if to himself, as he mounted his horse.

⌐———

ELLIS TURNED IN HER SADDLE AND WATCHED THE GREEN OF the hills merge behind her. The moist air carried the scent of pine and dogwood. A loon's cry echoed off a small lake, as the riders broke through thick brush. Beaver had partially dammed the stream, forming the lake, but allowing the river to continue on the other side where it tumbled over smooth rocks, creating a soothing voice to the rushing rill.

Further down the bank a thin wisp of smoke rose from a fire where Abe crouched, holding a pan in a gloved hand. Billie nickered and Ellis heard a muffled return. Abe looked up from the fire and waved. They had made camp on a small beach by the river. A spring flood might have swamped the site, but those rains had either already subsided or were yet to come.

Ellis and Miles dismounted and walked their horses down the bank to the beach.

George sat on a blanket on the ground, leaning against his saddle, smoking his pipe and reading a book through wire-rimmed spectacles. The other three horses were unsaddled, hobbled, and grazing on a patch of grass in a small clearing.

Miles unsaddled Smokey and Ellis followed suit, turning Billie loose with the others. She wondered where Libby was, but didn't want to seem too anxious to know. She was relieved when Miles asked.

"Where's LB?"

Abe looked up at him, then back at the pan that contained two small fish. "Libby's scoutin' down stream. Took a line and a snare." Abe looked at Ellis and nodded a greeting.

Ellis wanted to go after Libby, talk to her about what she was feeling. But would a fifteen-year-old boy do that? She reckoned she already looked weak to these men, and that weighed her spirits even more. She laid out her bedroll to sit on and draped a sweaty saddle blanket over the saddle, damp side up. Taking her journal from the saddle bag, she opened it, stared at the place where her pencil touched paper.

A darkness shadowed her as if a cloud had passed over, blocking the sun. She smelled the decay of the hollow tree, winced at the sound of a gun firing, smelled the smoking powder. She tossed the journal and stabbed the pencil into the ground, folding her body, hands behind her head, arms covering her ears, rocking on her haunches.

A loon called and Ellis imagined Earl riding in front of her. Another loon call caused her to unfold, looking for the bird, wanting it to be real. She saw Abe waving at Libby, walking up the shore. Libby carried a string of fish in one hand and two dead rabbits in the other.

"Well, well, I guess we'll eat good tonight," Abe announced, glancing at Ellis.

Ellis stared at Libby for a moment and then straightened. She picked up her journal and extracted the pencil from the sandy dirt, diverting her eyes to the blank page again. Libby's confident gait had emphasized Ellis's weakness all the more. She felt anxious and worthless.

Libby settled by the fire and handed Abe the fish, as Miles walked over and took the rabbits from her. Ellis watched him as he drew his knife from its sheath and settled at a large rock. He started the skinning process, slitting the belly from tail to neck. When he looked up and saw Ellis watching him, he moved his body, blocking her line of sight.

Libby walked up to where Ellis was sitting. She reached out a hand to check her shoulder, but Ellis waved it away, harder than she meant to. She didn't mean to at all.

Libby rose slowly and walked away.

Ellis quickly looked back at her journal and flipped through the pages to the back where she saw Earl's writing. She remembered him, when they were no more than five or six, snaring his first rabbit. He had been so proud when he presented it to Mama, but he couldn't bring himself to gut and skin it. Walter had laughed at him and did it for him, but made him watch. Earl fought tears, but she could tell he was crying.

The voices returned and she wrote what she heard. "... *come down to breakfast...mutual trust...cover your tracks...hold it like this...war's over...*"

Ellis felt a hand on her shoulder, but couldn't move away. The voices faded into the surging of the stream. The smell of gunpowder gave way to fried fish and roasting meat. She opened her eyes and looked up.

George handed her a plate. "Eat. And keep writing," he said.

Ellis took the plate and looked around to see who was watching her. But no one was. Abe and Libby sat next to one another, eating and engaged in a quiet conversation. Miles poured himself a cup of coffee. The horses were grazing and resting. The black gelding lying down, Billie standing over him. The scene was blissful, and yet Ellis felt anxious. Without appetite, she ate her food, hoping it would somehow displace what she was feeling.

George sat next to her. He seemed a man of few words and hadn't spoken much to Ellis at all since they met. She thought he didn't like her. "What you're going through—" he started, "—the voices, the visions. It happens to soldiers. I've been studying it. There's doctors studying it. Trying to find out if there's a way to bring men back, make them see the good in life after seeing the worst. It's not easy. No one wants to talk about it, but that's exactly what needs to be done. It's like when you have a bad dream, as a kid. You tell your Ma or Pa about it and it makes it better, you know?

"I used to tell my brother," Ellis said.

"Yeah, that's it," said George.

"He's dead," said Ellis. Her eyes dry, her face emotionless. She put down her plate and picked up her journal, hugged it close to her chest.

George swallowed. "You like to write?"

Ellis looked at her journal, opened it. What she had been writing was scratchy, almost unreadable. Vacantly, she looked up at George.

"Look, you just keep trying. Write whatever comes to you. If it's those voices, write them down. If it's a memory, write it down, if it's—"

"Get it out on paper," Ellis echoed her mother's voice.

"Yes, exactly," said George.

Ellis looked around the camp, picked up her pencil and turned to a blank page in the journal. For a while she just stared at it, listening to the sounds around her. The dying soldier's breath was drowned out by the gurgling creek. The crack of pistol rounds became high tree branches rubbing in the breeze, a squirrel dropping acorns and pine nuts.

*How I got through it and made it out alive, I'll never know. I do believe some angel watched over me. I don't know if that was Mama or Earl or… There's a sadness in me that I can't seem to shake. I fear if I was alone I'd simply fade away into it; let it all go. But when I think of those soldiers, fighting against all odds still believing they were right. They had to believe, didn't they. Why would they fight, kill, if they didn't believe they were right. If it was just self protection, then what were they protecting themselves from, if not just another scared soldier*

*protecting himself and another, and another after that.*
*On down the line and then where did it all start. Who is*
*responsible for the first blow. Who had the first thought to*
*replace his life with that other life.*

*No, there's something else in us. We're different than*
*a scared rabbit or a hungry wolf. Something drives man;*
*some sense of righteousness. That's what I saw during the*
*heat of battle. Pride, invulnerability. Those cut down died*
*with a look of utter disbelief on their faces. How could it be*
*possible that the invincible were mortal after all.*

Ellis stopped writing and felt a presence behind her.
Without looking she realized it was Billie. The horse sighed
and, with her nose, nudged Ellis's shoulder. For a few seconds
Ellis felt her sadness lift. She set her journal down and stood.
Putting her hands on Billie's back she felt the warmth of the
sun reflecting off her. She felt the life flowing through this
animal that was her companion in her most lonely times. She
looked up, over Billie's back, and saw Abe and Libby sitting by
the fire, George napping with a book open on his chest, Miles
salting the rabbit hides. The still water of the lake reflected
a tranquil blue sky and motionless trees, turning reality up-
side down; the dream and truth coexisting. But, Ellis thought,
which was which?

chapter

# FOURTEEN

ELLIS WOKE BEFORE DAWN. THE TEA LIBBY HAD GIVEN HER before bedding down had kept the nightmares away, but left her groggy. She stumbled her way to a secluded spot to relieve herself, hoping she wouldn't wake anyone. Bright moonlight filtered into the forest. Stepping back onto the sandy riverbank, she looked up and witnessed the full moon gliding into view over the tops of the trees on the opposite shore of the river. The light reflected off the surface of the water and lit up both shores. She watched the silver-white orb, and grew accustomed to the brightness. Downstream she saw the silhouette of horses drinking, their noses disappearing in a thin vail of fog around their feet.

Someone emerged from the woods near the horses. Ellis could tell by the way she moved it was Libby. Backlit by the moon, Libby removed the hobbles from her black gelding. The horse immediately walked into the stream and lay down in the shallow water. He rolled, scratching his back on the sandy bottom, and finally stood to shake off the sand and water. A spray of liquid stars scattered, veiling them in a mystical universe. The horse moved back toward the trees as Libby entered a deeper part of the stream. No flutter of a garment, Libby stood naked. Then like a forest nymph, she disappeared behind a leafy branch reaching over the water.

The forest nymphs of Ellis's childhood were just make believe; tiny creatures going about their business and taking the little girl Ellis was, in stride. Ellis crept down the riverbank, staying close to the shadow of the woods.

Libby had left her clothing on a large rock at the river's bend. From there, Ellis looked back toward the camp but saw no movement. She took off her boots, and as she started to unbutton her shirt she heard a light splash, a sigh. Startled, she hugged her shirt closed and moved from behind the rock toward the water's edge. She couldn't see Libby in the shadowy water below the low-hanging branches, but the reflection of the moon flickered over wavelets. Ellis heard a throaty gasp. She hurried toward the water and as her feet felt its coolness, the moon lit up the shadows. Its light touched Abe's muscular shoulder, his wet back glistening as Libby's fingers dug into him, her face in the crook of his neck.

Ellis drew in a quick breath. She meant to turn away. The slow, rhythmic movement of the couple caught her gaze and held it. The nighttime waters of the lake blanketed the lower half of them. Libby's legs wrapped around Abe's hips, her knees showing at the small of Abe's back, just above the surface of the water. They looked to Ellis like one strange being, breathing, writhing like a two-headed serpent.

Libby's eyes opened. They met Ellis's gaze, but softened and closed again. Ellis looked down into the center of the river. The moon glared back at her. She turned, grabbed her boots, and hurried past the horses, down the stream bank away from camp.

As the moon faded, a pink dawn lit the sky. Ellis stopped at an outcropping of rock shielding an eddy where the water slowed and stilled. A doe and fawn drank downstream. The doe looked up, stared as if to gauge Ellis's intentions, and then turned and quietly walked away, her spotted fawn following closely. The morning air grew thick and warm. The forest woke as Blue Jays gurgled greetings and sparrows chirped at chittering squirrels.

Ellis longed for a real bath with hot water off the stove and a warm room where she could sit in the tub soaking away the grime and guilt. In the fragrant forest she could smell the home-made soap of her childhood mixing with the wood smoke from the hearth, her mother's gentle hand rubbing her back. Long before the war she felt she had been too old for her mother's help with such things, but now a longing for that touch burned her eyes.

Her itchy skin brought her back to the river, and a surge of audacity encouraged her to disrobe. Naked, she walked into the stony-bottomed water and let the current rinse the dirt from her skin.

"You should keep that shoulder dry," Libby said, watching her from a nearby boulder.

Ellis dove for the pool, attempting to shield herself with the deeper water, cooling her embarrassment.

"Don't worry, I'm alone," said Libby, as she slid down the boulder landing quietly on the beach.

"Go away." Those were not the words Ellis wanted to say. Libby hesitated, then turned and started to walk away.

"Wait," said Ellis. Libby stopped but kept her back turned. "I'm sorry. You startled me, is all."

Libby hesitated, then turned back toward Ellis. She sat on the flat rock overhanging the pool and took something out of her pocket. She unsheathed her knife and unwrapped what she held in her hand. Ellis stood in the pool, the water just covering her petite breasts. Libby nodded questioningly toward Ellis's shoulder.

"It's pretty much healed over," Ellis said, glancing at the wound. "I just felt…so dirty."

Libby looked up at the lightening sky. "Might be a hot day." She looked back at Ellis. "Here." She tossed the object.

Ellis caught it as it started to sink next to her.

"Where did you find soap out here?" Ellis asked, rubbing it between her hands, smiling at the lather.

Libby shrugged. She threw Ellis's shirt and long johns to her. "Better wash those, too. They'll dry before we get back to camp."

Ellis scrubbed soap into the worn material and squeezed it into a lather, then rinsed it, rung it out and threw it up onto the rock near Libby. Libby spread the material out on the sun-drenched side of the rock while Ellis soaked and floated in the water.

Libby sat facing Ellis, but averted her eyes as she bathed. "You want to talk about…anything?"

After a pause, Ellis asked, "The others—do they know?"

Libby cocked her head. "They know Abe and me are… married," she said.

"No, I mean do they know about…me?" Ellis looked down at herself.

Libby smiled. "I guess they reckon a boy your age would've stripped naked and jumped in before now, but don't worry, they won't let on. They know how to keep a secret and why you'd want to."

Ellis rubbed the soap on her hair but kept dropping it, her healing shoulder still preventing full range of motion. Libby slid down to a ledge where she could sit to reach Ellis's head. "Here, let me do that."

Ellis moved close to the rock, gave Libby the soap, and turned around. Libby worked the soap into a lather and smoothed it through Ellis's hair. Her touch took Ellis's breath and a warm chill spread over her body.

"When they first found out about me, they never said nothin', still don't." She gently scrubbed Ellis's head. "So, what you saw back there..." Libby started.

"I know. I mean, I know some of what married folk do. It's just, well, I've seen animals...but never..."

"People," finished Libby.

"Yeah." Ellis was glad she wasn't facing Libby as they talked about this. She felt both comfortable and unnerved this close to her.

Ellis dropped her gaze to the water she stood in. "I guess I thought it would be different somehow, but..." She didn't finish her sentence and Libby didn't finish it for her.

"Rinse that off," said Libby.

Ellis wasn't sure why she thought breeding animals and people would be different, or at least she wasn't sure how to talk about it. She had understood a love and respect between her parents, but that kind of intimacy wasn't present when breeding horses. And although she had witnessed a love and respect between Libby and Abe, what she saw in the river seemed raw and basic; natural, not contemplated or thought out. She remembered what Earl had said about Walter—him trying to explain to her. But that had felt wrong. Witnessing Abe and Libby touched her in a way she'd never felt before.

Something deep inside her stirred, awakened. Libby turned Ellis's clothes over. They were drying fast in the morning sun.

Ellis dove into the deeper water one last time and then scrambled onto the rock to dry her skin in the sunlight. She and Earl had often swum naked in the river and ponds near the homestead. It never seemed wrong to them but at some point it seemed less innocent, and they stopped.

Ellis put her clothes on. The long johns and shirt were still damp, and they felt cool against her warm skin. She shook out her dusty pants before putting them on, pulled on her ragged socks and worn leather boots.

"Maybe I should wash these, too," she said, referring to her pants and socks.

"You'll be more comfortable if they're dry when we're riding. You and me are gonna scout ahead a ways. C'mon."

Libby had caught her horse and Billie, and walked them to where Ellis was dressing.

"I let Abe know we were going. Ready?" Libby jumped on her gelding bareback. Ellis's saddle was back at the camp, so she led Billie up to a rock and climbed on. Riding bareback, Ellis felt closer, more connected to Billie. The two of them had come a long way together and Billie's legs felt like her own. The horse seemed to sense Ellis's intentions, not just her movements. When Earl had told Daddy he preferred to ride bareback, Daddy said it might be okay to do sometimes, but for longer rides the saddle was easier on the horse. Add the convenience of mounting and carrying ropes, rifles and bedding, Ellis had almost always used a saddle.

The women followed a deer trail that meandered along the river a few hundred yards and then turned into the forest. Billie kept close to the black gelding's tail. As they rode, Ellis realized the trail wove in and out of the trees, following the hunger and thirst needs of the deer and other creatures. The path widened through a small meadow, where Ellis rode up next to Libby.

"How did you and Abe meet?" Ellis asked.

Libby looked sideways at Ellis, "He was helping some folks I knew. On their way up to Canada. The Pony Express was about to quit because of the telegraph. He, and those working with him, needed messengers. They knew we could ride, so they came through to the stations and offered us work." Libby watched ahead as she spoke. She seemed to be able to search her surroundings as she contemplated what to say. "You ever hear of the underground railroad?"

"I did. I wasn't supposed to, I guess, but I overheard some folks talking one day at the meeting hall. I think some of the elders were involved." Ellis paused, memories of home flashed through her mind. She felt the strong contrast of tranquil recollections and the harsh, soiled experience of what she'd been through in the past weeks. The sweet life she remembered became shallow and stained. A child never knows what a parent might be sheltering them from. Uncovering some of those things, and wondering what more might lie ahead—is this what growing up meant?

Libby wrinkled her brow. "Your family Quaker? You don't talk like others I've met."

"We lived in the community. Raised in their ways, mostly. My Ma and Pa were educated back east. Didn't believe in fighting. Moved west for a more private life and knew some folks they wanted to settle by. Probably would have landed in Missouri but something happened between my Pa and his brother there." Ellis shrugged. "Not sure."

A deer had been lying down on the edge of the meadow, hidden by the tall grass. As the riders came near it stood. Billie jerked sideways, but quickly settled. Ellis unconsciously moved with her, keeping her seat. She caught Libby smiling at her.

"What was it like? In the Pony Express. Riding like that?" Ellis asked.

"Dangerous." Libby looked pensive, then smiled. "Fun."

"Did they know you were a girl?"

"No. They would've got rid of me for sure. But I didn't stand out much. The boys were all young and lean. They wanted to keep the weight off the horses as much as possible. Just a bunch of scrawny orphans. Strong though, and good riders.

"Were you all orphans?"

"Far as I know. That's what they advertised for. I guess they thought they'd lose enough of us they didn't want family attached, you know?"

Another small herd of deer suddenly appeared ahead. They were moving quickly along the river in front of Libby and Ellis. The gelding picked up his head, ears pricked forward. Billie jerked to a stop, but then relaxed. Under the trees the air was still cool, but in the clearings, where the sun hit, it didn't take long for both women and horses to warm to a sweat. Relatively flat so far, the trail now meandered up the hillside.

Libby stopped and looked off to her right, away from the river. "This way," she said.

They rode a switch-back trail until it stopped near the top of the hill. Libby slid off her horse and loosely tied a rein to a sapling. Ellis jumped off Billie and dropped her reins.

"Where…" Ellis started, but Libby put a finger to her lips to signal silence.

Libby started hiking up the steep hill, having to pull herself up with her hands part way. Ellis followed her. Just before they crested the hill, Libby motioned to Ellis to keep her head down. Stealthily, Libby took off her hat and peeked over the top of the hill. After two more breaths Libby relaxed and motioned Ellis up alongside her.

"Come. Look," she said.

Ellis crawled up beside Libby and searched the horizon. A deep valley spread out before them. A larger branch of the river turned inward toward the valley center. Near the river a procession of wagons and riders snaked along for what must have been ten miles or more. A small herd of unsaddled horses followed the wagon train.

"Where do you think they're going?" Ellis asked.

"North. Union troops. They're going home," said Libby.

Ellis knew there was a lot of country between the east coast and here, but she couldn't help but wonder if her father might be on his way home from wherever he ended up. If he was still alive. If he did make it back to the homestead, would there be anything left? He might find Mama's grave. And if the house was still standing, he might find the letters, but he wouldn't know that his daughter was the only one of his family left. He wouldn't know where Walter's or Earl's graves were. He wouldn't know where she was. Just like she didn't know where he was.

She felt Libby's stare and looked away from the distant vision.

"You okay?" asked Libby.

"What about you and Abe. George and Miles? Will you be safe in town?"

"This is safer than where we've been before. We're careful, keep our heads down." She bowed her head a moment, then stared back into the distance. "Fences come down slowly. Others go up." She stood.

"I wish I had my spyglass," said Ellis, thinking she might be able to get a closer look. A breeze blew, carrying the sound of nickering horses in the distance.

"C'mon, let's get back. We'll be following them toward town."

On the ride back, Ellis started feeling anxious about getting to a town. Out here, in the wilderness, she was just starting to be able to ignore the demons that haunted her. Libby, Abe, George and Miles seemed to understand her and all she had gone through. They accepted her, allowed her to be who she needed to be.

She thought more about her father. Oh, was it possible he was still alive? Might he be closer than she could imagine? She felt a surge of energy as her mind filled with possibilities. If her uncle still lived nearby, perhaps he would have news, though she knew he and her father hadn't written for many years. Could it be that out of the ugliness of the war, some good shone through? Could it be that as much as it tore families apart, it might also bring some together?

Once they reached camp Ellis jumped off her horse, unbridling her as she dismounted. She hurried to her bedroll and sat down to write.

*Dear Daddy,*
*Today was the first time in ages I thought I might be lucky*
*enough to see you again. You won't believe what all has*

*happened, but I hope to heaven that I'll be able to tell you all about it when I see you. And I hope that is soon. Of course, I'm sure you have some tales to tell, yourself. I hope your travels have been easier than mine. But I reckon that can't be the case if you're with those cavalry troops I saw today. I don't know why I'm thinking you were with them. Maybe it's just wishful thinking, but I have a feeling. I'm hoping you're on your way to Uncle William's, too. That's where I'm headed. That's where Earl said to go. Oh, you don't know about Earl, well, I'll tell you all about it in person, when I find you. Which I think now will be very soon. We've lost a lot, Daddy, but we still have you and me. And I've still got Billie. She's doin' fine. You won't believe how she's managed.*

Ellis continued to write, her mind buried in putting words on paper. She didn't notice the others packing up. She didn't see George talking quietly with Abe and Libby. She had been so caught up with her own task, she didn't see them all unpack again and settle into the camp for another night.

Ellis slept soundly that night, from sunset to sunrise. She awoke more clear-headed than she'd felt in a while.

The riders carried on, constantly vigilant. The day's journey remained peaceful. The group noticed a few stray horses, boney and tuckered out, left behind by the wagon train Libby and Ellis had witnessed from the hill. Ellis wished Earl was riding with her, and she heard her mother's voice. After her father and Walter had been gone a year, her mother had said, *"this is just the way it'll be now,"* and went back to tilling her garden. Her mother was different after that; resigned, constantly sad. But Ellis had kept watching for her father.

Toward evening, the group spotted a good campsite. Someone had been there prior to their arrival, maybe by a day or two. They rebuilt a small fire near the riverbank. The river grew wider.

chapter

# FIFTEEN

ELLIS COULDN'T REMEMBER WHAT SHE HAD BEEN DREAMING, but she woke with alert excitement; the same feeling she had on the mornings she was due to wrangle a cavvy of horses with her father. She had tried not to think about her father since writing the letter to him. If he was still alive, why had he not contacted them for so long? But as she had come to see what the war had done to both sides, she realized how much more she still had to learn. About the war, about other people, about herself. And, finally, she found hope. That wagon train—crawling along the river—soldiers finding their way home. Her father could be alive. He could be with them or another group, or could even be wandering around alone, like Earl had been; like she had been. Today there were possibilities. Today she found something to look forward to.

Billie acted skittish, as if Ellis's excitement filtered down to the horse's demeanor. She didn't seem bothered, just giddy, as if the lively spring air provided a clean slate on which to create the day.

Ellis rode close to Libby, anticipating she would leave the group on a scouting venture, and she wanted to follow her. Just as those thoughts crossed her mind, Libby signaled to Abe that she was off. When Ellis loped after her, Libby stopped.

"What are you doing?" asked Libby.

"I'm coming with you. I want a closer look at that wagon train."

Libby looked back at Abe, then glanced at George and Miles. The men looked at each other, letting Miles make the decision. He nodded at Libby.

"Okay then," conceded Libby. "Stay close behind me." The women galloped off.

Ellis had to hold Billie back to stay behind Libby and the nimble black gelding, but soon the horse settled into a controlled lope. Although Billie was longer legged, the gelding was quick and agile. Ellis was glad to give Billie the outlet for the extra energy as the two kept pace with one another.

They rode through forest and meadow, mostly at a fast walk or trot. When a clearing stood before them and the surroundings grew still, they stopped. Listened. Now and then Libby would dismount and scour the ground. Ellis wanted to know what she was looking for, but didn't want to intrude on the quiet by asking questions, so she just observed and waited for any comment or instruction that Libby might give. Mostly Libby acted as if Ellis wasn't there.

Approaching a clearing, Ellis followed Libby's line of sight to a thin wisp of smoke. The women stopped their horses near a stand of trees. Libby dismounted and Ellis followed suit. It seemed to Ellis that Libby stood still for the longest time. Her horse seemed to know to stand still, as well. She hoped Billie would behave. Satisfied with the surrounding quiet, Libby took a step forward, paused and then took another step. From behind her, Ellis saw her shoulders drop, relax, and Libby walked forward, leading her horse, toward the smoke. When they got close, Ellis saw it was a campfire, or what had been a campfire. Someone had tried to extinguish it, but it still smoldered.

"They were here for a couple of days," said Libby.

"How do you know?"

"The ash. Makes it harder to put out the fire." Libby searched the ground, knelt and touched a rut in the dirt. "I'm pretty sure it was that troop we saw. There were wagons and quite a few horses. The timing would be about right."

"How did we catch up to them so quickly?" asked Ellis.

"They're traveling pretty slow." Libby looked around.

Imprints of bedrolls flattened the grass, footprints, and other signs. Billie lifted her head suddenly and looked toward the road. The women mounted quickly and rode back into the trees where they stopped and watched. But nothing happened. They rode back out tentatively. A horse stood quietly near a patch of grass on the side of the road. Another was laying down at its feet, flat out but its ribby sides still moved with breath. Ellis had seen horses guarding each other like this before. One down, while the other kept watch. Whether injured, resting or giving birth, this was a herding instinct.

"They look pretty tuckered out," said Libby.

"Do we just leave them?" asked Ellis.

"Yeah," Libby said sadly.

As they turned to go, the horse lying down raised its head. Ellis noticed something familiar. The wretched animal was dirty and skinny, looked close to dying, but Ellis recognized something. She dismounted and quietly moved toward the horses. The one standing pinned its ears and nodded its head as if to warn her away.

"It's okay," she said, keeping an eye on both of them. "I'm not going to hurt you." The reclining horse was a dark chestnut with a thin white blaze on its face. One ear looked shorter than the other. Lying on its right side, she could see a U.S. Cavalry brand on its left shoulder.

"What are you doing?" questioned Libby, "We should be getting back."

"I'm going to see if I can get him up," said Ellis.

"He's done, he's not gonna make it. Leave him in peace."

"Please, help me get him up." Desperation in her voice.

Libby sighed. "Get your rope on him."

Ellis put a loop over the horse's head and urged him up while Libby pushed and coaxed from the other side. They kept an eye on the standing horse, but it seemed too tired to do more than watch.

The chestnut finally struck its two front feet forward and grunted to standing. Ellis rushed to its right side.

"Nick," whispered Ellis.

Libby looked at the horse, then at Ellis. "You know this horse?"

"My Pa had three horses he rode. He'd interchange them, but mostly he rode one for training colts, one to gather cows, and one he liked best for long hauls when he had to drive a herd or travel for some reason. That was Nick. He named him that because he injured his ear somehow out on winter pasture. He came in that Spring with a big nick cut in it. It got infected, so they had to cut part of it off. See how it's shorter than the other one?"

Libby nodded.

"And this brand on his right hip. He didn't brand them all, but that's the Cady brand my Pa used sometimes. A "C" and waves from the river. Ellis felt tears building in her eyes, but a spark of hope, too. She had been separated from Billie and found her again. Maybe, just maybe... "He was going to put up a sign that said 'Cady River Ranch' when he got back..." Ellis buried her face in Nick's tangled mane for a moment. "There was no Cady river, but he thought it sounded nice and my Ma always talked about life being like a river, and ..."

"We got him up. He might be okay now. Those two will stick together. But we can't take him, you know?" said Libby.

"Yeah, I know. But don't you see? If my Pa's horse is here, maybe my Pa is, too. He might be with that group we saw. Maybe he's even headed for my uncle's place. The one Earl told me about." Ellis smiled as a breeze blew tears from her eyes, cooled moisture on her cheeks. She tried not to feel it, not to show too much emotion. It seemed each time she saw daylight, a cloud would wipe it away with darkness. Just when she'd think she had a hold of someone, they'd leave one way or another. But she couldn't hold back the words, "My Pa might be alive, Libby. My Pa might be alive!"

"We can't just go riding in on them. There's still laws against what we've been doing, and you..."

"I know... it's just..." Ellis saw the danger in coming face to face with a regiment of soldiers on either side, especially for Libby, Abe and the others. She wished it didn't have to be that way. When would this conflict end?

"Well, let's ride on a little more," said Libby. "See if we can tell how far ahead they are and if any split off."

Ellis removed the loop from the horse's neck. She rubbed on Nick's back and shoulder. He was skinny, but he stayed standing. He turned his head toward her and she smoothed his forelock.

"There's grass and the river's not far. They might be okay," said Libby.

Ellis gave Nick a final pat and mounted Billie. She looked at Libby and nodded a thank you. She needed to stay tough, ride strong, as Miles had said. She knew Nick had a fifty-fifty chance. The women rode a few more miles along the foothills, uphill from the main trail along the river; the trail that had been beaten out of the land by the wagon train and tired cavalry.

"We'll head back soon, but let's get to the top of that hill and see if we can see anything from up there," said Libby.

The horses loped up the hill, trying to keep forward momentum up the steep incline. Just before they reached the top, the hill leveled out and they stopped to give the horses a break. A footpath curled around the hilltop. Libby tied her horse to a downed tree and started up the path. Ellis took the spyglass out of her saddlebag and followed her on foot.

Crowning the hill the two women were struck by the vastness of the land before them. Green hills along the river undulated in emerald, sage and turquoise. Off in the distance, they saw a low cloud of dust. The wagon train.

"Look, over there," said Libby, pointing to the west. It looks like there's a fork in the river. The troops are staying on the main road, but it could be some of them went that way."

Ellis was already searching through the glass. "You're right, that looks like the same wagon train we saw before. Most of them are on the trail going north. I can't really tell, but I think maybe some of them are on that trail heading west." She lowered the glass to search more openly. A hawk circled above them and she looked up. "I wish I had your eyes," she said. Turning to Libby, "Do you know where that leads? That road?"

"North will eventually get to St. Louis. That western trail, I'm not sure. We've mostly gone north before we turn west, to get to St. Joe, where the station was. Never been west from here, but I'm pretty sure there's a town not too far down the river. Can you see anything through that glass?

Ellis searched again. Something in her wanted to find the town so badly, she thought she did see it. But something else stopped her from ever wanting to see a town again. Her life had changed. It was certainly different than what she had back in Tennessee, but different in another way here with Libby. Especially scouting. Just her and Libby and the horses. The world was quiet, the voices stilled. She saw something peaceful yet exciting in Libby's eyes. She felt a part of the land, an explorer. She was useful and each action she took had meaning. What would it be like to find family? How would they respond to her? What might they expect of her?

"Can I have a look?" asked Libby.

Ellis handed her the glass, hoping she wouldn't find anything.

"There, about a day's ride maybe. I think it's a town. We'll have to check with Miles. He has a map." Libby turned and started down the path back to the horses.

Ellis followed her back, panic thumping between her shoulder blades. How could she want to find her father, and family, but still want to be…Earl? Still want to be taken seriously and able to ride and work the way she wanted. How did Libby do it? Did people not expect anything from her? Or was it what Libby expected of herself.

"Libby, when we get to town, will you…?"

"Will I what?"

"Well," started Ellis as she glanced at Libby's yellowed shirt, worn dungarees and dusty moccasins.

"Dress different?" Libby filled in. She looked at Ellis a moment before she smiled. "I might find a washtub, but no. There was a time I thought I wanted to. When me and Abe got together. But I told him I'd never quit riding and I was comfortable like this." She looked wistfully at the landscape. "Honestly, I don't know what it'll be like when we settle down." She smiled. "If we settle down." Her face got serious again. "But I won't dress or act a certain way just because I'm a woman."

"But what'll we do when we're in town? How will folks find us?"

"They'll see me as black or Indian before they'll care about male or female, I've found. What you really want to know is how they'll see you."

"I guess."

"That's a decision you'll need to make. You'll pass for a boy, no problem, if that's what you want to do. But if you find family, well, have you thought about that?"

"No way I could fool my Pa, so I'd have to come clean when I find him. But I like riding, and these clothes are more practical for what we're doing. I feel more comfortable, more…natural."

Libby smiled at Ellis. The sun hung over the distant hills. A raven flew to a branch on a nearby pine and squawked a greeting as Libby untied her horse, closed her eyes, and faced the sun. Her sleek black hair moved in the wind like a bird's wing. She took a deep breath and pointed her horse back down the hill. "Let's get back."

The women mounted their horses and picked their way back down the trail to the river, then took their time returning to the men.

Evening shadows threw a rich light on the forest floor by the time they met up. The men were setting up camp in a clearing. It seemed to Ellis they were familiar with this place, they acted as though they had been here before.

Abe stirred a pot over some coals pulled to the side of the campfire. Miles dozed, leaning against his upturned saddle, his hat pulled low over his face. George read a leather-bound book, his hungry eyes gathering information behind the windows of his wire rimmed glasses. Now and then he'd make a note in a small journal.

Ellis unsaddled Billie and took her journal from the saddle bag. She sat on a log near the fire. Words and phrases flooded her mind, almost too much to write. She felt calm, but her hand shook.

For the longest time she watched the flames, contemplating the fiery life they represented. Sometimes they danced, sometimes they silently shouted. They beckoned and repelled. They surged and relaxed. The red coals and liquid gold flames contrasted with the dark wood yet to burn and the black charcoal, already done. Here, near the forest, the smell of the wilderness permeated the air, and yet the scent of the fire condensed the earthy odor to its own bouquet. Now and then a sharp crack would interrupt the purr of the fire, like a resting cat suddenly crying out. Sparks of exclamation celebrated this place of warmth in an otherwise cool night.

Ellis had watched this life line many times. How it starts slowly, accelerates, calms and dies. Something is always left behind in the ashes; clues to the life of the fire and who created it. A life is built, nurtured, kept alive while one needs the warmth, and then left to cool and disappear. Yet it's never really gone.

She wrote all this in her journal. She wrote until Libby handed her a plate of stew. The food nourished her words and she finished her plate and returned her hand to the page. In her mind, the others hadn't moved. If they had it didn't matter. She was lost in thought and words and hope. This fire and all the campfires she had watched and built, became her story. Distant fires encouraged her to leave home. Fire applauded when she found Earl. Fire warmed her in the cave. Fire was the source of each day into night. Fires along the river punctuated a journey of heat and cold, dark and light, life and death.

Like the river pulls forward, the fire burns upward. Always advancing, going somewhere, never returning. In that moment, Ellis knew she might wear different hats throughout her life, but she would always wear these clothes that were practical, comfortable, and naturally fit who she was. The world would have to see her as she saw herself.

She stopped writing, a smile crept across her face. She looked up and saw Libby watching her. Libby smiled, too.

*chapter*
# SIXTEEN

OVER THE NEXT TWO DAYS THE FIVE RIDERS DESCENDED
from the hills and converged upon the main trail. They stayed
vigilant, and Ellis hoped Libby had been right about being
far enough north now that they rode in safer territory. They
followed the tracks of the soldiers' wagons until those diverted
north toward the long ride to St. Louis. George had talked
about continuing that way alone, maybe catching up to them,
but then decided he'd stay with the group a little longer, for
safety and comfort. He wasn't sure his horse was up to much
more hard travel without a rest. Ellis was glad he was staying.

She knew they probably wouldn't all be able to stay together much longer. The others had lives they were trying to
return to. But she was in no hurry to see any of them take a
separate trail. With many boot prints, hoofprints and wagon
wheel ruts in the road, it was becoming more difficult to track
anyone in particular. The only way to know if her father had
veered west, was for her to go west, as well. If she found her
uncle, perhaps she would at least find news of her father. But
still, she didn't want to leave her traveling companions.

While clinging to this protective group, Ellis also felt vulnerable. She didn't understand these conflicting feelings. It was like returning to a new sort of battlefield. She felt the same surge of immediacy; caught up in an uncontrolled flow that created a focus, a fine point of awareness, that led a person to do things they didn't know they could. She didn't know if she should be wary or grateful.

When they rode up on a man limping down the side of the trail, Abe tipped his hat. The man glanced up at them with a fretful face; his eyes red, wincing like he was about to be hit. He looked like he might bolt into the trees, but he seemed too weary to try. Instead, he tipped his hat, looked back at the ground and kept walking. More socializing than that didn't seem called for, or welcomed.

According to Miles's map, the trail would pass through the small village of Jamestown, established by early settlers who wanted to stop short of the main road to Springfield. They rode by farmland where people toiled out in the fields. Sometimes the farmers stopped to look at them, but mostly they just kept on working; plowing fields and repairing shabby buildings. From the expressions of the workers, Ellis gathered it didn't seem all that unusual for a few Negroes to be riding into town. Relieved that her friends may be safer now, Ellis still kept her hat pulled down low and figured they thought she was one of them. Of the handful of other travelers they saw, no one was in uniform. If her father had gotten this far, surely he'd be at his brother's by now. If his brother was still in the area.

Abe and Miles rode out front, Libby and Ellis behind them, with George in the back. They didn't talk much but stayed close enough together to hear one another if words were uttered. "Looks like everybody's looking for work now that the war's over. There's more free men around," Abe said. Miles nodded.

Ellis hadn't thought too much about what kind of work she might be able to do. She wished the Pony Express was still running. "What are you all going to do?" she asked Libby.

"Well, George will be leaving us and heading back to St. Louis. Miles said he's headed west. Me and Abe will do whatever we can, probably building and cooking. Maybe find a ranch that needs help."

"You could train horses," suggested Ellis.

Abe turned and smiled at Libby as she said, "Maybe. If I could find someone that would hire…me."

"We'll get by," Abe said.

"If I can find my uncle, maybe he'd have work for all of us," said Ellis. Her father had talked little about his brother, William. Since she and her brothers were born, as far as she knew, neither had traveled to see the other. If her uncle had children, she didn't know it.

They were getting close to town now. Ellis could see the low outline of buildings in the distance. She didn't know why, but there was a part of her that was uneasy about seeing other people and a part of her that was excited about it. Her feelings kept flitting from one to the other, not knowing which to embrace.

Just outside of town the group climbed a hillock. As the distant buildings came into sight, they all stopped their horses to survey the view ahead. They took time to breathe and reflect on the situation. Minutes passed before Abe spoke, the sound of his voice a small shock to each of them. "Are we all ready for this?" he said, not really asking.

"Just remember," George said, "We're free but…we're still black. Some people see that differently than others. We're still meant to keep our place unless allowed otherwise, understand?"

Abe and Libby nodded. So did Ellis, but she really didn't understand. She figured if you were free you were free. What else was there? Her own light skin was just another part of her disguise. She felt like one of this group; not black or white, or even male or female. Just free, wanting to find a place to belong. They rode on into town and stopped in front of the Jamestown Hotel. It didn't look like much, but they didn't need much. A warm bed indoors and maybe a hot bath would be heaven, and a hot meal. But before they could dismount a man pushed open the front door, walked out from under the eve and leaned on a post, looking them over like he was sizing up a problem.

"You don't wanna stop here," the man warned. "Go on down two streets to a place called The Sage. There'll be a place for you there." George looked at him and then looked back at Ellis, Abe, Libby, and Miles. He turned back to the man, tipped his hat and said, "Thank you, sir." The group followed George down the street, but Miles looked back over his shoulder and scowled at the man in front of the hotel.

The Sage was in the middle of a cluster of shacks that looked like they were cobbled together from boards left over from building something else. Through an open window, they could see walls of the rooms were nothing more than canvas from old tents. They had all been sleeping in the same camp so sleeping more or less together under a dry roof might still be a step up. The keeper at The Sage, a black man with gray curls springing out from under a worn kepi, sat outside in a rickety chair that he had tilted back against the outside wall, his feet pushing against a wooden railing for balance. When the group rode up he let the chair drop to all four legs, stood slowly and scanned the riders without looking very closely at any one in particular. "Two bits each. Facilities are outside. Well's got good water," he recited. Then he looked a little closer to see if there were any takers. He addressed Ellis. "You, boy, what you doin' with these folks?"

Ellis wasn't sure what to say. She looked at Abe and Libby for help. Abe spoke. "We were working for the boy's folks. We all got separated during the fighting. Battle of Nashville. Made us promise to take care of him if anything happened to them. They got…burned out. We've been riding quite a ways to get here."

The man looked at them and then at Ellis. "That right, boy?"

"Yes sir," said Ellis. And then she took a chance. "I'm lookin' for kin. Would you happen to know any Cady's that live around here?"

The man squinted and tilted his head at her in a way that made her uncomfortable. "Cady, you say," he paused. "You don't mean James Cady…the man this town was named for?" The man snickered.

"Well, no sir. I'm looking for William Cady."

"That'd be his son. Well, I'll be. If you're a Cady, no sense you stayin' here. You'll find better lodging at their spread if they'll have you." The man still wasn't sure what to believe. "The old man—well, he was older 'n me—died a few years back, but William is running the place now."

"Where's his spread?" Ellis asked, the word "spread" made her wonder just who this William Cady was.

"About three miles out of town to the west. Just stay on the main road and you'll see the post with the KD brand on it."

Ellis looked at Abe and Libby. George stepped off his horse and said, "I think I'll stay here. Rest up for a couple of days. Then I'll catch the train in Springfield back to St. Louis."

The innkeeper said, "There's a stage comes through here for Springfield next week. Unless you want to ride that nag all the way."

George looked at his horse; patted his neck.

"Pete over at the livery might have a place for him if you want to sell him or let him rest up," the man said.

"Much obliged for the information, sir."

Miles had dismounted the same time as George. They each paid the man for a room and tied their horses to the hitching rail.

Abe slid off Smokey and stepped closer to Ellis who stayed mounted. "You go on and see if you can meet your kin. We'll be okay here," he assured her.

Libby, still mounted, nodded and said, "Go. See what you find."

"You won't leave until I get back?" said Ellis.

Abe nodded. "Go on."

Ellis gave them each a long look, nodded and turned Billie back down the road. She turned around once and saw Abe smile at her, Libby too. Something familiar crept under her skin; a feeling of loss, and independence.

The road out of town took her past a village of small clapboard houses, a church and a school house. The livery barn was the last building she passed. A giant of a blacksmith worked out front under an eave. His clear, black skin shone with sweat as hard muscle stretched and contracted. He hammered on horseshoes, the ring of metal on metal leaving an echo in the air. A mammoth draft horse stood calmly beside him. As Ellis passed, the smith turned away from her and she saw the scars furrowed on his bare back. She remembered moonlight glinting off Abe's flawless skin; his smooth back rising from the river. The blacksmith turned back and looked up at her as she rode past. She quickly looked away and forced her thoughts back to where she was headed. She chewed on the knowledge that Billie's shoes were wearing thin and wondered how much it might cost to get new ones. First she needed to find a place to stop. Maybe for a night, maybe longer.

During the three-mile ride, she tried to regain the optimism about finding her father. She had seen possibilities in the figures of returning soldiers, and then finding Nick. But her father had somehow been separated from one of his favorite horses. How long ago? Nick was in bad shape; her father wouldn't have let that happen. Her thoughts and expectations changed like the mud and dust of the trail. The sooner she learned the truth, the sooner she might be overjoyed, or overwhelmed with grief. The shedding of uncertainty, a small comfort.

Earl had wanted to go west. Ellis had been hesitant, wanting to return home. But Earl had convinced her there was nothing left for them in Tennessee. He was convinced, and had persuaded her, their life existed on the western trails, the zephyr trails, he called them. Zephyr, like his middle name. Ellis was on her own now, making her way along the western rivers. She'd check out the Cady ranch. If her father was there, she couldn't ask for more. If he wasn't, maybe they would have some word of where he was.

A fenced pasture came into view on the right side of the road. Two huge posts with a crossbeam over the top marked the entrance of a well-worn dirt road, wide enough for a wagon. The sign hanging from the crossbeam was branded, "KD." Ellis looked down the road where cattle roamed the new grasses on one side, a dozen horses in a fenced pasture on the other.

She urged Billie through the ranch gate and down the road that undulated through the open space. Riding up a shallow incline, she stopped at the top overlooking what she figured was the rest of the ranch land. A two-story house, painted white, and a large barn, painted red, appeared before her. Unpainted out-buildings, one with a long overhang and porch, populated the area next to the barn.

A drop of sweat touched the corner of Ellis's eye as Billie noticed the other horses. Between Ellis's nervousness and the animal's curiosity, Billie got a little jumpy. Ellis took a deep breath and rubbed Billie's neck. "I know, girl." She gauged her voice and realized she was now used to the lower tone. Maybe she could continue to pull this off.

As she rode closer, she noticed a windbreak of tall poplar and elm along the side of the house and a massive weeping willow in front. The trees were old and well-established. This ranch had been here a while.

Two men outside the bunkhouse were cleaning tack in the shade of the porch overhang, but they looked up when they saw her riding in. Two other men on the big wrap-around porch of the house, sat in rockers, talking and sipping drinks. When they saw her, they stood up. When she got closer she dismounted and led Billie up to where the men were walking down the porch steps toward her. One of the men looked a lot like her father, but older. Still, the sight of him took her breath.

"Hello, there. What can we help you with?" the other man said. She hadn't noticed until now that his right arm was missing from just below the elbow. He wore a gun on his left hip. He was looking at Ellis and she thought he glanced at the pistol holster she wore. Her father's look-alike was watching her too, and also giving Billie the once-over.

"Sir." Ellis addressed the man who spoke. "I was told I could find William Cady here," she said, glancing between the two men.

"That'll be me," the man who looked like her father said. "I'm William Cady. Who are you?" He was looking back and forth from Ellis to Billie.

"I'm El …Earl Cady. My Pa's…," she started.

"Thomas Cady?" The man declared. He took a closer look at her and Ellis was sure he'd discover her secret, but if he had, he didn't say. "That must make me your uncle, young nephew." He just stood there for a heartbeat and Ellis wasn't sure he was happy about making the acquaintance or not, but then a smile formed on his face and he stepped toward her with his hand out. "Well, Earl, welcome to Cady Ranch," he said. He shook Ellis's hand and put his other on her shoulder. He looked closely at her face. Ellis meant to look back at him with all the confidence she could muster, but she couldn't keep herself from looking away in case he was seeing the real her. She was certain, by his reaction, that her father wasn't here, but she felt the question form deep inside her. She tried to keep her disappointment at bay, but now she became uneasy. She waited for concerns about the rest of her family. But the man seemed distracted by Billie. "Nice mare you got there. Where'd you come by her?"

Ignoring the question, Ellis tried to keep her voice low and constant. "Is my father here?"

Bill paused and looked at the ground. "No, son…" Before he could continue, a woman stepped off the porch wiping her hands on an apron she wore over a clean calico dress. "Bill, who's this young man? I thought I heard someone ride in." William Cady put his arm around his wife and explained, "Maggie, this is Thomas's kid, Earl."

Ellis thought Maggie went pale before she spoke. "Well, I'll be. What are you doing out here? Oh, my word, child... did..."

Bill caught his wife's eye. "Maggie, the boy just got here. He looks like he could use some supper and a good night's sleep before we get the low down on the family." He looked back at Ellis. "I don't know how long you've been on the trail, but you must be tired and hungry, am I right?" He smiled.

"Yes sir," Ellis said. "I could eat. But I'd like to take care of my horse first if you have a place for her."

"Yes, you're a Cady all right," said the woman. Always thinking about the horses first." She chuckled nervously and glanced at her husband.

William Cady turned to the other man and said, "Kip, would you show Earl where to bed his horse down? And show him where the hay and grain is." Then he turned back to Ellis. "When you're done, come on in the house and we'll have some supper for you."

"Thank you, sir," Ellis said.

"You can quit with the 'sir' stuff. Call me Bill," he said.

"Yes sir...Bill." Ellis followed Kip to the barn.

Stone made up the lower half of the building, wood the upper half. Large double doors opened into a wide breezeway with eight stalls down one side. On the opposite side, a large tack room and grooming stall were flanked by six more stalls, three on either side. The roof was pitched longer on one side than the other, with a long hayloft stretching the full length.

A narrow staircase, not a ladder, led to the loft. Ellis had never seen such a fine barn.

"You can take that stall there on the end. Should be clean straw in it. Hay's over there and grain here in the bin," Kip said.

"Thanks," said Ellis, realizing she had been standing in the breezeway, awed, not moving. She led Billie to the stall.

She kept an eye on Kip, trying not to stare. The man seemed capable even with one arm. He was a handsome man, older than Ellis, but much younger than her uncle. Wiry, dark-skinned, and strong-featured, he looked determined and confident. If Libby had had a brother, she thought, he could be Kip. He picked up a pitchfork and entered the open stall next to the one Ellis stood in. He pointed to a cast iron water pump that stood over a metal basin.

"You can wash up over there when you're done." Kip looked Ellis up and down. "Before you go in the house."

Ellis looked at her hands and the front of her clothing. She wiped at her trousers and dust billowed in the still air. "Thanks, I'll do that," she said.

"You ride all the way from Tennessee by yourself?" Kip asked.

Ellis unbridled and unsaddled Billie, tossing the tack over the stall rail. "Pretty much," she answered. She put a scoop of grain in a bucket and some hay in the crib, filled another bucket with water. Kip continued to clean the stall next to her, but she felt his eyes on her. She needed to figure out the rest of her story. In the meantime she'd keep her answers short.

## chapter
# SEVENTEEN

ELLIS WALKED UP THE PORCH STEPS. SHE HOOKED A THUMB under the thin rope across her chest that secured the bedroll to her back. Her saddlebags draped over one shoulder. She turned at the top of the steps, looked down either side of the long porch and then squinted into the sunlight as she surveyed the property. Its stillness and seclusion calmed her, yet underneath her nerves felt stretched and taut. A sudden breeze stirred the hush, reminding her to move.

Opening the screen door she winced at the sound of its creaking hinges. A heavy wooden door was open to the inside, the KD brand burned onto it like the sign over the ranch entrance. As she entered the house, she took off her hat and habitually wiped her forehead with her sleeve. To her left a large mirror hung over a wooden sideboard. Her movement and image startled her. Even she thought she was looking at her brother, as she self-consciously smoothed her hair back with her fingers.

Inside the house she was afraid to move. She scanned the interior as if it was a new wilderness. The building was larger than her own family home in Tennessee, but similar in structure. Like a forked trail, a long hallway stretched ahead of her to the left, to the right a stairway led to a second floor. A parlor opened to the right of the stairs where light streamed in from a window, illuminating an upright piano partially hidden by a leather couch. The home felt comfortable but business-like, practical but with a woman's touch. The smell of leather, sweet tobacco and a good meal, calmed her like a fond memory. Framed photographs hung on the wall next to the mirror. Pictures of people and horses, but before she could look closely at them, Maggie came down the hall from the kitchen.

"Leave your things there." She pointed at the floor near a coat rack. "Your side arm, too. We don't allow wearing them in the house. Used to not allow them on the property, but that changed." Maggie looked down as Ellis unbuckled her holster. She had almost forgotten she was wearing it. She dropped her saddle bags from her shoulder and sloughed off her bedroll.

"Well, c'mon now, let's get some food into you." As she led Ellis down the hallway, into the dining room, Maggie kept talking. "My goodness how long have you been on the trail? You must have some stories to tell." But she didn't wait for Ellis to tell them, and Ellis thought that was for the best. In the dining room Bill sat at one end of a long table that could have seated eight people. Maggie pointed to an empty chair where, on the table, a bowl of stew and a thick slice of bread rested on a plate, a glass of sweet tea next to it. Ellis took her seat and Maggie sat next to Bill, a cup of tea in front of her. There would have been plenty of room at this table for Libby, Abe, George, and Miles. She wondered if they'd have been welcomed, but then she wasn't really sure if she was welcome yet.

"Now Maggie, let the boy eat, there's plenty of time for talking later," Bill said. He smiled at Ellis. His bowl was empty, crumbs on his plate. The stew was bland, but the sweet tea was a treat. Ellis had forgotten how hungry she was, and ate heartily. When her bowl was almost empty, she realized no one had been talking. She looked up and found both Bill and Maggie watching her. Her forgotten manners embarrassed her and she picked up the cloth napkin by her plate, wiped her mouth and slowed down.

"Sorry," she apologized. "It's been a while since I had a meal at a table."

Maggie smiled, blinked, waved off her apology.

"So, Earl Cady," Bill said, shaking his head. "So, my brother's kid. Didn't you have another brother. And a sister, too?"

"Yes sir." Ellis talked between bites. "I have…had an older brother, Walter, and…a twin sister…Ellis." That was a strange lie to tell. Her neck prickled and her stomach lurched.

"Do you know where they are? The damn war scattered so many people."

"Language, Mr. Cady," Maggie chastised.

"Oh yes, right, sorry Mrs. Cady." Bill looked at his wife sheepishly, but turned back toward Ellis and winked. "How'd you come to be out on your own?"

Now that Ellis was fed and Billie was safe, a weariness overcame her. She struggled to keep her head from spinning. She wanted to answer the questions and ask some of her own, but she couldn't find the words or the energy. She felt her face flush and tears welled in her eyes. She didn't want this to be happening, not in front of them. She braced herself, trying to steady her voice.

"My brother, Walter, was…killed…at Shiloh."

*Good shot, boy…keep those boy duds…no tellin what will happen…*

Ellis drank from the glass of tea, hoping it might quench her thoughts; the horses' and soldiers' screams. A door slammed and she jumped, squeezed her eyes tight, and when she opened them Kip was standing in the doorway at the far end of the room.

"Sorry to disturb your supper," he said. He had taken off his hat, and hung it casually over the stump of his arm, fingering the brim comfortably with his one hand. "Just wanted you to know that dun mare looks like she'll put it off another day or two. I'll keep an eye on her. The boys are done for the day."

"Thanks, Kip," said Bill. "We'll see you in the morning, then."

Maggie was watching Ellis with concern and, when Kip left, she exchanged a look with her husband. "Oh, Bill, let's let the boy get a good night's rest. We can talk about the family in the morning, huh?" She glanced at her husband, then back at Ellis. "C'mon, son, if you've finished your dinner I'll show you up to your room."

Ellis fought to keep the food down, wrestling with the sounds and images that finally faded. She stood. "I'll be fine in the barn. I'm used to bedding down with the horses," she said. How could she stay in this home when Libby and the others had been chased from the town's hotel to a hovel?

"Nonsense," said Maggie. "Come along with me."

Maggie led the way back to the hall. Just before leaving the room Ellis turned back and said, "I want to thank you, Bill, for letting me stay here tonight."

"Well, of course, son. You get some rest and we'll talk more tomorrow."

Ellis meant to acknowledge him with a "Yes sir," but it failed to form on her lips. She nodded.

She picked up her bedroll and saddlebags by the door, leaving her gunbelt on the rack, and followed Maggie upstairs. The woman stopped at a large dresser in the hallway, opened a drawer and took out a garment. They continued to a room across the hall that had a window by the bed just like Ellis's room at home. The window overlooked the horse paddock. A small desk and chair stood against the opposite wall.

"What might you need?" asked Maggie, hugging the folded cloth to her body.

Ellis turned her gaze out the window and then back toward the room. She tossed her saddle bags over the back of the chair and placed her bedroll on the trunk at the foot of the bed. She listened for the voices, but they had gone. "What?"

"Doesn't look like you have much in the way of clean clothes or night clothes," said Maggie.

"Oh, no ma'am, I guess I don't." Ellis looked down at herself and felt some embarrassment at her appearance. Bathing in the river had been refreshing on the trail, but that had been a few days ago now. It felt like ages since she'd been inside a house. "I…"

"Here, now, I got you one of Ty's nightshirts to wear. He was our boy. Lost him at Wilson's Creek." Maggie's voice paused. Go ahead and take off what you've got on and I'll get them washed and mended for you. In the meantime I'll find you some that might fit. I've put water in the bowl here so you can wash up, but I'm guessing you're gonna fall asleep before you get very far, am I right?" She smiled.

"Yes, ma'am, I think so," Ellis attempted a smile and stifled a yawn. She wondered how long it had been since the battle at Wilson's Creek. How long did it take a mother to get over losing a son in war?

Maggie stood there a moment and Ellis thought maybe she was waiting for her to get undressed right now. She froze. Both women stood looking at the floor.

"I'll just let you get some rest. When you do get out of those clothes, just put them outside your door and I'll get them." She smiled at Ellis and left the room, closing the door behind her.

Ellis sat on the bed and then got up quickly, realizing how dirty she was. She opened her saddle bag and found her journal and a pencil. Taking them out, Jack's small horse carving fell onto the floor. She picked it up and put it on the desk by the lantern. As if by habit, she sat down to write, but a dazed weariness kept her hand from moving. She stared at the paper but couldn't think. She took off her clothes, remembering the river and Libby's touch, as she washed up using a cloth and soap next to the basin. She put on the nightshirt. The flannel felt soft against her skin and smelled clean like the river in winter.

*Earl. I found our uncle, William Cady. It's uncanny how much he looks like our Pa. He lives in Jamestown, Missouri. The town was named after our grandfather, James. Bill and his wife, Maggie, seem like real nice people. I think you'd like them. They are a lot like Mama and Daddy. They've got a big ranch here with horses and cattle. I don't know why I'm writing to you, as I do realize you're dead. But it helps me sort through things writing to you and Daddy, and Mama...*

Ellis realized she had been sitting at the desk with her eyes closed for a while. She looked at the writing she'd started, closed the journal, and put it and the pencil back in her saddle bag. Too dark to write now and not wanting to waste a match, she shuffled to the bed, pulled down the covers and got in.

As her eyes closed, Ellis remembered her father coming home one day when she was about ten years old. Her mother had gathered her and Earl and Walter outside under the big oak tree, for a reading lesson. Earl kept climbing the tree and Mama kept telling him to get down and listen. "I'm listening, Ma," he'd say as he climbed higher. He hadn't seen Daddy ride up but he heard him yell, "Earl Cady, you get down here right now and sit still!"

Earl had almost fallen out of the tree, but had caught himself and swung down. He stood there for a minute waiting to see if there was punishment attached. Then he saw the foal. "Pa! What you got there?" Beaming he walked carefully over to the foal and took the lead from Daddy. No matter how clumsy Earl had been otherwise, he had always been careful around horses. He knew how to be with them.

Pa had said, "When you're finished with your lesson here with your Ma…" Earl had looked at Mama who knew she wasn't going to be able to contain him so she said, "Oh, okay, you're finished for now, but tomorrow we're back at it."

Ellis could see Earl's face so clearly and see that big goofy smile as he exclaimed, "Yes ma'am!" and led the foal to the barn.

Tonight her last thought before falling asleep was that there were no rocks under the blankets. The air was still. The pillow made her head feel like it was floating on a warm river.

Peaceful sleep didn't hold her for long. A flurry of nightmarish images invaded her dreams and Ellis woke, startled and sweating. For a moment she wasn't sure where she was, but as

the violent images faded, the comfort of the bed surrounded her with an almost overwhelming contentment she didn't
feel worthy of. She threw the covers off and stood, stretching
and catching her breath. She looked out the window into the
darkness, a low-hanging half moon to the east. She walked to
the door and listened. She wondered if Libby and the others
were sleeping peacefully.

Hearing nothing, she opened the door and saw a set of
clothing at her feet. She looked up and down the hall, carried
the clothes into her room and changed into them. The pants
were a little big, but they were clean and mended. She reckoned they must have belonged to the Cady's lost son. An image
flashed in her mind of soldiers pilfering clothing from the dead
on the battlefield. The cloth outlived the flesh. The clean wool
socks she pulled on now were a luxury. She carried her boots.

As quietly as she could, she crept down the hallway.
Halfway down the stairs she heard voices in the sitting room.
The house was dark and only a small fire illuminated the two
chairs in front of the hearth.

Bill Cady sat in the large leather chair in front of the fireplace, filling a pipe. The room emitted a smoky, sweet fragrance.
Ellis meant to sneak by unnoticed, but overheard her name.
She strained to hear the conversation, but some words were
clouded by the crack of the fire, some spoken in low whispers.

"So, what do you think of young Earl?" Bill asked his wife.

Maggie sat in the rocking chair, a bundle of sewing in her
lap. "Bill, I know we never saw Tom's kids since they were tots,
but, well…"

Maggie paused and Bill spoke.

"He's a little too fine. He's only, what, fifteen or so. Some
don't get their whiskers that early. If we weren't kin, I don't

think I'd have noticed, but then I don't think I shook the hand of a fifteen-year-old boy, and if I remember correctly, that kid's the spitting image of Elizabeth."

"If it is Ellis, why would she say she was her brother?"

"Maggie darlin', you and I have seen some terrible days the past four years. Lost a son of our own and most of our hired hands and house help. We've been lucky to hold on to what we do have." A match flared, smoke from his pipe drifted into the darkness. "Who knows what that child's been through. I believe Tom and his oldest went east with some horses at the beginning of the war. And now that letter we got. We're gonna have to piece this puzzle together."

"Seems everybody's been so busy fighting their own battles and trying to stay alive, we've all lost track. It's pitiful," Maggie sighed. "What do we tell the child? What do you suppose happened…to Elizabeth?" Maggie's voice cracked.

Ellis wasn't sure she was hearing things clearly. Did they know about her? Did they mention a letter? From whom? She felt caged—wanted to be alone with her thoughts, with Billie.

A long pause preceded Bill's reply. "Well, let's see what tomorrow brings, shall we?" A log shifted in the fireplace and the leather chair creaked. "Now, I know young Earl went to bed without dessert, but I'd love some of that apple pie you were making earlier today."

When Bill and Maggie moved to the kitchen, Ellis slipped out the front door, opening and closing it carefully, silently.

chapter
# EIGHTEEN

ELLIS SMELLED SWEET ALFALFA BEFORE SHE OPENED HER eyes to a stream of early morning sunlight, swirls of dust in its current. She felt Billie's breath on her hand, then the soft nudge of her nose on Ellis's foot. The horse turned and went back to feeding on hay and grain in the crib. Ellis stood and let the blanket fall away. She reached down, picked it up, and tried to remember where it came from.

"Thought you might get cold without it." Kip stood on the other side of the stall door. Ellis hadn't seen him, but his voice didn't startle her. He had a calm, soothing way that reminded her of someone familiar.

"Your mare's doin' fine. I could tend to her feet if you like. Her shoes are nearly worn through and she could use a trim."

As Ellis slowly reconstructed last night's movements, she remembered coming out to check on Billie. She must have fallen asleep. How could she have slept so soundly?

"I'd be much obliged," she said. But she wondered how Kip could shoe a horse with only one hand.

"They usually have coffee and breakfast at the house," Kip said, nodding his head toward the barn door."

Ellis folded the blanket and held it out to Kip. "Thank you."
Kip took the blanket and nodded.

Ellis felt a chill and folded her arms across her chest. She still wore the clean borrowed clothes, yet felt exposed.

Neither moved for a moment. Then Kip backed away from the stall door. "Don't worry, I won't let on." He lifted a worn woolen jacket off a hook outside the stall.

Ellis felt a spark of panic. She glanced at Kip. He smiled briefly. Suddenly she remembered the overheard conversation. Had she really heard it, or had she dreamt it?

"I think they'd understand you sleepin' out here with your horse. They know what it's like." He tossed the blanket over a saddle peg. "Or you could pretend you just came out here early. None o' my business." With his partial arm, Kip handed the jacket to Ellis. "Still kinda cool this morning."

Ellis breathed out, glanced at Kip as he walked away. She watched him grab a pitchfork and start cleaning stalls. Again she noticed how easily he worked with only one hand.

Ellis walked slowly toward the barn doors, calculating each step as she tried to anticipate what her aunt and uncle might ask, what she would say, how to explain.

Close to the entrance of the barn a doorway stood open to a room surrounded by bookshelves, a large oaken desk in the middle. The room was tidy, the desk neat and organized. An open letter the only thing out of place, left as if the person in the chair reading it had been called away. One short wall between shelves was pincushioned with newspaper clippings, sketches and notes. Ellis looked behind her, listened as Kip's work efforts continued down the stalls. She entered the room and searched the images.

Along with the clippings, certificates bragged of pedigrees and races won. A picture caught her attention. It was a blurry tintype, bent and faded, but showed a young man, who looked a lot like Bill Cady and her father, standing with a bay mare who looked a lot like Billie. A foal, on wobbly-looking legs, stood next to its mother.

"Recognize that foal?" Bill Cady stood in the doorway.

Ellis jumped.

"Sorry, didn't mean to startle you."

"No, I'm okay, I was just…. the mare looks a lot like Billie. The shape of her head, I guess."

"I'm pretty sure that's Billie's dam. And that would make that foal Billie. That's me in my younger days there holding her lead."

"Did my Pa buy the foal from you?" asked Ellis.

"Well, something like. When your Pa insisted on moving to Tennessee, I wanted to help him start his ranch. That was one of the first foals born here on this ranch. I wanted Tom to stick around and help manage this place, but he wouldn't do it. Had an independent streak, I guess."

Bill moved behind the desk to the chair, but remained standing. He looked at the open letter. Ellis's eyes went there, too, as Bill folded the letter and put it back in the envelope.

"We grew up back east as you probably know. Did he ever talk about why he moved to Tennessee?" probed Bill.

"No sir. I was born there, but…" Ellis remembered some bits of conversations she had overheard between her mother and father, at the same time remembering the conversation she'd overheard between Bill and Maggie last night. "He and Ma said a lot about just wanting to be on their own." Ellis looked up at Bill and suddenly felt scrutinized. He fingered the envelope in his hand.

"So, what happened to the rest of your family? Your mother? Do you know about your…"

Ellis looked down and shook her head. "I…"

Her words interrupted Bill's. She didn't want to hear any more questions. She had come out to the barn last night not only to look in on Billie, but to figure out the story she knew she'd have to share with these family members. That story wasn't yet clear.

"Ma had been real sick. It seemed like she was giving up on Pa comin' back. When she died…" Ellis's voice broke, she cleared her throat. "I guess I shouldn't have left like that, but…I didn't know what else to do."

Ellis felt her muscles constrict. Her legs weak, like they wanted to run. In her mind, a bizarre reality mixed with useless lies. A horse kicked in its stall. The sound, like a gunshot, shook Ellis. She heard Billie nicker and paw at the stall floor. She looked in that direction and rushed to Billie's stall. The horse had finished her feed and Ellis picked up a brush and started grooming and petting her, trying to calm them both.

Bill followed her. He stood at the stall watching. Ellis averted her eyes, but saw him touch the envelope that had been on the desk, now in his vest pocket. "Why don't you turn her out with the other mares," he said. "She's healthy, the grazing's good and she might like the company."

Kip walked up behind Bill. "I can take care of her feet and then turn her out for you. If that's all right with the boss."

Bill nodded.

"Much obliged," muttered Ellis, keeping her eyes on Billie. She also appreciated Bill wasn't pushing about more family information. Though she didn't understand why he wouldn't.

"Now, I don't think you've had your breakfast. Why don't you go on in and see what Maggie's got on the stove. I'll admit she's not the finest cook around, but she'll keep you from starvin'."

Kip started to chuckle but quickly stifled it and turned toward the tack room. Bill walked Ellis back as far as the office entrance. Ellis took another step toward the barn door, but then turned back. "Kind of funny. My Pa naming a horse Billie, you bein' Bill."

Bill looked down and smiled like he was remembering something. "Yeah, kind of funny."

⌒

ELLIS WALKED INTO THE KITCHEN THROUGH THE BACK door. Maggie stood at the sink, washing dishes. She looked up at Ellis, wiped her hands on her apron, and smiled. The gestures reminded Ellis of her mother.

"I saved some biscuits and bacon for you. Kept them warm." She placed the food on the table and Ellis sat down to eat.

"Thank you," Ellis said. She found it difficult to look at Maggie's face, though she could feel the woman's eyes on her.

Maggie poured two cups of coffee and joined Ellis at the table. "I'm afraid I'm not much of a cook. We used to have Annie." Maggie looked at her coffee and smiled. "Annie was a real joy around here. A good cook and a delightful woman. A good friend."

"Where'd she go?" asked Ellis, trying to fill the pause.

"Got married to a nice fellow who...came through one day." Maggie sighed. "They moved on, further north."

Ellis nodded as if she understood. Perhaps she did.

"It's been hard for people, this war. Even before the war it was hard for some." Maggie sipped her coffee and stared across the table, as if watching memories.

"Your boy, Ty? How old was he?" Ellis hoped her asking the questions might keep Maggie from asking more.

"Oh, he'd be twenty-three now." Maggie got a stern look on her face, as if she was about to scold someone. She looked hard at Ellis. "I'm going to tell you a secret, Earl." Her face softened. "My boy didn't die in the war. That's a story we came up with for when folks asked." She searched Ellis's face. "He wasn't a fighter, he was a peaceful man like he was raised." She kept looking at Ellis, the silence making her nervous.

"Then, how did he..." Ellis didn't know if it was right to ask, but she was curious and sensed Maggie wanted to talk about it.

"He was helping some folks through the woods to the north. We helped a lot of those folks." Maggie shook her head. "It was a matter of time, I guess, but we just thought...we prayed..." Maggie took a deep breath, breathed out, straightened up and smiled, tears in her eyes. "The folks got away. Ty was wounded. Hid out for a while and made his way back here just before he died. To keep everybody safe we told everyone he was wounded in battle. Those who knew us knew better, but the story worked for those who didn't."

Ellis put down her empty coffee cup. Felt Maggie's eyes on her.

"Lots of tales told over the war," Maggie said, her voice calm. "Folks just trying to keep themselves safe the best they can. I don't know what those battles must've been like. Hard to know how it would change a person. But I still have to believe people are good, want to be good. Wanna live, you know?"

Ellis looked at Maggie. There was nothing threatening in her eyes, maybe something pleading, searching. She thought Maggie might understand about Libby and the others. She felt something ease in her, yet couldn't quite find her voice.

"Yes, ma'am," was all she could say.

Maggie stood, cleared the dishes. Ellis rushed up to her room, before the first tear could fall. She wasn't sure why she ran up here instead of outside. She felt torn in two, wanting to be both places at once; on the trail on her own—or with Libby, and in this welcoming home. She was baffled they weren't confronting her with what they knew. Had she heard wrong last night? Did they not know? Did the letter on Bill's desk have nothing to do with her? Were those voices she thought she'd heard, coming from ghosts in her head?

She sat down hard on the bed's soft mattress. Then she realized the bed had been made. A coatrack that wasn't there before, stood by the desk. On it hung her mended vest and her duster brushed clean. She stood and looked out the window where she saw Maggie hanging the rest of her washed clothes on a line, alongside a dress, apron, and towels. She took off the jacket, splashed water from the wash bowl onto her face and smoothed back her hair. She fingered the new stitching on her vest before putting it on. A memory moved her hand to a vest pocket. She felt the tintype and relaxed a second before the anxiety crept back. Did Maggie see the picture?

Ellis stood before the mirror, tying a clean neckerchief at her collar. She looked hard at what she saw. The day she left the homestead she was a young girl, grieving but hopeful.

These few months later showed the changes she had seen in her brother. And she had been wrong. She didn't look like Earl. Earl looked like her father. She looked like her mother. She pulled the picture from her pocket. Virginia. Guilt coursed through her veins; and something else, maybe jealousy, as she looked at the alluring young woman. Again, she had a sudden urge to run outside. But a knock at the door stopped her.

"Earl, can I come in?" Maggie asked. "There's something I'd like to show you."

Ellis felt a strange annoyance that Maggie still saw her as Earl. If she knew, why would she pretend?

"Yes. Come in," she said, then, forgetting she had it in her hand, fumbled putting the picture back in her pocket.

Maggie walked in carrying a small box. She sat down on the trunk at the foot of Ellis's bed. "Come," she said, patting the space next to her on the trunk.

Ellis moved to sit by her. She smelled of lavender and coffee. She opened the cigar box that contained photographs, newspaper clippings and letters. Maggie picked up a loose picture and held it out to Ellis.

"Go ahead," Maggie offered, handing her the faded photograph.

Ellis took it, handling it carefully. The heavy yellowed paper seemed older than the tintype of Virginia and showed two people, a man standing behind a seated woman. The man was dressed in a suit and looked to be a businessman. It could have been Bill, but although younger and cleaner than the last time she saw him, she recognized him as her father. The woman, also much younger, but most certainly, Maggie.

"It's you and Pa?" guessed Ellis.

"Yes," said Maggie.

Ellis looked back and forth from Maggie to the picture, trying to figure out why they would be in the same photograph.

Maggie took a breath, let it out slowly. "We were still living back east then. Your Pa and his brother, my William, were both courting me." Maggie looked away. Ellis felt her embarrassment. "Your Ma and I were best friends. We were in college and organizing for suffrage." Maggie chuckled. "We were planning to change the world and didn't really want much to do with settling down just then. Thomas and William, well, they were both itching to go out west. They'd been raised here, near St. Louis, sent east for school. They were always telling stories about starting a horse ranch together."

Maggie's voice strengthened. "Oh, I thought that sounded like a dream. I loved horses, too, and loved to ride, though my folks didn't think it suitable for a girl. They were pretty strict about things, but they allowed me an education, which was rare in those days." Maggie's fingers searched through the box. "One day your Pa had a falling out with his father. I don't remember about what. Seems they were falling out a lot. Thomas announced to me he was going west and would I marry him and go too." She lifted a picture and held it out to Ellis; an advertisement for land west of the Mississippi, a drawing of a peaceful homestead. "He was all of twenty and I was barely nineteen, still in college for another year. Before he left he said he'd get settled and send for me. I agreed to it. But then I didn't hear from him for almost two years. Nobody did. William started courting me. He found out his father had bought a ranch and asked him to work it with him.

"This ranch?" asked Ellis.

"This very one." Before he left he asked me to marry him. You gotta understand, I loved both of them. And I thought by that time if Thomas was still alive, he'd forgotten all about me. So, I married Bill and moved to Missouri with him. A month later I got a letter forwarded from Thomas. Well, that's why your Pa and his brother never spoke much again."

"How come Pa never wrote to you for all that time?" More than ever Ellis felt the strength of letters, of heartfelt communication when people were apart. Hope depended on them.

"Seems he got involved in helping some Indian folks. The government had been relocating them for a few years and on his way out west he saw how they were treated and didn't like it. I'm not sure what all he did. I never got to talk to him about it. Next I knew he and your Ma were homesteading in Tennessee. I kept in touch with your Ma for a while, but the letters got more and more scarce and when the war started, well, they stopped altogether."

Ellis understood now why her mother stressed writing to sustain a feeling of connection. She wondered if her mother had known how much her daughter would need the ability to put feelings into words.

"How'd Pa and Ma get together?"

"Your Ma was on a train to St Louis, coming out to visit me. She ran into him there and they reckoned they still had some things in common." Maggie chose another picture from the box; a man and woman, the woman holding a baby. She held it out to Ellis. "Elizabeth sent this to me the Christmas after she gave birth to little Walter. Oh, she was so in love with your Pa. She admitted to me she always had been."

Walter looked innocent in the picture, like all babies do. Her mother did look happy, her father proud, and both of them so young.

"I remember Ma said they meant to have a picture done of all of us, like they could do back east. Joked they'd never get us to sit still long enough." She paused, then looked at her aunt. "Do you know anything about my Pa? I thought maybe he'd found his way here, but…" Ellis saw Maggie take a letter out of her pocket. It looked like the same letter that had been on Bill's desk in the barn.

"I haven't had anything to add to the box in a while. I was going to put this in there, but I think you need to see it first. Oh, I hate to bear this news, dear." She handed the wrinkled envelope to Ellis. "It doesn't say much. Just his name and dates."

Ellis read the address on the stained and folded envelope. It was addressed to her mother at the homestead in Tennessee. Government stamps and forwarding notes covered the envelope. She unfolded the letter gingerly, as if her father was inside. Maggie was right. It didn't say much, just the name Thomas Cady and the date he got there, to Andersonville prison, just after he wrote that last letter to Ma. A chill severed Ellis from the warm room, but her eyes stayed dry. She felt the hope that came with knowing just a little bit more, and a determination she wasn't sure she could harness.

"It doesn't say he died there. Just that he was there?" Ellis asked.

"That's right," said Maggie. "Bill tried to find out more, but kept running into dead ends." She looked down and Ellis thought she looked like she was praying. She took a deep breath and looked back at Ellis. "We thought sure he'd get in touch if…" She couldn't continue.

Ellis saw the resolve on Maggie's face. She nodded. "If someone wanted to find somebody, how would you go about it?"

"Well, Bill and I were in touch with a newspaper fellow in St. Louis. Some people put ads in the papers, but he let us know that was a long shot, especially from so far away. He reckoned in time we'd hear more as places recovered, but well, he wouldn't encourage us. He'd heard a lot about that place. None of it good. Some things you just couldn't find out and others you didn't want to."

"But...," Ellis started, "he wasn't killed, he was captured." Ellis stood quickly. She was smiling and animated as Maggie's face showed only anguish. "He's alive, I know it."

chapter

# NINETEEN

THE NEXT MORNING, ELLIS WOKE UP IN HER BED. ALTHOUGH she had slept soundly after a day of working horses and fixing fence, she woke with a start. Her foggy mind was still trying to sort through vivid dreams and memories. She looked at her journal on the desk and thought about sitting down to write but she needed to check on Billie first and she'd promised to help Kip with the morning feedings in the barn. She hurried into her work clothes, rushed down the stairs and out the door. After detouring to the outhouse, she remembered Billie was in the pasture, sporting new shoes and bickering with the other mares. If her father was alive—if only he could see Billie in the pasture, living the life she was born to. Ellis longed to talk to Libby. About the horses, about the letter.

Before entering the barn, she walked over to the pasture fence where Billie was sidled up to a fat black mare, looking like it was about to foal. Ellis climbed onto the wooden fence and whistled. Billie looked up and started to move toward Ellis, but then nudged her companion and they both continued grazing. It was good the horse had a friend, though Ellis couldn't help but feel ignored. She jumped off the fence and walked to the mares.

"You deserve some peace and quiet," she said, as she rubbed Billie's head and ran her fingers through the horse's mane. The black mare reached over in between bites of grass and nipped at Billie's rump. Billie moved over but kept grazing.

"Hey, you behave," Ellis scolded the mare. It would take some time for Billie to be fully accepted by the herd.

Yesterday nothing more had been said about her family after Maggie had showed her the pictures and the letter about her father. Her aunt and uncle continued to call her Earl and she worked alongside the other men. Maybe she had dreamed that conversation in the parlor.

"There you are." Bill leaned on the fence and smiled at Ellis and the horses. "You're missing your breakfast again."

Ellis gave Billie a final pat and walked back to the fence, climbing over to the other side. "Sorry, I just wanted to see how she was doing. When's that black due to foal?"

"Any day now. We're watching her pretty close." Bill nodded toward the horses. "Looks like they're getting along pretty well."

The two stood watching them for a few minutes. The rising sun warmed the pasture, backlighting small swarms of crane flies and midges. The growing buzz accompanied soft snorts and swishing tails of contented horses.

Bill sighed and Ellis saw a sad but easy look on his face. She reckoned her father would look older now. She hoped he could be as content.

"Kip said you might be a little short-handed," she said. "I know a couple of folks who could use work. One's really good with horses and the other's a decent cook. I rode with them on my way here and they helped me out. I could ride into town and ask them, if you're interested," she said.

"Tell you what," said Bill. "You go get some breakfast and I'll get the buckboard hitched up. I was on my way into town for supplies anyway, if you don't mind giving me a hand. Maybe I could meet them then and we'll see."

Ellis smiled. "Yes sir."

BILL PULLED UP TO THE FRONT DOOR IN THE BUCKBOARD drawn by two mules, a dun and a sorrel. Their sizes and confirmation were well matched. Ellis walked up to the dun and rubbed its head.

"Careful of the sorrel, she nips sometimes," warned Bill.

As if on cue, the sorrel reached out its nose to nip at Ellis's arm. She moved her hand in a way that smacked the mule's nose, but then petted its head. "You just want some attention, too, don't you," she said. She climbed up onto the seat next to Bill.

"I never worked with mules before. Is it much different than horses?"

"Well, they're a little smarter I think, some folks say stubborn. If something startles a horse it might react first, and ask questions later. With a mule, they're more apt to look at the problem and try to reckon the danger before kicking or leaving. I don't know, I think that's smart." He smiled and looked at Ellis. "They're not as fast as a horse, but they can handle more of a load, and these two have been a pleasure to work with, except for the nipping. But once you pass her test, she'll be alright."

They didn't talk much more on the way to town. Bill seemed to be okay with not talking much unless it was important, which mostly meant the conversation would center on horses. Ellis remembered her father's company the same way.

On the edge of town Ellis pointed toward the back streets. "They got rooms over there when we came into town."

"Over there, you sure?" asked Bill.

Ellis hoped she wasn't wrong about Bill. She watched the man, his brow wrinkled with concern. She thought he looked like he was weighing what to do next. He stopped the wagon.

Why don't you hop down and see if you can track them down. I'll go get what I need and meet you back here."

Maybe his hesitation was just about getting done what he had come to town for. Although it seemed strange to her, she realized she fluctuated between feeling a part of this family and being cautious of them. "Sure, okay," said Ellis.

Bill urged the mules down the main road toward the center of town, and Ellis walked a quarter mile of back streets to The Sage. As she got closer, she saw Abe was holding Smokey's lead, standing at the horse's shoulder and talking to a white man, dressed in fancy clothes, who looked like he was admiring the horse. Libby watched from the porch, adjusting a strap on her saddle slung over the porch rail.

"No sir, sorry sir, he's not for sale," Abe was saying.

"I don't know what you're doin' with that horse, boy, but I'll give you a fair price," said the man.

George and Miles exited the inn and stood behind Libby. They exchanged looks and stepped to the edge of the porch, closer to Abe and the man he was talking to. Ellis watched Miles cross his arms in front of his chest. She noticed now what an imposing figure he made, tall and muscular. She knew of his kindness, but it didn't show on the outside.

When Abe saw Ellis he said to the man, "Sorry sir, he's not actually mine to sell. He belongs to this young fella." He looked at Ellis.

The man squinted at Abe, raised an eyebrow to Ellis. "Is that right, son? Is this your horse?"

"Yes sir, my...he's mine." Ellis tripped over the words, kept her head down.

"Well, then. Do you want to sell him?" asked the man.

Ellis looked at Abe, then at Miles and George who were standing, unmoving, staring at the man. She glanced at Libby who pulled her hat lower, still fiddling with her saddle. "No sir," Ellis said. "Not for sale. Sorry, sir." Ellis stared at the man.

The man looked around at the group quietly glaring at him. Finally he tipped his derby and said to Ellis, "All right then, you all have a nice day." He looked back at Smokey, rubbed his hand over the scar on his flank and said, "Fine looking animal," and walked away.

Ellis watched him leave. She turned back to Abe who was rubbing Smokey's neck, but watching the man leave, too.

"Bill Cady, my uncle, wants to meet you and Libby. He might have work for you if you want it," she said. She looked at Miles and George. "Might be work for all of you."

George and Miles untied their horses. "Thanks, but we're heading north. Family to get back to," said George.

Miles nodded. "We'll be picking up a few supplies and heading on."

Ellis imagined her friends returning to their families and was happy for them. But she was sad to see them go. Goodbyes could mean forever these days.

George walked up to Ellis and held out his hand. Ellis shook it, held on. "It was good riding with you," he said. "You take good care, now. Keep writing."

"Maybe we'll see you all again," said Miles. He tipped his hat and the two men walked off toward the dry goods store, leading their horses.

Miles's confidence sparked a timid smile on Ellis's face.

Abe looked up at Libby as she spread her horse blanket over her saddle, brushing it clean. "There's a train just north of here. We thought we'd head up to St. Louis with George and Miles to find work. Once we save up enough we want to head west."

"It's a nice ranch," urged Ellis. "He raises horses and cattle. He's been short on help since the war. His wife does the cooking, but I can tell she's not used to it. Your campfire grub was as good or better." Ellis searched Abe's face. He smiled a little. "And wait till you see the horses." She turned to Libby. He's got a strong herd." Libby looked at Ellis, then at Abe as she lifted her saddle off the porch rail, walked down the steps and saddled her black mustang.

Abe spoke first. "Does he know we're…he would take us on?" Abe seemed more doubtful than he'd ever let on while on the trail.

"Did he actually say he'd give us work?" Libby asked.

"Well, he wants to meet you, but he knows you helped me get this far. There's other folks there. There's been all kinds. Some are just passin' through and he could use some extra hands. He's okay. They're good people."

Ellis panicked at the possibility that Abe and Libby might be leaving. She had been so certain they'd want to work at the ranch. The trail had brought them close. "Just come meet Bill. I think you'll like the ranch. And maybe you could make your money there and then head west." Ellis noticed the pleading in her own voice and wondered who she was trying to convince.

Abe looked at Libby. Libby nodded.

"Well, okay, we may as well meet the man," said Abe.

Relief overcame Ellis as she watched Abe tie his bedroll onto Smokey's saddle and Libby do the same with her gelding. The three of them walked toward the meeting place, leading the horses.

They arrived at the corner just as Bill Cady was pulling up. New wood planks covered the bed of the wagon. Sacks of grain, and a few crates of groceries sat close behind the wagon's seat, holding down the boards. The smell of pine and burlap hovered over the buckboard. Once he stopped the wagon, he looked over the group and settled his attention on Smokey.

"Bill, this is Abe and Libby. They're the ones I was telling you about," said Ellis.

Bill tipped his hat. "Glad to make your acquaintance." He hardly paused before he said, "That your horse?" Both Abe and Libby looked at Ellis.

Ellis said, "That horse belonged to Ea…" she faked a cough. "…that horse belonged to my brother. After he died I kept him with me for packing, and let Abe ride him when we met up." She hoped the story worked but wasn't sure the way Bill was scrutinizing all of them. Abe and Libby were hushed by the lie.

"I see," was all Bill said. "And you, sir?" He addressed Abe. "You good with horses are you?"

Libby and Ellis looked at Abe and then at each other. Ellis chuckled. "Bill, Abe here's a really good cook. You'd be surprised what he could make over a camp fire. It's Libby that knows horses."

Bill looked shocked and started to shake his head. Then he looked at Ellis. He chuckled and conceded, "Oh, all right, c'mon let's get this load home. We'll see what we can do about jobs for you."

Abe tied Smokey to the back of the wagon and jumped on, preferring it over the saddle. Libby mounted the black. Maybe to show Bill that she was, indeed, a horsewoman. Ellis sat on the wagon seat with Bill. He gave her a long hard look and Ellis tried not to let him see too much of her. But at least now her friends were with her.

Before Bill could encourage the mules, George and Miles rode by, they lifted a hand to wave goodbye, and Miles stopped his horse. He looked at Bill, and Ellis could see they recognized one another. They both smiled, tipped their hats.

"Good to see you made it back," said Bill.

"Yes, sir," acknowledged Miles. And the two rode off.

Ellis thought she heard her uncle say "Silas" under his breath.

"You two know each other?" she asked.

"Mm, worked with me a while back," her uncle said, striking a match and lighting his pipe. They continued to the ranch without more explanation.

When they reached the gate to the ranch, Abe and Libby looked out over the pasture. Dozens of horses grazed quietly. Ellis took a better look at them this time, too. Some looked like they were in good shape but she now saw some were thin and scarred. She ventured a question.

"Bill, did you breed all these horses?" She was pretty sure he hadn't.

"Some, but most of them were rounded up along the trails." He saw Ellis's questioning look.

"I guess a lot of the big battles were going on in the east. News was hard to come by for a while. But there were fights going on out this way, too, in Missouri, Illinois, Arkansas." Bill looked pensive but continued.

"Here in Missouri it was hard to know which side you were supposed to be on. But we weren't fighters. Back then there were no Friends halls out here, but like your Ma and Pa, we were raised to be peaceful folk. Troops came through, both sides, and took horses. All of 'em eventually."

Ellis stared at her feet. She nodded.

"I thought we were done and then Kip rode in one day. Him with one hand missing and riding a washed out mule." He looked at the team, waved a hand toward the dun. "That mule there. We nursed him back to health and he's earning his keep. Kip's doin' okay, too." Bill smiled.

"We'd find some animals still alive along the rivers and creeks where at least they had water. It didn't take much to rope them or herd them back to the ranch. We lost a few, but mostly they've come through okay."

Ellis remembered finding Nick, but couldn't bring herself to tell the story. She wondered if he'd be lucky enough to turn up on a ranch like this.

Bill stopped the wagon and pointed to a roan horse munching grass near the fence. He was thin and weathered. "See that horse there?" Ellis nodded and Libby rode up to where she could hear what they were talking about. Abe was napping in the back of the wagon. "How old would you say that horse is?" he asked Ellis. Ellis scrutinized the horse. He looked starved for both food and attention. He raised his head as if about to bolt.

"He looks old," said Ellis. "But there's something about him…"

Libby dismounted and tied her gelding to the rail on the wagon. She walked over to the roan. Bill watched her and waited to say more.

When Libby got to the fence, the horse squared up to her. Ellis expected the horse to run off as Libby climbed over the fence. When she jumped down the horse startled, but Libby walked away from him and he followed her. She turned toward him and rubbed his nose.

"Well, I'll be," said Bill. "That guy won't let just anybody close to him. Kip has some trouble with him."

Libby climbed the fence again and the horse went back to grazing. She looked up at Bill and Ellis and said to Bill, "He's a young stallion. Maybe three or four."

Bill smiled. "Where'd you learn to be like that around horses?"

"My family. Raised with them."

Ellis was stunned the horse was so young. "What happened to him?"

"Don't really know," said Bill. "The army went through a lot of horses. He may have been green broke or not even. He had some bad wounds on him he either got in battle or by someone trying to break him rough. Either way, he's been through some fights and doesn't trust men much. But I think he'll come around. And I think there's some good blood in there." Bill looked at Ellis and Libby, glanced at Abe dozing in the wagon. "He had to be pretty tough and courageous to make it this far."

Libby mounted her horse and Bill got the wagon moving again down the road and toward the house. When they passed the bunkhouse Kip and another man were standing outside smoking. Bill stopped the wagon by the feed barn.

"Kip, Joe, come get these grain sacks off the wagon."

Abe was awake now and jumped down and started helping unload the sacks.

"Not you," instructed Bill. "They can do that. I need to get you up to the house to meet the missus if you're going to be cooking for us."

Kip and Joe looked at each other. Abe looked at them and shrugged.

"Yes sir," he said to Bill. And got back on the wagon.

Maggie sat in a rocking chair on the porch with some sewing in her hand when the wagon pulled up. Libby dismounted and Abe joined her. Bill and Ellis climbed down. Bill said, "If you could bring those boxes in to the house, Abe?"

"Yes sir," he said.

Libby started tying her horse to the hitching post.

Bill said, "Earl, why don't you show her to the barn where she can tend to the horses. I think there's an empty stall across from where you put Billie."

"Okay." Libby led her horse and Ellis led Smokey to the barn.

Libby looked around at the barn and the few horses in stalls. Most were outside grazing.

"How'd you do that?" Ellis asked. "What you did with that colt out there?" Libby didn't answer right away. She unsaddled her horse as Ellis pitched some straw in the stall.

"You know how," she finally said to Ellis. "He was in a pasture. He knew he had open country. I wasn't giving him anything to be afraid of. No rope, no bridle, no whip. Just me. I didn't care if he stayed or left, though I was hoping he would stay."

"He squared up to you. What my Pa would say 'hooked on'. Why would he do that?" Ellis unsaddled Smokey and brushed his back.

"He had a herd of geldings out there. I guess he liked me better." Libby said this with a straight face. But soon she and Ellis were laughing.

"That's probably about right," Kip said. He had a habit of appearing without being heard. "You know horses then," Kip addressed Libby.

Seeing them side by side, Ellis smiled at the similarities between Kip and Libby.

"We get along," Libby said rather coyly.

Kip continued, "They used to have a bunkhouse full of wranglers here before the war. Now it's just me and a couple of guys passing through on their way north. You fixin' to stick around?"

"Don't know yet," said Libby.

"Well, if that husband of yours cooks better than Miz Maggie, I'll sure hope you are." Kip smiled. "It's safe here. Just so you know, used to be a candle in that window every night."

Libby looked at Kip and smiled.

Once the horses were taken care of Ellis and Libby walked toward the back door of the house to the kitchen. On the porch they both turned around and caught the sun low in the sky, silhouettes of horses in the pasture. The air smelled fresh and horsey, clean and maybe about to rain. For Ellis it was a peaceful, calm feeling and one she hadn't felt in a while. One she still didn't quite trust.

"What did he mean," she asked Libby, "about the candle?"

"A signal of a safe house on the railroad. A candle or a lantern out front. That's how we knew we could trust the con-ductors and the station."

Ellis looked puzzled.

"Your people here," said Libby, "I reckon helped a lot of folks on their way north. Like we did. Like your brother did."

Maggie opened the screen door. "You two wash up. Your man, Abe's, cooked up a fine supper for us looks like."

In the kitchen Abe looked over at Libby and smiled at her. Then he said to everyone there, "Food's on the table."

"Well c'mon then all of you, let's sit down," said Maggie as she went into the dining room. Abe and Libby paused, not knowing if they had actually been asked to sit at the table with everyone.

"C'mon," said Ellis.

They walked into the room and stood behind the chairs meant for them.

"Now," said Bill, "If you're gonna be working here with us, you're gonna eat. The boys usually eat out in the bunkhouse but that's just because they don't want to have to be polite. They'll join us in here on Sundays mostly." He looked at them as Abe and Libby still stood there. "Sit," he insisted, nodding at their chairs.

"Shall we take a moment, Bill?" prompted Maggie. They bowed their heads, Maggie held her hands palm up, closed her eyes. Ellis was reminded of home, and Abe and Libby glanced around the table and waited. After only a few seconds of quiet, plates and bowls were passed, silverware clinked against ceramic dishes.

"Why, this is a fine meal," said Bill. "If the two of you want to stay on here a while, that would be fine with us. Were you headed anywhere special? Got family somewhere?" asked Bill.

Before they could answer Maggie offered, "There's an extra room here, just off the kitchen. Annie stayed there before she got married and left. We were sorry to lose her, but what did we go through that darn war for if not the ability to do just that?"

Maggie looked at Bill, maybe for approval. He nodded slightly.

"You two can have that room if you like. It's warm and cozy. A sight better than the trail, I'd guess," said Maggie.

Abe said, "We thank you, ma'am. That will suit us just fine for now. But I can't promise how long we'll stay. We did have plans to see some folks in St. Louis, but I don't even know if they're still there."

"Well," said Bill, "As long as you want to stay, if you keep cooking like this we'll give you room and board. And a good wage for a good day's work." He looked at Libby. "Maggie always liked to ride, and she's good with horses, but…well, I confess, I never saw anyone do what you did with that injured colt today. You've got a way and if you want to, I'd give you a chance."

Libby looked at Abe and then at Bill. "Yes, sir, I'd like that."

*chapter*
# TWENTY

ELLIS SAT AT HER DESK, THE SWEAT OF BAD DREAMS SLOWLY drying on her nightshirt. She struck a match; the sizzle and smell of sulphur brought back memories and a surge of emotion even though she realized it was not her last match and now there would be plenty more. Visions of the cave and camps along the trail faded as a quiet light crept into her room from the lit candle. Dawn whispered from the open window.

> *I still feel skittish every morning when I wake up. At first a feeling of joy washes over me; knowing I'm alive for a new day. That Libby and Abe are safe and still near me. That George and Miles are on their way home where they belong. Then I remember what I was just dreaming and I realize it wasn't a dream, not really. It was a memory. Mama really is buried back home. I may never see her grave again. Walter, drowned in a sea of scattered bodies in a mass grave. Earl, buried in the wilderness, his bones maybe scattered by wolves. Lost graves no family will ever be able to find. But I don't cry any more. Sadness seems to have withered like a plucked flower. I'm still here.*

209

*I can still feel joy, even if for just a moment before I re-*
*member. Remember to feel guilty. For killing, for want-*
*ing to kill. Remember those left behind. Virginia. Did she*
*meet someone else? Did she marry someone else because her*
*soldier never returned? Because of me. Pa. Oh, Daddy,*
*where are you?*

Ellis felt a twinge in her gut. A warning of her monthly
bleeding. She laid the pencil in the crease of her journal, took a
deep breath and sighed. She reached over and rubbed the horse
carving between her fingers before standing and looking at her
face in the mirror over the wash basin. Although she wouldn't
be growing a beard, her face was tanned and toughened beyond
what most fifteen-year-old girls' would be. Her hair was still
relatively short. It stuck out in places on her head, reminding
her of her twin. She poured some water from the pitcher into
the wash basin. The water was tepid; warm compared to river
water. She walked to her closed door, listened and opened it to
peek into the hallway. She heard no stirring, no creaking footsteps. Closing the door, she returned to the mirror, removing
the night shirt she was wearing, and stood back so she could see
her whole body. Startled at how thin she was, still she approved
of her taut, lean muscles. Her breasts nettled her this time of
month, but she could still conceal them under her shirt and
vest. She examined the mark on her shoulder where she had
been wounded. It seemed strange to see the puckered pink scar
where there was no longer any pain. Like a brand.

Holding her head above the basin, she poured water over
her hair. She lathered on some soap and scrubbed her head.
She wondered if the smell of soap would always remind her

of that day at the river with Libby. Of her mother. Memory atop memory.

She washed the rest of her body and rinsed her hair before toweling herself dry, slipping into her clothes, and folding a clean rag to place between her legs. With a dirty shirt she rubbed her boots clean and put them on. She combed her hair back with her fingers. Folding her dirty clothes, she set them at the foot of her bed but then remembered Earl's room back home. She picked them up again, shook them free and tossed them on the floor.

In the barn a couple of the men were feeding horses and cleaning stalls. Billie nickered when Ellis walked in.

"She's been waitin' for you." Kip said. He was bent over a horse's hoof, aligning a new shoe. He didn't look up.

Ellis watched him as he plucked a nail from the corner of his mouth, held the hoof between his knees and placed the nail, hammering it home with his good hand. When the last nail was set he gently released the hoof and straightened up, rubbing the horse with the stump of his forearm as if there was still a hand attached. When he looked at Ellis, she caught herself blushing and turned toward Billie's stall.

Ellis opened the stall door and rubbed Billie's neck. "Hey girl," she cooed. She fed Billie hay and grain and brushed her while the horse ate.

"I meant to leave her out in the pasture, but she insisted on coming in with the dam, so I put her next door."

Ellis looked up and saw the pregnant mare standing with its head lowered. "Will she foal soon, you think?"

"I reckon so," said Kip. "Tonight or tomorrow, I'd say." He moved to the other side of the horse he was shoeing, eyed her legs and led her into a stall. "Yours is a good looking mare," he said. "Do you know her breeding?"

"No, but I think Bill does. She was just a weanling when Pa came home with her, but I think her dam was bred here."

"You train her?" asked Kip.

"My Pa and brother started her. They thought I was too young to be working with her, but she seemed to like me best," Ellis smiled and then remembered who she was and wiped the smile from her face.

"Yes, sometimes they do play favorites," said Kip.

"Well, I thought I'd find you out here." Bill Cady interrupted. He shot Kip a friendly glance and then looked at Ellis rubbing on Billie. "Kip, you gonna work with the colt today?"

"Yes, sir, thought I might have Libby help, since he seems to like her so much."

Bill looked at Kip, nodded and smiled. "Better get to it, then."

"Earl, come walk the stalls with me," said Bill.

"This gelding just came in last week." They were standing in front of a stall where a bony, mud-brown horse was foraging through his hay."

To Ellis he looked sad and weak.

Bill anticipated Ellis's questions. "He actually looks better now. The sores on his back are healing and we're hoping the hair will grow back. It'll be a while before we can put a saddle on him, but once he gets some weight on we'll start with some ground work and see where he's at."

They walked stall to stall like this, looking at a half dozen horses in the barn instead of out in the pasture.

"We keep them in until we're sure they're healthy and can hold their own in a herd," Again, Bill seemed to have read Ellis's mind.

They came around to Smokey's stall. He was just finishing up his breakfast.

"Libby's been putting an ointment on his cuts and sores. Don't know what it is, but he doesn't seem to mind it. That must've been quite a graze he got on his flank a while back," Bill said.

Ellis nodded, looked at the c-shaped scar and didn't know if she should make up a story or stay silent. Earl hadn't gotten around to giving her many details about Smokey other than he might have stolen him.

"Why don't you go give them a hand in the round pen," said Bill, "I think after dinner they're gonna ride out looking for mustangs."

Just outside the barn was a small round corral, built so as not to have any corners where a horse could get stuck. Ellis remembered helping her father train horses in one just like it on their homestead. The new sun shone through the dust the colt kicked up, making his hooves sparkle. Libby stood in the middle of the pen, centered on the colt, now and then smacking the coils of the rope she held, against her thigh. She'd repeat this, getting the colt to move out and then stopping and drawing its attention to her. The young horse would look at her and sometimes take a tentative step toward her, but then Libby would move him out again. Eventually when Libby drew the horse's attention, the horse squared up its whole body to her, like she was all he was interested in. Then Libby turned away from him and took a couple of steps. The colt followed her and came up behind her. Libby turned and gently rubbed the horse's nose, then slowly, its head and ears.

"He seems fine with that," said Kip. "Nice job."

As Libby moved her hands to the colt's withers, he stiffened and his ears flattened. "He doesn't seem to want anyone getting near a mounting position on him," she said. She moved back in front of him and shook her rope. The colt stepped back and turned away.

"Get him moving and then try again," said Kip.

Libby repeated the pattern until the colt seemed more relaxed with her at his side.

"I think we should stop now and let him think. Turn him out maybe," she said.

"Agreed," said Kip.

Ellis admired the way Libby and Kip were working together. Their subtle movements with the colt, just at the right time and with just enough energy to move him but not startle him. An unexpected flood of emotion spread over her, making her eyes water. She took off her hat and wiped her eyes and forehead as if dust had blinded her.

"I've got a few to ride today," said Kip. "You feel like putting some rides on a couple?" He was talking to Ellis.

"Sure," said Ellis. She wanted to ride Billie, but was happy to let her get some much deserved rest in the pasture.

"I'll bring out the mustang. I could use a rider on him while I get him used to a rope." Kip jumped off the corral fence and went to the barn. Libby had turned the colt out with the geldings. Now she stood next to Ellis.

"You gonna keep pretending to be your brother?" asked Libby. "I'd bet they'll be okay with you being yourself."

"Yeah, I don't know. It's just, maybe if they knew they'd be different toward me, you know?" Ellis kicked the bottom log of the pen with her boot. "It's just, well, I like wearing these clothes and handling the horses."

"Well they seem to be okay with me. Why would it be different for you?"

Ellis shook her head. "I dunno. Family's different maybe. And besides, I've been pretending for so long, I'm not sure I know how to stop," said Ellis. That was the truth of it.

They spent the rest of the morning working with the horses in the round pen and then riding a couple out in the large paddock. Libby, Ellis, Kip and one of the hands, Johnny, saddled up another bunch to take on the trail. They had seen signs of a troop traveling north not far from the ranch. They might be able to pick up some more strays. Ellis wondered if there was any chance her father might be in that group.

They left after dinner and had been riding a couple of hours when they climbed up a rise that overlooked the valley road. "There!" observed Kip. "I thought it was a small troop but that looks like the wagons and all."

Ellis couldn't believe what she was seeing. A line of cavalry, maybe fifty men, followed by a line of wagons trailing behind them for a dozen miles. They were traveling at a good rate of speed, horses walking out or trotting. Behind the wagons a small herd of loose horses, following on their own.

"C'mon," said Kip.

As they got closer, Ellis watched the trailing herd through her spyglass. Some of them looked fresh and although they were very lean they looked a lot healthier than the others just barely able to keep up.

"Let's hold up here for a while," Kip said.

"What are we waiting for?" asked Ellis, thinking they might be able to talk to someone; ask about her father.

"We can't go in like horse thieves," warned Johnny. "They don't care about the ones left behind, but we can't be too eager. Bill doesn't really want them seeing us."

Through her glass Ellis watched one of the soldiers dismount and another soldier bring up a fresh horse from the rear of the wagon train. The soldier took his saddle and bridle off the horse he'd been riding and put it on the fresh horse. He mounted again and they both rode off. The unsaddled horse stopped, laid down and rolled. They watched as the troop disappeared down the road.

"Let's go," said Kip.

When they got to the downed horse Ellis could see raw sores on its back. The horse was sweaty and lathered. It wasn't laying flat out, but with its legs tucked under it and its head up. It nibbled on the wispy grass surrounding it.

"That's a good sign," said Kip. He dismounted and walked up slowly to the horse as it lay there. Reaching out carefully he rubbed its head, talking softly to it. Handling the rope from his saddle he put a loop over the horse's head and coaxed the horse back onto its feet. He mounted his saddle horse and led the other one behind him. "Let's get him over to the river. He needs water."

When they got to the river there were two other horses there, grazing on the grass at the river's edge and drinking.

"Got 'im," said Johnny, as he gently threw a loop on one.

Ellis untied her rope from her saddle. Her father and Earl had taught her how to rope, but she never had to use it much. These weren't exactly wild mustangs, and they seemed to want to be caught, so she didn't have much trouble getting a loop over the third horse's head.

"Let's start back," said Kip. "Libby, ride behind us just in case one of these balks. They're pretty tuckered out.

They rode slowly but steadily, stopping here and there for the horses to graze and then move on. Ellis noticed the sores on the backs, and at the cinch. The horses' heads were raw where the bridles had been.

"Why don't they stop and rest their horses?" Her voice incredulous.

Kip looked at the horses and then ahead at the trail. "They have to get where they're going. Sometimes fast. But those men treat their horses as good as they can under the circumstances. They know they mean life or death to them. I've seen lots of 'em climb off their horse and carry their own saddle and walk them for a ways just to give the beast a rest. They'd do more if they could, but they're under orders."

Kip and Ellis were riding side-by-side now.

"Where were you in the war?" she asked Kip.

He didn't answer right away and Ellis wondered if maybe she shouldn't have asked. Kip scouted ahead and then looked down at the ground. He rubbed his horse's mane frequently and Ellis was again reminded the man only had one hand. His reins were tied and hung loosely on his horse's neck. The lead of the rescued horse was dallied around his saddle horn and he held the end in his hand. He was riding with his legs and seat.

His voice pierced her thoughts. "I was with an outfit near St. Louis. We transported horses back east to Washington. The government was buying all the horses they could get their hands on. We herded them to the railway station, loaded them onto the cattle cars and off they went." Kip shook his head. "It was hard on those horses to travel by train like that, but most of 'em made it. Anyway, when they started takin' black soldiers I joined up."

"That wagon train we just saw was nothin'. During the worst of it those trains were thirty miles long. The wagons carried food for the men, but also feed for the horses. And medical and vet supplies, too. The war was only supposed to last a few months. After a couple of years, most of the grazing along the way was done."

Ellis hesitated, knowing some questions don't want answers, but her curiosity prevailed. "How did you lose your hand?"

"Hmpf." Kip glanced at his arm. "Those cattle cars? Got caught in the door."

"An accident," affirmed Ellis.

"Not exactly." Kip got a far away look on his face. He looked sad, then changed the subject. "I remember, just before I ended up here, I was riding that sorry mule and I came upon a troop of about ten soldiers. They'd been marching a while I think, and were pretty beat up from battle. They were so tired, they were fallin' off their horses. But they saw a pasture that still had some grass on it and rode out into it. They got off their horses, tied the reins to their wrists, and laid down on the grass. The horses grazed around them while the soldiers slept. When they left the next morning there were these little soldier-shaped patches of grass all over the field." He smiled.

Ellis was trying to picture this in her mind. Then she smiled, "Oh, you're kiddin' me, right?"

"No, I ain't. That really happened," said Kip, but they both laughed.

*chapter*
# TWENTY-ONE

*Every day on the Cady ranch is about the same. Me and Libby and Kip, and whoever's handy that day, work the horses in the morning. The green ones we gentle. Libby's especially good at that and at dealing with those damaged as much mentally as physically. We have breakfast cooked up by Abe, and talk about plans for the rest of the day. Fixing fence, herding cattle and working more with the horses. Lately we've had to ride farther to find strays.*

*I've learned a lot about remedies for saddle sores and getting a mare in shape for breeding. We fixed a lot of horses that had seen too much war and I wondered what the men who rode those horses were going through if they lived. Was there someone fixing them? Earl, I wish you and I would've had more time. I don't want to write let-ters to you anymore, it keeps you too close. Everything I write is like you're right here beside me.*

*Billie is in her best shape ever. Bill and Maggie go off to Sunday morning meetings, but we ride the trail to the lake most Sundays just like you and me used to ride to the river back home. Sometimes Kip or Libby and Abe come along, but often it's just me and Billie. She isn't too keen on leaving the herd anymore, but she will and once we're out of earshot it's just our breathing and the wind in our ears. It's like we're back on the trail again. No word of Pa yet. I miss you. It's like half of me is gone.*

THE END OF THE DAY WAS ELLIS'S FAVORITE TIME. SHE turned her horse out to pasture, put up her saddle and bridle and stretched her tired muscles beneath gritty skin. It felt good, natural. Billie trotted over to her favorites in the herd and grazed near them. But the tranquility of the scene contradicted the struggle in Ellis's heart and mind. An on-going struggle as big as that damn war.

"You just gonna stand there staring at the herd all night or you gonna come in for supper?" Ellis hadn't seen Libby walking up behind her, but she wasn't startled. She had gotten used to Libby's ability to appear, unheard. She expected it.

"Did you ever think you'd find a place like this to be?" Ellis asked her.

"Most of the time I didn't much think about where we were going. We just had to go." Libby climbed up on the fence and looked out at the pasture. "Then we got here and, well, I just kept waiting to get pushed on but we weren't." The young women sat side-by-side on the fence. "Abe and I've been talking. We're not sure if we should stay here or move on, but comparing this place to St. Louis, I'd vote for here if they'll have us." She looked at Ellis. Ellis looked down and nodded. Libby surveyed the pasture. "We can be ourselves here, doing what we're good at. If this isn't freedom, I don't know what is."

Libby nudged Ellis with her elbow. "What's got into you? You like it here, don't you?"

"I do…of course I do. It's just…I don't know. Look at Billie; she's got a herd, good feed, a job to do, everything she needs; and I do, too. But it's like there's this itch I can't scratch and it won't leave me alone."

"And you're not the scrawny *boy* you were when we arrived, huh?" said Libby.

Ellis's hand rubbed her chin and then smoothed the shirt under her vest. "I keep thinking I should feel good here, like I belong. But even though it's my family, I don't. I mean all that's true but still there's something missing." Ellis searched Libby's face for an answer.

"Maybe it's time you let them know who you really are," said Libby. She nodded toward the horses. "Billie's living her truth, nothing to hide. That's a peaceful place. You could use that, too."

Ellis shrugged, knowing maybe Libby was right, but not sure it was the answer she'd been looking for. She didn't want to struggle like her mother had. Her mother was smart, educated, and so in love with a man that she changed her life for him. She loved books, and music, and horses. She died scratching in the dirt for potatoes.

"You know, my Ma had the farm, the horses, us kids; she loved my Pa. And all she had in her pocket when she died was two letters." Ellis looked away. "Earl thought he could find Pa and piece everything back together. He learned different."

Libby sighed. "You asked me a while back how I do what I do with the colts. Remember that young roan when we first came here?"

Ellis nodded. "He's come a long way with you working him."

"He'd been struggling, fighting probably most of his life. He didn't know how to have it good, how to not be scared that every minute he might be hunted down. I had to give him more time when he wasn't chased, but helped. I had to balance his past abuse with more kindness." Libby paused, glanced at Ellis. "Maybe you've been through enough you don't remember how to have it good, peaceful, like here." Libby took off her hat and rubbed her arm over her forehead. She sat staring at the hat, fingering and twirling it. Then she looked up at Ellis.

The women's eyes met. Ellis searched Libby's dark eyes, a strand of her hair lifted by a breeze. She felt a warmth, as if a surge of strength had been passed between them. She couldn't help but wonder if the horses felt something similar when Libby worked with them. Her mind reflected on when she first met Libby. Her hand touching Ellis's wounded shoulder, the grace with which she mounted her horse, her fingers rubbing soap into Ellis's hair. She smelled the campfire and the river.

A horse snorted in the pasture, nipping at another, bringing Ellis's attention back. "Yeah, maybe," Ellis muttered.

Libby got a sly look on her face and said, "Look, you can stay 'Earl' as long as you want maybe or you can settle down here and let them know who you are. You'll find a husband, raise a family and maybe take this place over one day."

Ellis frowned as she realized the truth of those choices. If they knew who she was, that would be exactly what would happen. Or at least what they would mean to happen. She couldn't stay here if she wanted to be Earl. And if she was Ellis, another life might be rolled out for her because she was a woman. She heard Bill's voice. *Mares are for breeding.* He was all for breaking them to ride and being useful, but bottom line was populating the herd. Did he feel the same way about people?

"Hey you two, come on in to supper!" yelled Abe from the back porch.

Ellis and Libby glanced at each other, then jumped down from the fence and walked to the house, brushing the dust from their clothing. Just before the door Libby whispered, "Don't leave without the truth being out." Ellis heard the words, but more than that she felt Libby's warm breath on her neck.

MAGGIE AND BILL WERE ALREADY SEATED AS ABE BROUGHT in food from the kitchen. Kip joined them at the table, passing a plate of steaks. The smell of roasted meat and something sweet still baking in the kitchen fostered smiles all around.

"Well, how'd it go with that new gelding we brought in yesterday?" Bill asked Kip.

"He's pretty sore, but I think he'll be all right with some of Libby's tonic," said Kip.

"That gouge on his shoulder looks like a bullet graze. I thought the war was over. It looks pretty fresh." Libby said.

"War's over, doesn't mean the fighting's stopped," said Bill, with a sideways glance at Maggie.

Ellis remembered hearing those words before. They echoed in her head, but she was getting better at keeping the visions away.

"Yes, well…" Maggie stuttered, and then hurried to say, "I think we have something to celebrate tonight, don't we?" She looked at Ellis.

Ellis looked around the table. Everyone was looking at her, smiling and acting like they all knew the joke but her. All except Libby.

"Earl, Bill found a letter your Daddy wrote some fifteen years ago. Son, didn't you know today's your birthday?" Maggie smiled at Ellis.

Ellis looked dazed. She remembered all the birthdays she and Earl had celebrated together. The new journals from Mama and being relieved of their chores for the day. She and Earl would take a long day's ride together. A special cake after supper. When she last saw Earl he had whisker stubble on his face, was a good hand taller than she was, his callused grip like her father's. At fifteen she was strong, but smooth-skinned, her breasts were swelling and her trousers fit differently. It seemed all these changes happened overnight.

"No Ma'm," she choked out.

"Well, it is, and we're gonna celebrate..."

She couldn't do this. These people had been kind to her, accepting her into the family, and yes, she was family, but not the member they thought she was. She couldn't lie anymore. Libby was right.

"No, Ma'm...I mean no, well, I guess it is my birthday, but..."

"Well the letter..."

"It's not right because... I'm not Earl." She awaited the repercussions. Her mind flashed back to the battlefield; she fired the gun and everything slowed down until the bullet struck and the soldier fell. She put down her fork and sat back in her chair. She wanted to get up and run, up to her room or outside to the barn. But she couldn't move. She took cover by sitting there in her chair as still as she could be.

"What do you mean, son?" asked Bill.

"Child," coaxed Maggie, "are you all right?"

It took Ellis a moment to find her voice, but then she calmly stated, "I'm not Earl, I'm Ellis, Earl's twin sister." She waited for the fall. Nothing. Then she heard a sigh, two sighs. They were not sighs of disgust or shock or disappointment. They were sighs of relief. She looked at Maggie and Bill. They smiled at each other and then at her.

Maggie spoke first, "We know, dear. We wanted to give you time. We don't know all you went through with your family and during the war, let alone getting here."

"We figured it was easier for you, and probably it was," said Bill. "But you don't have to pretend anymore. You can tell us everything, the truth. You're family and we want you here. We can give you a home."

Ellis felt heat behind her eyes. Her mind spiraled back to the last time she saw Earl alive. She strained to keep the memory of his dead body out of her mind. She felt relief and sorrow, anger and gratitude. She winced as she imagined what horses felt when the saddle was pulled from their back after too long. The hide stripped. A tear fell and then another, but she didn't break.

Maggie came to her and put her arm around her. "Oh, honey, it's okay, you're safe with us here."

"I...I really need to be alone right now. I'm sorry. I'm sorry you went to all this trouble..." Ellis didn't want to leave Maggie's embrace. She felt like she was in a dream, as she watched herself stand and walk up the stairs to her room.

*Earl. As long as I was you it seemed okay to be here, to be doing what I'm doing. But now I don't know. They all know I'm Ellis and not you. I just want to be who I am, but I don't know who that is now. It was feeling so real, so natural, but now folks will be expecting other things of me. Daddy used to talk about horses having an instinct.*

*They're built to be with a herd and need to have a pur-
pose, a place. I feel that for myself, too, and I was thinking
this was the place, these people were my herd, but...I don't
know. It's like there's something else out there drawing me
and I don't even know what it is. It's kind of like when
I left the farm to find you. Maybe it's what it was that
made you leave to find Daddy. I was scared to go, but felt
like I had a halter on my head and someone was pulling
on the lead. I'm sure Mama and Daddy would want me
to stay here, but I keep thinking about what you would do.
I know you had a crazy notion to head west and I think
I have that notion, too. God, almighty, I wish you were
here to go with me.*

Ellis didn't hear the knock on the door until Libby tried
again louder. "Yes," she called.

The door opened and Libby stuck her head in. "Okay if I
come in?"

"Sure." Ellis stayed seated at the desk. She took out her
knife and whittled a new point on her pencil.

Libby sat on the trunk at the foot of Ellis's bed, as Maggie
had when she showed Ellis the pictures.

"You've lost a lot of kin and seen things no girl or boy
should at your age or ever. But we've all seen those things or
something like it. Those people downstairs, they understand.
They can accept...whoever you are."

Libby stopped talking and for a while they both sat silently. Ellis heard her words repeat in her head. She felt Libby's
voice touch her as clearly as if it was her hand. Her strong
gentle fingers caressing her heart. She rose from her chair and

watched herself move to where Libby sat at the foot of her bed. She watched her own hand reach out, met by another.

Libby stood. "I should…"

"No. Don't go," whispered Ellis. She leaned in close to Libby's face. She could feel her breath, a warm, moist sweetness. Their lips touched, and still, for a moment, Libby didn't move.

She lifted her hand, stroked Ellis's face, then turned away. "I should go." She moved toward the door. "They all hope you'll come back down. The food's good and…they have a gift for you." She paused at the door. Ellis stood watching her from the bed. "Will you come?"

The women looked at each other across the room.

"In a minute," said Ellis.

Libby closed the door behind her.

chapter

# TWENTY-TWO

ELLIS SAT ON THE BACK PORCH BENCH, LEANING AGAINST the wall. Her legs tucked up, she hugged her knees and readjusted the blanket wrapped around her. She stared into the distance, waiting for the sun to come up over the hills. Watching the shadows rise and the pastured horses come into view, helped to wrestle her from dreams and nightmares into the joy of morning.

For weeks no one had said much about who Ellis was. She dressed the same and worked the same as she had been. They called her "Ellis" now, but no one seemed to expect anything different from her. Libby treated her like nothing had happened and Ellis began to think maybe nothing had.

Now that autumn embraced the air, the early morning fog lingered, clinging to the tops of the cottonwood. Yellowing leaves dropped on green pastures as the days heated up for a few hours in the afternoon, but the air felt different, softer. Ellis had been waiting for Libby to come out of the house, as she usually did, to sit on the porch with her and watch the birth of the morning. They shared no more than the warmth of a blanket and silent appreciation for a new day. Their connection helped heal a wound left raw by her twin's absence.

Nickering from the barn alerted her as she realized Libby might already be out there. She sloughed off the blanket and hurried to the barn.

Still dark inside except where the high windows let in the dawn light, Ellis followed the rustle of fresh hay and the soothing clucks and whispers Libby used with the horses. The sounds came from the foaling stall. An old mare, a straggler they'd rescued from the fields, had been close to giving birth for a few days.

"Has she…" Ellis started and then saw that, indeed she had. The mare was standing, but the foal hadn't gotten up yet.

"She was having a little trouble, so she let me help. But I think nature will take over now," said Libby.

The mare turned to her foal, licking and nudging it, encouraging it to stand. The foal, dazed and unsure, raised and lowered its wobbly head and finally got its newborn legs under itself and stood. The mare nickered. Libby moved to the stall door and came out and stood next to Ellis. They watched the colt take its first steps toward its mother's milk. The colt's legs were crooked and his head seemed too big for his body; his nose too long.

"As beautiful as they turn out, sometimes colts are just plain ugly," said Ellis.

"He'll grow into himself," said Libby. "I've seen the ugliest ones turn the most handsome."

Libby and Ellis looked at each other and chuckled. Libby turned back to the mare and foal, but Ellis kept looking at Libby. They stood shoulder to shoulder and Ellis was struck by the piney, earthy scent of her.

"The mare's a good mother. The colt will be a good addition to the herd. Maybe a stud." She glanced back at Ellis who was still watching her. "What do you think?"

Something caught Ellis's breath. She turned away suddenly. "Uh, yes...he's...I think we should let Bill and Kip know." She started to walk away.

"Kip knows." He was standing at the bottom of the loft stairway. Half dressed, his shirt hanging open, he yawned and scratched his head. He finished buttoning his shirt as he walked over to the stall. "I stayed with that mare until late last night. Didn't look like it was going to happen yet, so I went back to bed. Just like her to have it while I was asleep." He looked into the stall. "How'd you know?" he asked Libby.

"Just luck I guess," said Libby.

Kip stepped in between Libby and Ellis. The three of them stood at the stall door, arms touching, enjoying the sight of new life and the familiarity of each other. Ellis was reminded of a time when she and her brothers watched a mare and foal, back when they were all young enough they still enjoyed each other's company. She noticed that male smell on Kip. It felt both comforting and disquieting.

"Well," Kip yawned, "I'll go let Bill know you two have things under control here." He left the barn and Libby moved closer to Ellis.

A strange awareness overtook her. The sibling feeling when the three of them were standing here changed to something else. Something she couldn't name. Something that both attracted and scared her. Libby nudged her arm and a nervous shiver rattled Ellis.

"I guess we should get some work done, huh?" said Libby.

Ellis caught Libby's gaze and found it hard to move. "What? Oh, yeah, I guess so."

"Are you okay? You look a little flushed," said Libby.

Ellis let out her breath she now realized she had been holding and looked back at the mare and foal. "Sure, it's just… this is such a miracle, isn't it?"

Libby looked at the horses. "Yes, that it is." And she walked away.

———

AT THE MIDDAY MEAL, ABE SET UP A TABLE OUT BACK AND served up beef sandwiches, pickles, and strawberries. Maggie brought out coffee and sweet tea. Kip and the wranglers ate on the bunkhouse porch. Libby and Ellis joined Maggie and Bill in the shade of the main house porch eaves, and once everyone got their food, Abe covered the leftovers with cloths and sat down with a plate next to Libby.

Bill spoke in between bites. "It's a bit late for that foal, but that one wasn't up to us. I like to get them out to pasture for the first few months, but if the weather comes in we'll have to keep them in the barn. Besides, I don't want any chance of that mare getting bred during her foal heat. Better to wait until spring." Bill smiled and looked at his sandwich. "Gosh, this sure is fine cooking you're doing, Abe. I do hope you and Libby will stay on through the winter, at least."

Ellis hadn't thought about the weather turning. She had thought about leaving— thought she'd be gone by now. But as much as she wanted to go, something held her back.

"Well, sir," said Abe, "Libby and I were talking and we'd like to stay on a little longer. That would suit us just fine."

Ellis realized Libby had as much as told her this, but hearing Abe say it shocked her.

"Glad to hear it!" said Bill, and Maggie nodded in agreement.

"Ellis," Maggie said, "We sure hope you'll make up your mind to stay, too."

Ellis didn't know what to say. She wanted to stay, knowing Libby was staying, but before she could stop herself she said, "I need to move on." The words seemed to come from someone else's mouth, and she looked straight across the porch at Libby. "I'm not sure, I..."

"You don't have to make up your mind now," interrupted Bill. "We sure hope you'll think about it. Winter will be here before you know it and you won't be able to get far. Might as well be here with us than waiting for spring in a strange town."

"That's right," said Maggie, "Please say you'll think about it for now."

Libby observed Ellis with a strange, questioning expression. Ellis looked around at the others. Abe glanced at her, grinned and chewed. Kip appraised her with a stern but friendly eye. Libby looked back down at her plate and took another bite of food.

"Okay," said Ellis. "I'll think about it." Although she didn't have much of an appetite, she went back to eating, too.

THE RANCH HANDS HAD GONE BACK TO THEIR AFTERNOON chores. Libby returned to the barn, and Ellis helped Abe bring in the dishes. She watched the ground in front of each step, mired in thought about staying or going. She wiped her hands on her trousers and was heading out to the barn when she caught sight of Maggie. Her aunt, silhouetted by the kitchen window, was reading a letter. The woman's butternut hair, graying at the temples, was pulled back loosely in a chignon at the nape of her neck. She wore her favored outfit of a homespun shirt, a vest and a long riding skirt. Ellis admired the woman who reminded her of her mother, yet possessed a toughness her mother never achieved. She couldn't help wondering if Maggie was truly satisfied with her life here.

Maggie looked up from the letter. Her eyes met Ellis's the way they had when she was showing her the pictures of her father. Not taking her eyes off Ellis, she folded the letter and put it in her vest pocket.

"Is it…my father? Is there word?" Ellis felt a slow blush of hope.

Abe was cleaning dishes and preparing food for the evening meal. He kept his head down.

"No dear. Not really. Come, let's sit in the parlor." Abe looked up and smiled at Maggie as she walked by. Ellis glanced at them, feeling like words were passed but not heard.

The women walked through the hallway to the front parlor. Maggie sat on a wingback chair. A small table, holding a short stack of books, sat to the side of the chair. The simple sophistication of the room appealed to Ellis, but she felt out of place in her dusty work clothes and hesitated to sit down. She had never seen the ranch hands enter this room and hadn't visited it herself, but she had seen Maggie reading in the chair. And some evenings, on the way up to her room, she had heard her playing the piano. The tunes were sweet and melancholy.

"It's okay, dear, please, sit here so we can talk." Maggie motioned for Ellis to sit on the sofa. "Do you remember me telling you about that news writer from St. Louis. The one who wrote about…the prison?"

"Yes," said Ellis, her heart sinking.

"Well, I wrote to him. I told him about you, because I thought maybe, if he did hear any more about Thomas…about your father, I wanted to make sure he'd let us know." Ellis thought Maggie seemed nervous the way her voice hesitated.

"I, well, I feel badly I didn't ask you first, but I didn't want you going…going to St. Louis. I want you to stay. But I know that's your choice. Anyway, it looks like Mr. Bilford is coming here. He wants to talk to you."

"Why would he want to talk to me?"

Maggie reached for the books on the table next to her. She handed one, a journal, to Ellis. "You left this on the bench this morning. I found it out there a few weeks ago, too. Sunday, when you rode out to the lake by yourself. I only read a little. I'm sorry, I couldn't help myself. I thought it might help…"

Ellis felt her cheeks flush. She wasn't angry. She was embarrassed. She never meant for anyone to read her journals. She never thought anyone would want to.

"Oh, honey, I'm sorry if you didn't want me to read it, but I told Mr. Bilford about your writing. You're a good writer, Ellis, and you've got a story to tell. I've been writing all my life and can't turn a phrase like you do." Maggie searched Ellis's face.

"Lucas Bilford, he's an honest man and wants folks to know the worth of women. He reckons the more folks know how women played a part in the war, the easier it'll be to achieve suffrage and property rights." Maggie searched Ellis's unchanging expression.

"Your mother and I knew Lucas's father before the war. Before we left Philadelphia. When Lucas senior died, his son took over their printing business." Maggie paused waiting for Ellis to say something. "Your Ma would be so proud of your writing. I know she encouraged you."

Ellis looked up at Maggie. "She did." She rubbed the leather journal with her thumb. "She never read it." Ellis remembered the shelf of journals she left behind on her desk in Tennessee. "Any of them." She wondered, doubted. "At least she never let on she had." Silence echoed between the women. Ellis thought of her mother; how she would gently reprimand them during their lessons and always praise them for their try. How her health slowly waned with each day of her father's absence.

"I remember reading to her when she was sick. You know the book, *Wuthering Heights*? I thought it was sad, but she loved that story. She said she named me after the author, Ellis Bell. I didn't know until later it wasn't the author's real name. That writer died just a year after her book was published. A tragic thing, Ma said. All that talent gone to waste." Ellis stood and walked to the front window, caressing her journal. She noticed a candle in a brass holder on the windowsill. "I remember now. Ma said, 'Ellis, promise me you'll never waste your God-given talents.' Huh, I thought she was talking about horses, and riding." Maggie stood and Ellis turned to her. "I guess it won't hurt to talk to Mr. Bilford."

"Well," said Maggie, dabbing an eye with her handkerchief, "good, that's good then."

"When's he coming here?"

"Tomorrow."

ELLIS CAME DOWN FROM HER ROOM AND STEPPED INTO THE parlor. She had heard a carriage drive in as Maggie was playing the piano. To Ellis, the parlor felt familiar today. It felt like a place of change, a starting point. She heard footsteps on the porch and Bill opened the door before the visitor had a chance to knock.

"Well, glad to see you again," said Bill.

"And you, Mr. Cady," said Lucas.

Hearing the voice of the stranger, Ellis felt like bolting. Maggie turned and rose from the piano bench, reached out and touched Ellis's arm and smiled at her. Ellis relaxed for a moment, before flinching from the voice at the parlor entrance.

"Hello Mrs. Cady," said Lucas. He fingered his hat nervously, but stood with confidence. He was a handsome man, a bit taller than Ellis. His brown hair was full and unruly. He wore a friendly expression and smiled at Ellis without staring. He held out an ink-stained hand to Maggie, which she took confidently.

"Hello Lucas, so good to see you." She stepped toward Ellis. "I'd like to introduce you to our niece, Ellis. Ellis Cady." She said the name proudly and Ellis heard it as if for the first time. "Ellis, this is Lucas Bilford." Lucas held out his hand to Ellis and she wondered if the ink was dry or if it might rub off onto her hand, staining it as it had once been, so long ago. She longed for the familiar smudge. She shook it strongly then quickly checked her hand, hoping no one would notice. Lucas smiled, embarrassed.

"Hazard of the trade, I'm afraid." He shrugged. His teeth were straight and white, one dimple showed on the left side of his mouth. It made him look mischievous and reminded Ellis of Earl.

"Glad to meet you—sir," she said.

"Oh, please, call me Lucas. Sir ages me more than I care to be."

"You two sit down and talk, I'll get some lemonade. Or Lucas, would you like something stronger?" said Maggie.

"No, please, lemonade would be just fine. Thank you," said Lucas.

Maggie left the room and Ellis and Lucas stared at each other for a moment, each waiting for the other to speak.

"Like I said in my letter, I really want to hear your story. I've heard some talk about, well, about women who fought in the war, but didn't really know anyone until you. Well, I don't know you, either, but, well, I think we have a friend in common. You know George Adams I understand." Lucas waited for a reaction he didn't get. "He teaches at the college and he told me about you."

"George Adams?" Ellis didn't recognize the name at first, but then realized who it was. "Oh, I never knew his surname. You know him? Did he make it back to St. Louis? Is he all right?"

"Yes, yes, he's fine. Back at the college and doing fine. Full of stories himself. In talking to him, and then hearing from Maggie, uh, Mrs. Cady, well that's how I found you."

Ellis stared at the floor, looking perplexed.

"I'm sorry, do you want to tell your story?" asked Lucas.

"Mr. Bilford…Lucas, this is all a little…I'm just trying to piece it all together. You see, sometimes I remember things that don't feel quite real. Like I read it in a book instead of lived it, you know?"

Lucas looked at Ellis like he understood, but didn't say anything.

"What is it you want me to tell you, Mr. Bilford?"

"Lucas, please. Miss…er…Cady, I know you did what you did out of necessity, and I think others may have done, too. I'm a writer and I'd like to write that story, but I think it would be better if you wrote it. How you left your home and fought as a…man. Miss…Cady…"

"You can call me Ellis."

"Or maybe we could write it together. Ellis, Mathew Brady and some other photographers have brought the reality of the war into peoples' homes like nothing ever seen before. And for folks to know it wasn't just men, but women…well, suffrage was put on hold for the war, but it's a prevalent topic now. You might be able to help it forward by letting people know just what women can do, how strong they can be. Wouldn't you want to be a part of that?"

"Well, sir, I don't know how my story will help that. I know some exceptional women, but I wonder if most don't really want to do the things I've done. I didn't want to do some of it. And I don't especially want to do the things they've done."

Shadowed images crept into Ellis's mind. Filthy soldiers in camp, the dead woman soldier, the smell of gunpowder. And then, her mother reading her father's letters, teaching her and her brothers under the sycamore tree.

Ellis shook her head. "But I know my Mama and Maggie wanted something else for women than what they got. And the war put a halt to that." She took a deep breath and let it out slowly. "If you think my story might help change things, then…"

"Wonderful!" Lucas beamed momentarily, before his face again turned serious. "There's another reason I wanted to talk to you. I know your aunt's been looking for your father, Thomas Cady."

Ellis brightened.

"I don't know where he is, but I think I know where he's been," said Lucas.

"They told me about the prison," Ellis said, deflated.

"Yes, well, I'm finding out not all of the survivors went north. They spread out, lost track of a lot of them and, well, if a man wasn't sure where he was going, there was a lot of reason to go west. And if a man was to go west, chances are he'd start in St. Louis."

"Lucas, do you have some reason to think my father's alive?" Ellis felt hope creeping back to her but held it at bay.

"I don't know. I don't want you to expect too much. Maggie said you have a letter your father wrote…to your mother."

"Yes."

"Would I be able to see it?"

Ellis shrugged. "I guess so, but why?"

"I've been contacted by a friend of mine in Washington. They're in possession of some prisoners' diaries. They're still sorting through them, but they didn't want them going to the families. Not yet. It might take a while, but I've asked some be sent to me. The ones they might not be able to place." Lucas waited for a response from Ellis's troubled expression. "I thought if we could match the handwriting, or maybe you could, well, tell by what was written…"

"Do you think one could be my father's?"

"I don't know. And I need you to know the things I've heard about them, the writing, might not be what someone wants to know about their kin."

"I…I'd want to know. When can I see them?"

"It could be weeks, maybe months before I get them. Honestly, I wouldn't have said anything, but Maggie thought it might help, give you some hope to know some people made it out of that place." Lucas shook a pained look from his face. "I hope that's the case."

Ellis straightened and nodded. "Yes. I want to know as soon as you have them."

Lucas smiled. "And in the meantime, will you show me your journals? Will you trust me with your story?"

# EPILOGUE

DAWN CREPT OVER THE TREES IN A QUIET MIST. ELLIS watched Billie grazing, the horse keeping a sensitive eye on the herd. It was hers now. An ear twitched, a blink, her head moved imperceptibly to the side; tiny movements that spoke volumes to the other mares. Billie had found her place.

Ellis checked the bedroll on the back of her saddle. The young buckskin gelding stood quietly. A light rain dulled the air where she stood and the pasture where Billie grazed. She closed her eyes and smelled the distant fields rife with early crocus and daffodils. The horse flicked its tail bringing her senses back to creaking leather and musky saddle soap. A clear patch of sunshine illumined the hills to the north.

She patted the buckskin and left him there as she walked over to Billie. She'd said her goodbyes already, but couldn't resist another moment with her hands tangled in the mare's mane. Ellis climbed the fence and walked up to Billie. She saw her again as that filly her father had brought home. The one that would change their lives. Or save them.

"You relax, girl. Have lots of beautiful babies like Daddy planned. This is where you belong."

Billie stopped grazing and turned her head toward Ellis. The girl rubbed the horse's head, put an arm around her neck.

"Don't worry, I'll be back." The words echoed in Ellis's ear. How many times had she heard someone say that? "I will," she whispered.

She returned to the buckskin, mounted, and held up a hand to those watching her leave. A smile on her uncle's face, a tear in her aunt's eye, Abe's face, confidently beaming. She rode past the barn and stopped where Kip stood. He handed her a small package of brown paper, leaning in close to her horse's neck. "You know how Ace here likes his sugar cubes."

Ellis pocketed the gift and looked toward the pasture. Billie grazed. Content.

"Don't worry, she'll be fine."

"I know she's happy here. It's just...hard to leave her."

Libby waited at the corral gate, holding the reins of a paint mare. When the women's eyes met, Libby swung up onto her horse bareback.

"She wanted to ride with you to the end of the property," said Kip.

"I don't know what the fuss is about. I'll be back. I'm just going to see that diary he's got. See if it is my father's. At least I'd have...something."

Kip nodded and stepped back, watching the two women gallop off.

———

THE GRAY-HAIRED MAN LOOKED OUT THE WINDOW OF THE train. A leather bag sat to his left, on the bench. His right hand held an ironwood cane, a carved horse head as its handle. He wondered why he looked out the window. He didn't remember knowing anyone in St. Louis. No one would be meeting him here. He stepped off the train gingerly, but with dignity; a man used to wielding a cane as if he didn't need it. He quickly glanced around the station and limped off toward the city.

His fingers found the note in his pocket. He unfolded it as a wagon hurried by, stirring the breeze enough that he tightened his grip on the paper. He searched for the address of the printing office. "Bilford News and Printing Company" was two blocks down the busy city street.

He stopped before a red door with the address painted above it and stepped back to peer up at the windows on the second floor. Two young children ran toward him, laughing, and playing an unknown game. One bumped into him, knocking the paper out of his hand.

The look on the man's face startled the boy, but the boy stopped and picked up the dropped paper, holding it out to him.

"Sorry mister. Here, you dropped this."

The man stared at the boy before taking the note. Something in him stirred to see the boy's blond hair curling from under his hat, a familiar mischievous look in his eye.

The other boy looked annoyed at the man with the cane. He nudged his playmate. "C'mon. Let's go."

As the man watched them run off, his eye was drawn to a sign hanging on a storefront. "Bookstore." Just inside the window was a display of a new book. The title was burned into the tooled leather cover. *Ellis River.* The longer he stared at the book, the deeper he felt it was here he would find what he was looking for.

# ACKNOWLEDGMENTS

Real experience is the catalyst for story, and I have many to thank along my journey to this first novel. Some of the best experiences that contribute to these pages were had with equine friends and acquaintances, most memorably:

**Bayja**—the first horse I actually owned. Please forgive me for leaving you on that farm by yourself, and thanks for going with me to watch Knevel try to jump the canyon, **Babe**—the horse love-of-my-life. We had the best adventures and never did I feel more connected to and loved by an equine, **Red**—the round-up sure was fun even though the dogs did most of the work, **Flash**—for introducing me to Ray Hunt, saving both our lives, **Mocha, Hank & Moon**— my beautiful babies; I hope you had beautiful lives, **Squirrel**—for tempting me back into the saddle after all those years, **Trigger**—the hard-headed trickster that got me out of that forest in one piece, **Mia**—best borrowed horse, ever. And last but not least, **Cider**—who taught me and re-taught me what it is to be in a horse's life.

Beta readers: Cathy Jaeger, Llynn Bennett Huntley, Nancy Owen James, Elizabeth Mullins, and all of the folks in Henry Marchand's creative writing classes who were kind enough to give me honest critiques.

Horsemanship mentors: Ray Hunt (Idaho 1979—where I rode with the Zen master of horsemanship as he saved lives both equine and human), Kristi Fredrickson (I cherish our friendship and your ability to instill confidence), Buck Brannaman (for keeping the teachings alive and spreading them to riders far and wide), Ricky Quinn (how are those boys doin'?), Nick Donohue & Amelia Maloley (for giving Cider a chance at a better life). May horses always unite us.

To all my English and Creative Writing teachers: know what you have done, and still do, makes a difference. Especially: Bonnie Mottar Farrington, Linda Kimble Mitchell, and Henry Marchand.

To my editor, Laurie Chittenden, who helped make this book the best it could be by asking unanswered questions and wanting to know the colors of the uniforms even though I didn't want to say. (Any lingering errors are my own.)

As a book is judged by its cover, my designer, Danna Mathias Steele, who deftly captured the essence of the book I wanted to hold in my hands.

Untold help from: Independent Book Publishers Association, Reedsy.com, Writer's Digest University, and IngramSpark Academy.

If I missed thanking someone in my excitement to get this book published, please forgive me and I will thank you later. In gratitude...

# ABOUT THE AUTHOR

*Photo credit: Cathy Jaeger*

NICKI EHRLICH GREW UP IN Southern Illinois before attending college at the University of Denver and later, Idaho State University, where she graduated with a B.A. in Philosophy/English. After living ten "horse-rich" years in Idaho, she moved on to Oregon, and later Washington, where she realized she had unwittingly traveled the Oregon Trail.

While living in the Pacific Northwest, Nicki continued to write fiction, non-fiction and poetry. She has won awards for her poetry and creative writing, including the Writer's Digest Annual Poetry Awards and the Ray Fabrizio Memorial Award. Her writing has been published in Scheherazade, the literary magazine of MPC, among other magazines and newspapers. Nicki holds a Certificate in Creative Writing from Monterey Peninsula College and is a member of the Central Coast branch of the California Writers Club. She also holds a Coast Guard Captain's License and currently lives on California's inspiring central coast where she is at work on the sequel to *Ellis River*.

You can find Nicki at: NickiEhrlich.com, Facebook, Instagram, and Goodreads.

Made in the USA
Coppell, TX
16 November 2023

24335849R00152